PAPER WIFE

ALSO BY LAILA IBRAHIM

Yellow Crocus

Living Right

Mustard Seed

PAPER WIFE

LAILA IBRAHIM

This is a work of fiction. Names, characters, organizations, places, events, and incidents are either products of the author's imagination or are used fictitiously.

Published by Lake Union Publishing, Seattle

www.apub.com

ISBN-13: 9781503904576
ISBN-10: 1503904571

Cover design by Shasti O'Leary Soudant

Printed in the United States of America

For my parents, Hilmi Ibrahim and Margaret Loughlin, whose choice to immigrate to new lands gave me the wild and precious life I'm so immensely grateful for.

I am satisfied the present Chinese labor invasion (it is not in any proper sense immigration—women and children do not come) is pernicious and should be discouraged. Our experience in dealing with the weaker races—the negroes and Indians, for example—is not encouraging.

—US President Rutherford B. Hayes

CHAPTER 1

Ancestral village
Guangdong Province, China
March 1923

Before opening the door, Mei Ling turned back for one last look at her family. Swallowing hard, she studied them, burning the tableau of faces into the folds of her memory. Soon they would be separated, perhaps forever.

Jah Jeh, Mei Ling's nineteen-year-old sister, perched like a prized bird between their parents. A fancy comb pulled back her shiny black hair. The bit of red in her pale cheeks was the only hint of turmoil on her smooth, calm face. Fuchan's weary dark eyes told of defeat, while Mah-ma's held a steely pride.

A single glance around this room told how far her family had fallen. Their glossy black lacquered table sat on the old, dusty floor like a jewel in a pig barn. Elegant scrolls hung on roughly finished wood walls. As with countless other families in Guangdong Province, the triple devastation of war, famine, and disease had chipped away their family's fortune until all they were left with was this, surrendering their beloved Jah Jeh to a stranger.

Years ago, Mah-ma had set a foundation for a different path for her daughters. She faced the contempt of her neighbors by leaving their feet unbound, allowing the girls—born so close to one another they were mistaken for twins—to run freely through childhood.

She insisted that her daughters be educated as well as her sons, going so far as to send them to school when they lived in the city. That had been a radical choice too. They didn't know if that long-ago decision would increase or decrease their chances for fortuitous marriages.

As their fortune fell over the last two years, the questions in their family mirrored the battle in their land: Keep the old ways or adapt to the new? Fuchan, a scholar and teacher, fell back to the Confucian practices of his childhood, believing his ancestors would intervene if he held true. With each setback he burned more incense and gave more offerings. But ghosts were no match for the gunpowder of the power-hungry warlords or the greedy foreign invaders who carved up China for profit. All her father's petitions to their ancestors were nothing in the face of a singular devotion to the wealth that came from controlling the import and export of goods.

So it had come to this: Fuchan would go through the charade of negotiations with the matchmaker waiting behind the door. But when you are out of options, there is no debate, only the opportunity to accept the terms offered to you.

Mei Ling thought she'd already lost all hope, but a single silk strand of it still danced in her soul. This moment held the possibility Jah Jeh would stay in their lives, that she would marry into a family that lived nearby and would permit her to visit them.

Ahma, Fuchan's mother, stared at Mei Ling. Her white hair was pulled back into a tight bun and her dark eyes were surrounded by wrinkles. They took one breath in unison, and then Ahma nodded. It was time for Mei Ling to open the door.

~

March was the most beautiful month of the year, but the spring morning framed in the doorway held no joy for Mei Ling. The cool air that blew in with the matchmaker didn't clear the chaos in her heart. Mei Ling stood by the open door and bowed to welcome in the destructive savior. The woman, knowing she had no business with Mei Ling, strode past without acknowledgment.

Fuchan's hand trembled as he gestured to the place of honor for the old woman. Mah-ma poured fragrant tea into two cups. Mei Ling stood by Ahma's chair and breathed in the enticing scent. She imagined her youngest brother was listening from the kitchen where he couldn't be seen. At ten years old he understood this was important family business but not the full implications of this meeting.

Mei Ling's eyes traveled to Jah Jeh's face. There was fear in her sister's eyes but also acceptance, resignation. She looked at the matchmaker. The old woman sipped her tea and nodded with a tight smile. The silent waiting was unbearable.

Fuchan cleared his throat. The woman arched her right eyebrow. Mah-ma suddenly bobbed her head in understanding and flicked her eyes downward to Fuchan's hand. He looked lost, as he had the day Mei Ling's eldest brother took his last breath; then Fuchan grasped her mother's meaning. He pulled a coin from his pouch and placed it on the black surface. They had to pay simply to learn of the offer.

The old woman cradled her tea against her chest with both hands. She shrugged while barely lifting two fingers from the cup. Fuchan sighed and placed another coin on the table in front of him. The woman stared at the coins across from her. When he didn't move, Mah-ma leaned forward and slid them to the matchmaker.

With the coins in her grasp, the woman's demeanor immediately changed and she declared, "I bring good news to your honorable family."

"We are grateful for your services," Mah-ma replied. "Please tell us your news."

"I have found a fortuitous match for your eldest daughter. He is a recent widower in search of a new bride."

A widower. He might be old with many children. Mei Ling searched the woman's words and expression for meaning.

"He has only one son, two years in age. His wife died . . ." The woman hesitated as she chose her words. "Very recently."

Only one child meant he was most likely young.

"He was born in the year of the Ox, which makes him the most suitable husband for your Rabbit." The woman smiled.

Mei Ling calculated. He was either two years or fourteen years older than Jah Jeh; she could not entertain the idea that he was twenty-six years older, but that was not unheard of. She studied the woman's face, trying to discern more information about her sister's fate.

Where does he live?! Even with modern forms of transportation and the dream of the end to the wars, distance mattered as much as philosophy. Once they were married, many women saw their own families rarely, if at all. Traditional mothers-in-law demanded their new daughters act as if their original family had died. Mei Ling prayed that Jah Jeh's new family would not require her to have a singular devotion to them.

"He is a merchant," the woman declared, clearly pleased to reveal this detail.

Mei Ling's mind flashed to the most likely places for his residence: Shanghai or Hong Kong. Please let it be Hong Kong, only two days' journey away, and not far-off Shanghai. Though many merchants preferred their families to live in their ancestral village with their elders, rather than with them in the bustling cities.

A challenge entered the woman's voice and she said, "He is a *Gam Saan Haak*."

Mei Ling's stomach dropped. *Gold Mountain*. He lived in California.

"Perhaps our daughter will stay in his village in Guangdong Province, as so many Gam Saan Haak choose?" Mah-ma spoke out loud Mei Ling's fervent hope.

The woman shook her head, looked at Jah Jeh with some sympathy in her eyes, and said, "He has three return tickets from Hong Kong to the United States."

An audible gasp escaped from Fuchan, Mah-ma's face tightened, and pain flashed in Mei Ling's sister's eyes.

California. A lifetime away.

The old woman explained, "The Americans have changed their laws in order to restrict Chinese men from traveling back and forth to visit their families. There is a rush to bring wives and children to California before the law is enforced. The long-held practice of families here and husbands there is ending."

Sorrow and fear gripped at Mei Ling's throat. Her sister was leaving China, likely forever. She grew so dizzy that she reached for the back of her grandmother's chair to steady herself. She felt her Dragon rumble inside her. She took a steadying breath to calm it.

"When . . . ?" Jah Jeh burst out, breaking protocol.

"The ship leaves in ten days," the matchmaker replied. "You must decide today—right now."

Mei Ling grabbed her grandmother's shoulder. A cool hand patted her fingers.

"I have an appointment with another family should you turn down this match. As you can imagine, he is eager to have this settled."

A gloomy silence filled the room. Mei Ling's stomach filled with mud. When she could stand the unbearable silence no longer, she finally asked a respectful question: "What is his name?"

The woman turned her head, looked Mei Ling up and down as if seeing her for the first time, and replied, "Chinn Kai Li."

Strong start. It was a powerful name, fortuitous for Jah Jeh, her timid Rabbit of a sister.

"There is another issue to which you must agree." The woman turned her attention back to Mei Ling's parents. "She must be a paper wife."

Fuchan's face pulled inward in anguish. *Paper wife.* Her sister would have to take on the identity of a stranger, officially become someone else to live in California.

The matchmaker explained, "The United States' restrictions on Chinese immigration go into place in May. Because he is a merchant, he was able to get a visa for his wife and son at considerable expense. Unfortunately his first wife died while he was journeying here. The name on the visa cannot be changed before the ship sails. For immigration purposes, she must pretend to be Wong Lew She."

Mah-ma's eyes darted between the matchmaker and her older daughter.

Fuchan asked, "She must give up her name?"

"Only for the paperwork," the woman reassured. "It means nothing."

"Are you certain the American officials will be fooled?"

The woman's eyes flashed. "I assure you I know my job! If you do not trust me, then we are through here." She started to rise.

"Please . . . ," Mah-ma begged. "We are only worried parents. Forgive us."

The woman sank back into the chair, satisfaction written all over her face. She knew she'd achieved her purpose. Pain in his eyes, Fuchan slowly transferred eight coins to the table and pushed them to the woman. She nodded slowly.

"I will share the good news with Chinn Kai Li. He will be satisfied with this match. Flat feet and the ability to read are an asset in a wife in San Francisco. This will be a successful match. I will return in two mornings to accompany her to Guangzhou for the wedding."

Two days! The speed was not surprising; it was commonplace for marriages to happen so quickly. But it was hard to accept how soon Mei Ling's life would permanently change. She looked at her sister. Jah Jeh's cheeks were flushed red with emotion. California was a nearly mythical place. Mei Ling wasn't sure she believed any of the stories about it—the far-fetched tales of easy wealth or the dramatic reports of mistreatment. But she knew it was most likely that she would never see her sister again, which made her nauseous.

The matchmaker finished the last sip of her tea. She set the cup down carefully and rose to leave. Mei Ling crossed to the door to open it for the woman who was both destroying and assuring her sister's life.

The woman stopped in the doorway and said, "He is Christian, so the wedding will be in a church. If need be I can explain the protocol as we travel. I will not lie to him about your faith, but you will be wise to keep your beliefs private."

After delivering that final blow, she departed from their lives for the time being.

~

Jah Jeh rose without speaking. She walked away from the family and disappeared into their sleeping room. Mei Ling bore the silent inaction for only a moment and then rushed to find her sister.

The lid to the battered wooden trunk was open; its previous contents were on the bed in neatly folded piles. Jah Jeh stared at the pile, though she must have felt Mei Ling's arrival. She turned to the cabinet and pulled out slippers, her trembling hands and flushed cheeks revealing the intensity of her feelings.

"Jah Jeh." Mei Ling's voice broke immediately.

Jah Jeh glared Mei Ling into silence. "I accept this is my fate," she said. "I ask no less of you."

Mei Ling nodded and blinked back tears.

"I will have a very comfortable life as a merchant's wife," the elder sister explained, sounding as if she were convincing herself as much as Mei Ling. "I am fortunate. When national tensions decline, I will have the means to return for a visit."

Mei Ling cleared her throat, nodded, and pulled her lips into a tight smile. "As always, you are the wise older sister," she replied.

A tear escaped from Jah Jeh's right eye. She ignored it, but Mei Ling crossed over to her and wiped it away with her thumb. Her fingers rested on her sister's black hair.

Mei Ling whispered, "I will miss you."

Jah Jeh took Mei Ling's fingers and squeezed. "I will miss you more." Tears filled the eyes of both sisters. Jah Jeh shook her head, wiped at her face, and said, "You must not reveal the pain in my heart to our parents . . . or grandmother."

"Of course not," Mei Ling assured her sister, annoyed but not surprised by Jah Jeh's need to tell her something she already knew.

The sisters worked in silence, carefully fitting Jah Jeh's life into a small metal-bound container. Clearly she had been planning for this day, because Jah Jeh did what needed to be done with little hesitation, separating what to keep and what to leave behind, until she came to her statue of Quan Yin.

The statue resting in her two hands—the goddess of compassion and mercy—looked up at Jah Jeh. She squeezed her eyes tight and then placed Quan Yin back on her shelf.

Mei Ling gasped.

"I will do what I must to make a harmonious marriage," Jah Jeh insisted.

Mei Ling nodded as if she agreed, but she would not have been able to make the same sacrifice. Through the hunger and the deaths, there were times when she could not express her fear and sorrow even to Jah Jeh, but she always shared her burdens with Quan Yin. If Mei

Ling were the one being sent to a foreign land with a stranger, she would have needed Quan Yin's strength and compassion to survive.

~

As most of the family rushed to prepare for this upheaval, Fuchan escaped into his mind by reading one of his few remaining books. Mei Ling stared at him, contempt burning alongside pity in her heart. The defeated expression on Fuchan's face reminded her of their last days in Guangzhou.

Nearly one year ago they had moved permanently to the village, but it seemed like another lifetime that they had lived in Guangzhou. Following the fall of the Qing dynasty in 1912, China had been in chaos. Fuchan had placed his faith, and their future, with the wrong man. Sun Yat-sen, the leader of their region, had raised an army to fight for control of a reunified China. As an outspoken supporter of Sun and the Kuomintang, Fuchan believed he would become part of the leadership of a prosperous and modern China. When the Kuomintang forces fell in 1922, Sun abandoned the families that had allied with him and fled to Shanghai.

Various warlords fought for control over Guangzhou, battling through the city's districts. Last June, soldiers from one faction had pounded on their door in the middle of the night. The image of the young men holding lit torches high above their heads still haunted Mei Ling. They were fortunate to have been woken up. Some families were not so lucky.

Mah-ma and Ahma, fearing an attack, had packed their trunks and moved them outside each night for many weeks. It felt foolish each morning when they brought them back in. But when the fateful night came, they were grateful for Mah-ma's foresight.

They fled their home in minutes, their tears hidden in the dark night. Mei Ling never learned whether their home had been burned.

She preferred to imagine that it still stood and that a small piece of her was in it somewhere: a strand of her hair, a slip of paper with her writing, or a length of bright embroidery floss.

Fuchan, a respected and prosperous enough teacher in Guangzhou, did not have the skills or temperament for this new life. Education was a luxury not prioritized in a time of war and famine. No one in the village had extra chickens or crops to pay for their children's educations. Like Mei Ling's family, they needed every bit of sustenance just to survive.

The garden provided the family with some food, but not enough for six stomachs. Mah-ma and Ahma pretended to eat, but Mei Ling saw that they had lost much of their flesh to keep the younger generation healthy. They would not survive another winter without more food or fewer mouths.

Mei Ling and Jah Jeh were more burden than support. At eighteen and nineteen years old, it was time for them to marry, to make lives of their own outside of their childhood family. They could delay no longer.

Mei Ling walked past her father without comment. She joined the women in the kitchen, preparing rice and vegetables for a midday meal. Like Mah-ma, Ahma was hardly hampered by her lotus feet. She toddled around the kitchen, bearing any discomfort without complaint as she had for most of her life. Mah-ma considered killing one of their precious few chickens but decided to wait until tomorrow, Jah Jeh's last day with them.

"It is a bitter and sweet day," Ahma acknowledged with a kind pat on Mei Ling's shoulder.

Ahma was attempting to be a comfort, but Mei Ling could not believe there was anything sweet about this day. She had not grown up expecting that she or Jah Jeh would be lost entirely to their family once they were married. Mah-ma did not want them to share the fate of so many Chinese women. They had believed they would marry progressive thinkers in Guangzhou—businessmen or scholars—who would be proud to have educated wives with natural feet.

Leaving their home because of the warfare was tragic, but the deaths were a devastating loss that Mei Ling could not accept. Cholera was a common companion of war—and far more fatal than metal blades or bullets. Months before the soldiers forced them to leave, Dai Low and Mui Mui, Mei Ling's eldest brother and younger sister, had succumbed to the disease in a matter of days as the family helplessly watched them become dehydrated and then die, leaving only three children in the family: Jah Jeh, eldest sister, Mei Ling, and Dai Dai, youngest brother.

Ahma interrupted Mei Ling's thoughts. "She will adjust, as Rabbits do, darting quickly in a new direction to keep safe."

Unspoken was the warning that Mei Ling would be wise to mimic her sister. Now that Jah Jeh's future was secured, Mother and Grandmother would scrape together the gold to find Mei Ling a husband, but it was common knowledge that female Dragons were challenging wives. Mei Ling would need to keep her fire contained if she wanted a harmonious marriage.

CHAPTER 2

Ancestral village
Guangdong Province
March 1923

Mei Ling woke up in a sweat. It was still dark out, so she did not rise but rather breathed deeply to calm her beating heart. *Our last full day together,* she thought. She and Jah Jeh had slept in the same bed for as long as Mei Ling could remember, and tomorrow they would say a forever goodbye. Mei Ling did not share her sister's conviction that she would return to China in the future.

Mei Ling rolled over carefully so as not to disturb her sleeping companion, but she needn't have bothered. Jah Jeh's face shone with a glaze that came from a high fever. Mei Ling sat up and placed her hand on her sister's red and sweaty forehead. She was burning hot. She thought back to yesterday. Her sister had not complained of stomach pain, a headache, or weakness. She hadn't coughed in the night or soiled herself. Her heart shimmied between hope and fear and landed on the side of hope that Jah Jeh did not have a life-threatening illness, but that this fever would prevent her sister from traveling tomorrow.

Though it was early, Mei Ling rose to stoke the fire for tea water, but Ahma was already tending to the task when Mei Ling came into the kitchen after relieving herself outside.

"You cannot change her fate," Ahma reminded her, as if she read Mei Ling's thoughts.

"She is ill, with a high fever."

Ahma nodded as if her granddaughter had just confirmed something she already believed, then left to check on Jah Jeh and returned without comment.

They worked together in silence, warming rice porridge and boiling tea. Her grandmother pulled out the medicine for a fever, a foul-smelling and fouler-tasting mixture from the herbalist in the neighboring village.

Mei Ling was slowly spooning the concoction into her sister's mouth when Mah-ma came in to check on Jah Jeh. She touched her daughter's warm body and then sighed. Mei Ling could not make out the words between her mother and grandmother, but she suspected they were discussing the merits of sending for the herbalist. They had stopped paying for his treatments as their income ran out. He would most likely be unwilling to come now.

Mei Ling looked at the trunk sitting in the corner of their room. The thought *It might be unpacked tomorrow* jumped into her mind, causing her heart to flutter with desire. Perhaps her sister's fate was going to be in China and not the United States.

No one called for the herbalist. Instead they spent the day in quiet whispers and prayers, caring for Jah Jeh. When the fever did not go away by bedtime, Mah-ma sent Mei Ling to sleep with Ahma. Mei Ling willed herself to lie quietly, but agitation and uncertainty filled her body and her dreams. In the morning nothing had changed.

By the time the matchmaker knocked on the door, Mei Ling was confident her sister would not be leaving with the old woman.

~

Mei Ling welcomed the tingle of the cool breeze on her face as she opened the door. The matchmaker marched in, but stopped suddenly when she saw the empty space between Fuchan and Mah-ma. Mei Ling felt a deep satisfaction that this woman was about to be delivered some bad news.

Her mother poured tea as the tension built in the silence. When cups were settled in their rightful places, Fuchan was the first to speak.

"A tragedy has befallen our family."

The woman arched her brows, silently encouraging him to proceed.

"Our daughter is too ill to travel," Fuchan continued. "We are sorry, but we cannot fulfill our contract. Fate has another plan for our Jah Jeh."

Mei Ling sighed in relief at these words spoken out loud.

The woman looked around the room, incredulity covering her features. "Where is she?" the woman challenged.

Mah-ma rose and the woman followed her to the bedside. Jah Jeh was curled on her side, sweat glistening on her slack face. Her breathing was shallow, and she showed no awareness of the world around her. By all rights Mei Ling should be filled with worry for her ill sister, but she was more relieved that her dearest companion would be remaining in their home.

The matchmaker returned to her seat, a steely anger covering her face.

"We are an honorable family but cannot argue with the fates. Please, we must have a refund," Fuchan declared. "You may arrange the marriage with the other household."

The woman slowly shook her head. "It is too late."

Mei Ling's Dragon stirred. Fire flared in her chest and an argument clawed at her throat. How could the matchmaker refuse their fair request?

The woman looked directly at Mei Ling, assessing her up and down like something to be purchased. Panic overtook her anger; her Dragon wings beat hard, urging her to take flight.

"What is the day of your birth?" the matchmaker demanded.

"No!" Mei Ling responded without thought.

Mah-ma looked worried. She stared at the woman, then at Fuchan.

Fuchan whispered, "November 1904."

"Dragon." The woman shook her head. "You must not reveal your actual birth date. He is expecting a Rabbit, so a Rabbit you must be. But otherwise you will do."

Her body rebelling, Mei Ling's knees gave way. She braced herself on Ahma's chair. She swallowed hard and shook her head.

The woman glared at Mei Ling and threatened, "If you do not trade identities with your sister, you will not be given another offer for marriage—nor will she. No matchmaker will work with your family again. Your fate and your sister's future require this of you."

Mei Ling looked at her family. Fuchan stared at the floor, defeat on his face. Mah-ma bit her lip and nodded to Mei Ling. Was that reassurance or encouragement? Either way, she was agreeing to this contract. Ahma whispered up to Mei Ling, her voice tight but definitive, "This is your destiny."

It hit Mei Ling with sudden certainty: each of them had anticipated this exchange. Her Dragon roared in protest.

She looked at her family, pain riddling each of their faces. But strong feelings did not change their situation; it was time for her to leave home. They each knew this day would come, just not today in this way.

Mei Ling took a deep breath to calm her Dragon. She would not add an emotional outburst to the pain.

Through the screeching in her mind she faintly heard the woman explain, "You have one hour to prepare. I will wait at the temple for you." Then the matchmaker rose and walked into the morning that Mei Ling had so recently welcomed in, unaware of the danger and disruption that it was springing upon her.

~

For once, Mei Ling was frozen. Her mouth could not form the jumbled words in her brain. How . . . ? What . . . ? *Now?!* Her eyes stung.

Mah-ma jumped into action, disappearing into their bedroom. Fuchan patted Mei Ling's shoulder as he shuffled by. Mei Ling gave in to gravity, her legs so weak it was a relief to collapse into the chair still warm from the woman who was destroying her life.

Ahma opened her hand, revealing a jumble of gold coins. Mei Ling gasped. She hadn't seen that much money for many years. Ceremoniously, Ahma slipped them into a small, flat pouch of fabric, lifted the hem of Mei Ling's skirt without saying a word, and started sewing the pouch into a fold of Mei Ling's dress with a threaded needle that seemed to appear out of nowhere.

"A wife obeys her husband, yes," Ahma instructed. "But a wise woman earns her own money and saves for the emergencies that a husband cannot see coming. Give him most of your earnings but hold back a portion. A mother protects her children—always." Ahma's voice cracked, sending a lightning bolt of sorrow through Mei Ling.

"In case he has no elders: Xinyi for your son; Jingyi for your daughter."

Mei Ling was confused, but then understanding took hold: her grandmother was naming her future children.

Tears pushed at the corners of Mei Ling's eyes. She was shamed by her public display of emotion but helpless against the force. This was all too much to take in. She wanted to protest, to find another path, but the certainty in her mother and grandmother pushed her along.

"Do you really believe I can find joy in children born so far from home?" Mei Ling asked, her voice tight.

Ahma replied, "For centuries women have borne the burden of leaving all that they love to begin a new life. You are stronger than most. There is no reason that you cannot make a harmonious life."

Her grandmother came close and gently cradled the sides of Mei Ling's face, her gnarled thumbs wiping at Mei Ling's tears. Ahma leaned over slowly and planted a kiss on the crown of her granddaughter's head. Mei Ling breathed in the feeling of her elder. Ahma tipped Mei Ling's head back to look into her face. Mei Ling resisted looking directly at her grandmother, afraid she would break down altogether. But Ahma did not let her hide. When they were looking eye-to-eye at one another, Ahma said in a hoarse voice, "And now I will tell you what my grandmother said to me the last time I saw her."

A wave of sorrow crashed over Mei Ling.

Ahma whispered, "Every time I see the moon, I shall send you a blessing, knowing the same moon will soon shine my blessing down upon you."

Mei Ling sucked in a jerky breath and nodded. She tried to smile but her cheeks were too tight. Her jaw was locked and would not form words. She hoped her grandmother could feel the unspeakable pain in her heart. Ahma nodded back, kissed her crown once again, and released her.

As soon as Ahma walked away, Fuchan shuffled up, a book in his hand.

Mei Ling was still reeling from her grandmother's words when he declared, "For you."

Mei Ling was confused. She thought this book had been sold with most of the others.

"I saved one for each child. *The Analects of Confucius*. Wisdom that will guide you in living a righteous life."

"Thank you, Fuchan." Mei Ling swallowed hard and bowed. "I will treasure it for always."

"Write when you are able. Please." He set paper, ink, and a pen on the table in front of her.

Mei Ling nodded.

Without a break, Mah-ma grabbed her hand and led Mei Ling into the kitchen. She must have been waiting for Fuchan to finish speaking with her. "You shall take my Quan Yin," she declared.

"What? No!" Mei Ling replied. This was her mother's most precious object.

"Yes," Mah-ma insisted. "We will trade. You will have mine, from my mother. I will have yours. When your sister leaves, we shall trade. She will have yours and I will have hers. By this we will all be connected . . . across the miles and hours." Mah-ma exhaled and then went on. "I never saw my mother again, but I carried her with me always."

Mei Ling nodded, her throat unbearably tight. Mah-ma's words of wisdom sounded calm and measured, but Mei Ling heard the emotion underneath.

"We do not know our fate. This may be a forever goodbye; it may only be for years. My love for you will never waver, however long or however far."

Mei Ling did not bother to wipe away the tears that streamed down her face. How could she possibly walk away from her family forever? Her mother and grandmother had done it. She'd heard them speak of it, but never imagined them this scared and frightened or young. In the stories they'd seemed so old. Had they felt like this?

Mah-ma coached, "It will seem impossible to take the first step. But on the second step, since you already did one, you know you can take another. Then another and another. Before long you will have walked into your new life. Do not believe you are betraying us by loving your new home," Mah-ma said, her voice quavering as her emotion broke through finally. "I—we—will celebrate your happiness. And do not hide your sorrows too deeply from us."

Mei Ling nodded, working to take in her mother's words, not just feel her emotion.

"I asked my husband to teach my daughters to read and write so we would know one another should we be parted."

Mah-ma unwrapped a bundle of cloth to reveal bright-green plant stalks.

"Two chrysanthemum," she said, her voice tight. "And two peony. May they take root in your new life, bearing you beauty and comfort for years to come."

Mei Ling sucked in her breath. These stalks descended from the plants her mother's mother had given to Mah-ma on the day she had left home. For decades their family drank chrysanthemum tea and enjoyed flowers in the spring from the mothers of these cuttings. Mei Ling took the stalks with a small bow, her hand shaking from emotion.

"Work hard, be kind, be humble—and you will live a harmonious life." Mah-ma pronounced the familiar refrain, the advice she'd given her daughters for as long as Mei Ling could remember.

Mah-ma led Mei Ling to her bedroom. A red silk skirt and tunic plus an exquisitely embroidered red jacket lay on the bed next to Jah Jeh. Mei Ling's lungs caught.

"Change into your wedding attire, and then say goodbye to your sister," Mah-ma said in a flat voice.

Mei Ling inhaled deeply. Her knees felt weak as she removed her plain black tunic and pants. The silk clothes were smooth and lovely against her skin, yet foreign, as if she were putting on a costume. Mah-ma helped her into the jacket, even fastening the frog enclosures like when Mei Ling was a child.

"You are ready." Mah-ma patted Mei Ling's shoulder. Tears glistened at the corner of her mother's eyes. Mei Ling didn't feel ready, but saying so wouldn't change anything.

She went to her sister's side and took Jah Jeh's hand in her own. It was limp and warm. Her face was still shiny and slack. Her unresponsive sister would awaken to a nightmare: her path taken by Mei Ling. It was hard to know how she would feel: perhaps a measure of relief along with a huge dose of fear and sorrow about her own uncertain future. Or righteously angry that Mei Ling had taken her dowry funds and her turn at a first marriage.

"I will think of you every day," Mei Ling whispered through a tight throat to the sleeping young woman. "Thank you for being my Jah Jeh."

Mei Ling squeezed her sister's hand and then let go.

The trunk sat on the dusty floor in the living room, no longer filled with Jah Jeh's belongings. Mei Ling felt ill seeing her own neatly folded clothes inside. Mah-ma placed the jade Quan Yin, wrapped tight in an embroidered silk cloth, followed by the paper, ink, and pen in the trunk. On top went the picture of the family—from before, when Dai Low and Mui Mui were still alive. The book and the cuttings were slipped down one side; her embroidery set was slid into the other edge. Then Mah-ma closed the lid on Mei Ling's life.

Mei Ling gestured to Dai Dai. Her brother walked to her with his head bowed down and his face hidden. She bent over and whispered into his ear, "I will think of you from across the ocean. Be an obedient and helpful son. Soon it will only be you to care for Fuchan and Mah-ma."

He gave a quick nod. She held out her fisted hand, turned it over, and slowly revealed a jade turtle.

She explained, "This was Dai Low's treasure. And now it is yours to remember him . . . and me." She swallowed hard. She wished she could give him a reassuring look, but she kept her eyes averted rather than let him see the distress in her soul.

Ahma walked to their family altar. Fuchan, Mah-ma, and Dai Dai joined her. Mei Ling took her place by her younger brother. They kowtowed in unison, each bending all the way to the ground, inhaling deeply, and then standing again. Three times in all. Mei Ling bit her lip hard to hold back the force of sorrow that pushed at her throat.

When they were done, she bowed low to Ahma and then Mah-ma, her eyes downcast. She could not possibly look directly at them; otherwise her emotions would increase the suffering of the day. Mei Ling paused at the threshold to take one last look at this house that would no longer be her home. Once she was married, she was supposed to give up her own ancestors out of loyalty to her husband's. But she vowed as she left that her devotion to her own family would never end.

~

Mei Ling followed her father and brother along the narrow muddy walkway between the houses. Fuchan and Dai Dai carried her trunk between them. Great Auntie stood in the doorway, baby Low Fun in her arms. The old woman used the girl's arm to wave goodbye. Smiling, she shouted, "Congratulations."

The woman's excitement for her was a sharp contrast to the dread inside Mei Ling. She looked around for other friendly faces but saw none. Apparently no one else cared to see her off.

Her home was in the fourth row from the street in their small ancestral village—seventeen dwellings in a neat square except for the single house in the fifth row. In just a few minutes they were at the compact dirt road. She looked to the left toward the temple. Down the road, a crowd of people surrounded the wagon. Her village *had* come out to wish her farewell.

They turned away from the gathering of people, to the right, toward the eastern exit of the settlement. Fuchan stopped before their village god to pay tribute by burning paper and incense. *May they be safe from all harm. May they be free from all suffering. May they know joy,* Mei Ling asked for her family, though she knew it was an impossible request even for a god.

They walked a hundred paces to the entrance to their village, to the wagon parked in the middle of the crowd in front of the temple. Sorrow pressed down on her heart with every step. She pinched the inside of her left arm hard, using the sudden pain to chase away her despair, a trick she'd used many times before to hide her feelings from the world.

The crowd parted. The familiar faces of her neighbors watched Mei Ling. Little girls bowed. Renshu, the boy too shy to speak with Jah Jeh, gaped at her. Blessings from aunties filled the air, but she couldn't discern who spoke them. She heard a shocked whisper echo through the crowd: *It is Mei Ling, not Yu Ling.* Someone patted her back. Many times she'd been on the other side of this particular ritual. She'd envied the young women who were being celebrated and cheered on, entirely unaware of their terror.

Her father and younger brother placed her trunk on the back of the wagon. A curtained palanquin, large enough for two, sat in the center of the wagon bed. A small stool waited for her weight.

Fuchan turned to Mei Ling. With a slight nod he indicated she should go with him into the temple. No one followed.

She stopped half a length behind her father in front of the altar. They knelt in unison and bowed all the way to the ground. Mei Ling exhaled deeply as her cheek hit the floor. *Surrender.* Her mother's familiar instruction echoed in her mind. At this moment it was comforting. They stood up and repeated their full kowtows two more times. Fuchan placed a food offering on the table before they returned outside.

She stopped at the palanquin, her legs frozen and resistant. Suddenly someone grabbed at her waist. She spun around, ready to strike the attacker. She halted her arm midmotion. It was Dai Dai, his face buried into her belly. She knelt. Wrapping her arms tight around him, she felt his small, precious body. She would miss so much of his life. Soon he would be the last child left in the household. Her heart couldn't lie about this loss; it swelled up in pain. She squeezed hard. Still unable to look directly at him, she stood, tousled his hair, and kissed the top of his head. Mei Ling turned away, parted the curtain, and ducked inside.

The matchmaker joined her inside the palanquin. The woman signaled and the wagon jerked forward. Mei Ling turned her head away to face the curtain, hiding her face from the woman who was bringing her so much pain. She could not bear to look outside, to watch her world grow small behind her. Mei Ling pinched her arm again, but her sorrow wouldn't be chased out. She switched to her calf, squeezing as hard as she could. Her body jolted at the sudden infliction. She'd achieved her goal; anger and alarm overtook her despair.

CHAPTER 3

Guangzhou
March 1923

The journey to Guangzhou would take six hours if all went well. Mei Ling gazed out the window at the familiar road. Travel in this direction had been a journey toward their *real* home, their modern house in a new neighborhood of Guangzhou. The village had been their ancestral home, worthy of visits for festivals and holidays, a return to simpler, backward living. As a young child she loved visits to the village, running through the fields, giving honor at the little temple, and playing with the animals. Over time she'd grown disdainful of the simple rural life and was mortified when they were forced to move there permanently.

They'd been fortunate to have a home in a village when the soldiers came. Mei Ling and Jah Jeh had assured one another it would only be a temporary move, that they would return to the city . . . their real lives. She might have fought harder to stay in Guangzhou had she known that life would lead her to this: marrying a Gam Saan Haak and sailing away to a foreign land.

The matchmaker interrupted her thoughts. "If we arrive when I expect, we will go directly to the church. You will walk between the chairs to the front, where you will stand for the entire ceremony. It will be very fast, so you won't tire. The minister will ask you each questions. You will agree. Then you will sign papers and it will be over. I will stay until then."

Mei Ling gave a single nod. Then she sat back and closed her eyes, hoping the woman would just leave her in silence. Hours later Mei Ling opened them when she heard noises from outside the palanquin. She peered out of the curtain.

Her heart leaped at the sight of this city, her city. Guangzhou—Canton to the Westerners—was buzzing around her. She was home, if only for a day.

~

Motorcars, rickshaws, and carts filled the packed-dirt street. Containers of water, oil, and nuts dangled from poles slung over the dark-brown shoulders of thin men. Some vendors weaved in and out of the traffic, hoping to make sales from drivers and passengers. Mothers with filthy babies sat on the ground with begging bowls. *May they be safe from all harm. May they be free from all suffering. May they know joy,* Mei Ling chanted to herself. That was a sight that Mei Ling didn't miss. No one in the ancestral village begged to eat.

They turned off the main street, and too soon they stopped in front of a simple building with the Christian symbol, the plain white cross, on the front. He was in there. Chinn Kai Li, the stranger destiny was tying her to. Mei Ling took in a shaky breath in a futile attempt to calm her heart that was beating so hard and fast that it hurt.

The matchmaker got out and whispered something Mei Ling couldn't hear to the driver. The man disappeared. The woman returned to Mei Ling with some fabric in her hands.

"You must wear this on your head, covering your face until the ceremony is over," she explained.

The old woman's swollen hands shook as she fastened the translucent white material on Mei Ling's dark hair and then pulled the bulk of the cloth forward over Mei Ling's eyes. Her body tensed reflexively against the assault of the fabric. Mei Ling closed her eyes, took a deep breath, and reminded herself that it was only temporary. She slid her hands up against the netting to pull it a few inches away from her face. The lightweight fabric was scratchy and rough. Looking straight downward, she could see clearly. She focused on the colors in her skirt and ignored the misty white shroud obstructing her vision.

The old woman climbed out again. Momentarily she reached through the curtain next to Mei Ling, offering a palm to assist her from the palanquin. Mei Ling ignored the hand and instead used the wooden side to steady herself. She followed the woman into the church. Using her small slice of clear vision, she trailed the woman's black shoes along the tiled aisle.

When the woman stopped, Mei Ling did too. Suddenly the matchmaker grabbed her right wrist and lifted her forearm up, placing Mei Ling's hand into a man's. Mei Ling nearly pulled away but stopped herself. Warm, moist fingers barely held her palm.

Mei Ling looked through the gauze to study his face. In this dim place it was hard to make him out clearly, but he was young, close to her age. That was a measure of solace. He was dressed in Western clothing, a merchant's suit. She couldn't read the expression on his face—perhaps he felt leery, or tired, or nervous.

The minister's words floated by Mei Ling. She struggled to understand the Westerner's Cantonese through his thick accent. He was asking her a question and wanted her to agree to something, along with Chinn Kai Li. Before long the robed man congratulated them loudly, declaring them man and wife. Without warning the veil was lifted.

Mei Ling looked at her new husband for an instant before averting her eyes. His smooth and round face confirmed that he was well-fed and didn't labor outside. Her first impression was that he might be handsome.

She felt Chinn Kai Li studying her face. Her heart pounded fiercely. He released her hand and turned away. She looked up slightly. He was standing to the side with a modern fountain pen in his hand. After he marked his name on the paper, he offered her the instrument.

The first words Mei Ling's husband spoke to her were a question: "You can write, correct?"

Mei Ling nodded.

"Only make an *X*," he told her. "Wong Lew She cannot write . . . couldn't write."

Mei Ling took the pen and finalized her marriage, hiding herself for the first time. Out of the corner of her eye, she saw her husband hand a pouch to the matchmaker. They bowed to one another.

And then the woman who had permanently altered her life left it forever.

~

Kai Li took a few steps toward the outer world. Mei Ling supposed she should follow him, but she hesitated, uncertain how far behind him she should walk. He paused, turned to face her, and motioned with his head without speaking. She stepped closer. One step, two, three. When she was less than a full pace away from him, he started walking again. They had much to work out, but it seemed he expected her close to his side—further confirmation that he was from a different world.

They walked along an unfamiliar street for several blocks. Thin men pulled rickshaws with well-dressed Chinese and White people. Lovely palanquins, carried by four men and balanced between two long poles, hid travelers. In her previous life Mei Ling had been carried in a palanquin on a few special occasions. And she often rode in rickshaws back then. Though they were walking now, perhaps her status as a merchant's wife would allow her to be carried around once again in San Francisco. Mei Ling got a chill when the familiar and haunting sound of a ship's horn floated up from the river.

Mah-ma loved that sound. She had rarely walked to the Pearl River, but commented on the beauty of the water whenever she heard the echo of a ship's horn. *It's all still here, Mah-ma,* Mei Ling telegraphed. She thought of Jah Jeh and wondered whether she was recovered and aware of her changed circumstance, but then realized it hadn't even been eight hours since she'd left her sister. Her fever wouldn't have broken yet.

Kai Li turned into a narrow alleyway. Mei Ling nearly missed the change in direction, but she rushed to keep up with her husband. This was an unfamiliar neighborhood, but the delicious smells in the alleyway were tantalizing. Mei Ling inhaled the fragrant scent of ginger and garlic sizzling in woks and smiled. Chinn Kai Li noticed and acknowledged her appreciation with a small nod and a smile of his own. Mei Ling flushed.

She was taken aback when Chinn Kai Li entered a dilapidated Western-style building. Mei Ling had imagined that a merchant would stay in finer accommodations. But she reminded herself that he was still young. At the beginning of his career a man was wise not to expend money frivolously. Ahma would approve.

They climbed five stories on worn stairs to the top floor. Chinn Kai Li opened the door to a dingy, windowless space. The room was in no better repair than the building.

A very young child sat alone on the bed. Mei Ling was startled but shouldn't have been. This must be his son, Bo, who wouldn't be three years old until August, according to the matchmaker. She looked for a caregiver, but there was none. He'd been left alone to fend for himself. Her impulse was to go to him, but instead she focused on her husband. He pointed out the stove and water basin that were so close as to be impossible to miss against the forward wall. Then he walked to the other side of the only bed to show her that her trunk was already here.

Kai Li bowed low enough to show honor but not subservience and left Mei Ling alone with the boy who was now her son.

~

Mei Ling took in a steadying breath and pushed down the insult that her husband had left without the courtesy of introductions. She did not know who was not worthy of that honor—the boy or herself. Perhaps both of them.

She wanted to dig through her trunk to confirm that her coins were safe but decided to greet the child instead. The little boy looked even more scared than she felt. His pudgy hand was clutched around something. She looked closer and saw two long brown ears poking out: a carved rabbit. She approached the bed and sat close, letting their bodies touch. His shoulder flinched, but he didn't turn away.

"I'm your new mother," Mei Ling said carefully, studying his narrow face for a reaction. He stared at the floor, his expression flat, unchanged.

Mei Ling probed, "What do you like to be called?" The boy's dark-brown eyes slid sideways to look at her without turning his head, but he didn't reply to her question.

"You can call me . . ." Mei Ling stopped, uncertain, her throat tightening. She didn't know what she was to this child. Her lungs pulled in tight. Suddenly this dingy room felt suffocating and small. She left the boy to open the door for fresh air. The stuffy hallway was barely an improvement. She leaned her head on the door jamb, overwhelmed and alone.

Out of the corner of her eye she saw a movement. She looked over. The boy was lying on the bed now, curled up in a ball, his back to her. Shame welled up in her. This little one was her responsibility. She owed it to him to be a good mother.

She exhaled, walked back to the bed, and squatted by the side, her head close to his.

"You may call me Mah-ma," she told him. "I'm your Mah-ma now."

He looked directly at her, his eyes intense and uncertain, and gave a tiny nod. She nodded back with a small smile despite the pit of doubt in her stomach. Mei Ling touched his back gently. He flinched but didn't pull away.

She smiled again, and said, "Hello, little rabbit. Do you have a name?"

Bo looked at his hand, then back at Mei Ling.

"May I pet Rabbit's ears?" Mei Ling asked.

The boy nodded, nearly imperceptibly. Mei Ling gently rubbed the figure in his hand. She smiled at Bo, but he was looking down. She sighed at her failure and stood up.

She explored the tiny kitchenette. A dented wok sat on a hot plate. Two bowls and two sets of chopsticks were stacked up neatly. The only food she could find was a small bag of rice. She craved tea, but had no means to make any.

A throat cleared behind her. She spun around to see Chinn Kai Li framed by the doorway, a bag in each hand. He crossed to the table where she stood and opened one bag. He unloaded tofu, bok choy, and black bean paste.

"I . . ." Instead of finishing his sentence, he raised a finger slightly. He opened the other bag and pulled out a bowl and a third set of chopsticks. Then he reached in and brought out a small sachet of tea. Peony. A tea of celebration. Wordlessly he set it on the table and turned away.

She was touched by the offering. He seemed to feel as uncertain as she did. Mei Ling looked at the simple foods on the table. She'd use them to do her best to make a meal for her new family.

~

She served her husband first and then the boy. When the child dropped a chopstick, she offered him one of her own. He stared at her outstretched hand, then reached for it tentatively. When his bowl was empty the little boy managed a surprisingly long sentence in his small voice: "Bo is pleased. Thank you."

Mei Ling smiled at him. "You are most welcome, son." And in that moment she felt pleased too.

But anxiety quickly returned. She was trepidatious about being a physical wife, and dread rose in anticipation of what was to come that night. While washing up after dinner and preparing for bed, Mei Ling felt her heart racing hard in her chest and her breathing growing shallow. She did her best to hide her anxious feelings and was grateful that Chinn Kai Li didn't expect conversation.

Mei Ling took Bo to queue up in the hall so he could relieve himself before going to bed. After a twenty-minute wait, they squeezed into the small space. It was disconcerting to be so intimate with a boy she had just met and yet comfortably familiar to care for a young child. When she was eight years old, Dai Dai was entrusted to her care soon after his red egg party a month after his birth. She doted on him, and then her precious younger sister, as much as her mother and her Jah Jeh did.

After finishing in the bathroom Mei Ling encouraged the boy to lie on the bed. She lay down next to him to tell him a story, just as her Mah-ma would when she was sick or especially frightened.

"Do you know the Rabbit Moon story?" Mei Ling asked. The boy looked at the wooden rabbit clutched in his hand.

"When the moon is big and round, we can see the rabbit. I will show you next time he is there," Mei Ling said. "Would you like to hear the story?"

Bo nodded without speaking.

Mei Ling told the story just as her mother recounted to her:

Every night Change, the goddess who lives on the moon, looks down on Earth to see how her animals and people are doing. She smiles to see them resting after a hard day's work. She winks at children as they fall asleep. She hovers over rivers and lakes, lighting the waves and the shore, helping animals to find their way home safely. Then she sails on to other lands to do the same for the children and animals that live there.

One night long ago, Change watched the Jade Emperor disguise himself as a starving old man to test the kindness of the animals in the forest.

He walked through the trees until he came to the clearing where Monkey, Fox, and Rabbit lived. When the creatures saw him, they looked up at him with bright, shining eyes.

"Good day, sir," Rabbit said. "How do you do?"

"Welcome to our forest," said Monkey, and Fox bowed low.

"Oh, friends," the Old Man said, leaning heavily on his walking stick. "I'm not doing well. I am old and poor, and I am very hungry. Do you think you could help me?"

"Of course we'll help," Monkey chattered.

"We always help our friends," Fox agreed.

"We'll fetch some food for you," Rabbit added, and without a moment's hesitation, the three ran off, each one in search of food to offer the poor beggar.

The Old Man sat down and leaned against a tree. Looking up into his sky, he smiled.

These are good animals, *he thought.* And I am curious to see who is most generous.

Before long Monkey returned, carrying an armload of fruit.

"Here you are," Monkey said. "The bananas and berries are delicious. And take these oranges too, and these pears. I hope you will enjoy my gift." He laid his fruit before the beggar.

"Thank you, my friend. You are kind," the beggar said. Before he had finished speaking, Fox raced into the clearing. He carried a fat, fresh fish between his teeth, and this he laid before the beggar with a bow.

"My friend," Fox said, "I offer you a fresh fish to ease your hunger. I hope this will satisfy you."

"You also are kind," said the Old Man. "I never knew how kind the forest animals were."

"Of course we are kind," Monkey said proudly.

"And we are skilled at finding food," Fox added.

Then all three sat waiting for Rabbit to return. Meanwhile, Rabbit dashed this way and that through the forest, but no matter how he tried, he only found grass for the beggar. He was disappointed in himself because he knew that a human's hunger would not be satisfied by grass. At long last he returned to the clearing.

"Friend," Monkey cried. "You have returned!"

"I have," Rabbit said sadly. "But I must ask you to do me a favor, dear friends. Please, Brother Monkey, will you gather firewood for me? And Brother Fox, with this firewood will you build a big fire?"

Monkey and Fox ran off at once to do as their friend asked, and the beggar sat quietly by, watching in wonder.

When the fire was blazing, Rabbit turned to the beggar. "I have nothing to offer you but myself," he said. "I'm going to jump into the fire, and when I'm roasted, please feast upon me. I cannot bear to see you go hungry."

Rabbit bent his knees, preparing to jump into the fire. In an instant, Chang'e flew down from the moon and scooped up Rabbit before he reached the flames.

"Don't be afraid," Chang'e said. "I am the moon goddess, and I have seen that you are the kindest and most generous animal of all. I will take you home with me, where you can help me watch over the children and the animals on Earth to make sure they are never harmed."

The goddess lifted Rabbit and carried him up to the moon. Monkey, Fox, and the false beggar watched in amazement and gratitude.

If you look carefully, when the moon is full and bright, you will see Rabbit living there in peace, watching over all of us. So you can sleep peacefully knowing that you are being kept safe.

Half asleep, Bo smiled with drowsy eyes at the end of the story.

"Roll over. I will rub your back," Mei Ling instructed.

He blinked at her, but then did as she said. Within moments he was asleep on the bed.

Mei Ling sighed in bittersweet satisfaction. All the tricks she'd learned to take care of her Dai Dai and Mui Mui were working on her new son. *May they be well.* She sent a blessing to the two little siblings who were lost to her—one by distance and the other by death.

She looked up to see Chinn Kai Li watching. He nodded, indicating his satisfaction. She gestured back, though all the confidence she felt with Bo melted away at the prospect of what was to come.

Since Bo was asleep on the bed, Mei Ling wondered if she might delay the rite of marriage her mother had told her and Jah Jeh about. She indicated that she could sleep on the floor, but Chinn Kai Li shook his head. Gently he scooped up the sleeping child and moved him to the ground.

It was time for Mei Ling to get into bed with her husband. She considered getting under the blanket just as she was, in her red wedding tunic and skirt, but fear of ruining them overtook her modesty. She dug through her trunk to find her sleeping gown. She bowed to her husband and went through the door to find the bathroom. Mei Ling exhaled hard once she was in the hallway.

Keeping the red silk off of the dirty floor was a challenge, but Mei Ling managed to change without sullying it. She returned to the small room and lay down on the bed. Chinn Kai Li left, presumably to wash up in the bathroom, returned a few moments later, and climbed next to her.

Chinn Kai Li pulled up her skirt until it was above her knees. She lay still, frozen with discomfort. He climbed over her, pushing her legs apart so he could fit between them. He buried his face in her neck, nuzzling her skin with his lips. She flinched at first contact, but when she relaxed it wasn't uncomfortable; in fact it was almost tender. Without thought her hands went to the back of his head. She petted his hair as if he were a child. Soft sounds came from him, and then he entered her suddenly. She tensed up and squelched a cry of pain. Her shoulders pulled up to her ears. He rocked back and forth for a few minutes and then shuddered. Collapsing, his body weighed down her right side. She thought it might be over.

He lay so still she wondered if he was harmed, but she could feel his warm breath against her skin and he was quiet, calm. Over the fabric of her gown, he petted her arm slowly. She felt a drop of moisture fall onto her shoulder. She couldn't tell if it was sweat or a tear. The idea of one repulsed her; the other raised tenderness.

He patted her cheek and then rolled away. It was over. She had done it. She'd imagined a kiss, like in the Western movies she'd seen, but otherwise it was fine. She was proud and relieved to have this rite of passage behind her.

She rolled to her side, her heart and her mind racing. Bo's soft sounds floated up from the ground. Mei Ling peered over the side of the bed. The little boy was curled up on the hard, dusty wood, his carved rabbit clutched in his hand. Kai Li watched her as she rose, picked up the child, and placed him in the middle of the bed; wordlessly he nodded his consent.

She lay back down, facing away from Kai Li and Bo. With nothing to distract her, the image of Jah Jeh alone and fevered in their room popped into her mind. Worry filled her heart, making it nearly unbearable to stay in bed, but she didn't want to disturb the quiet night. She forced herself to lie still and breathe deeply to calm her Dragon.

Mei Ling begged Quan Yin, *Please show mercy and compassion to my Jah Jeh and the others in my family.* She looked at the dirty walls that trapped her, wishing there was a window so she could see outside. Mei Ling consoled herself by imagining the world past this room. She conjured up the moon in her mind, picturing its light radiating down to her family in the village. And then she imagined the moon's blessing pouring down on this building, through these walls, onto her and this new, fragile family in Guangzhou. *May I learn to be a calm and yielding wife so that we may have a harmonious marriage and family.* She fell asleep with that petition in her mind.

CHAPTER 4

Guangzhou
March 1923

In a dream Mei Ling fell, hit the ground hard, and then startled awake. Disoriented, she lay still though her heart was beating fast. She felt the small warm body nestled against her back and remembered it wasn't Jah Jeh.

Quietly she rose from the bed. She studied Bo's face. His lips pulled up in the corners and his eyes moved side to side under his lids. She looked at Kai Li's mussed hair, his back to the boy who lay between them.

She prepared a simple breakfast and then pulled out her writing instruments to wait for her husband and son to awaken. She would use the quiet of the morning to update her family.

She sat at the worn wooden table and wrote home.

My dear Jah Jeh,

Were you relieved or angered when you realized that I took your place? Mei Ling longed to learn but didn't ask.

> Guangzhou remains as we remember it. Colorful costumed acrobats, enticing food vendors, and the bustle of movement fill the busy streets. The most notable change is the number of motorcars zooming around donkey carts, rickshaws, and palanquins.
>
> Your sister's marriage to Chinn Kai Li is complete. Three of us will leave Guangzhou today for a two- or three-day journey to Hong Kong by donkey cart. Our ship, the *Persia Maru*, is scheduled to sail on March 31.

I am frightened and miss you more than you can imagine, Mei Ling thought, and then wrote, knowing that Jah Jeh would read this letter to the entire family.

> I am following your wise words and doing what I must to make a harmonious family.

Before she finished her note, Kai Li sat up in bed. She rushed to his side, carrying his breakfast of tea and rice. He accepted it with a nod. She returned to finish her letter, hoping her husband did not mind that she was distracted, but she wanted to get it posted before they left Guangzhou so her family would be reassured as quickly as possible that she was well.

> Bo, your new nephew, is a quiet two-year-old. He is most polite and cooperative and has yet to make a demand of his new mother.

> My new home is called 8 Brooklyn Place in San Francisco. It has a lucky number and a lovely name.

We will not arrive for nearly two months, but I await your news.

Please honor our parents and Ahma and give Dai Dai a hug on your younger sister's behalf.

Your devoted sister, Mei Ling

As she signed her name, Kai Li set something down on the table next to her.

"For you to study," her husband said.

Flooded by the reminder she was a paper wife, Mei Ling leafed through papers tied together with string in a makeshift book. Intricate details about a family and a village filled the eight pages. A map showed the layout of the village with one house circled. That house had its own page, labeled in great detail with notes, including one that said *mention the skylights*.

Mei Ling looked at Kai Li, an unspoken question on her face.

"When you are on Angel Island they will ask you many, many questions. Your answers must match the information in this book or they won't let you land in San Francisco."

"This is your ancestral village?" Mei Ling asked.

A wistful look crossed his face. He must miss his Chinese home.

"Can we visit before we depart?" she asked.

"We have no time." He shook his head as if to clear his thoughts. "If you study, we will have success. Do you understand? It is very important. They don't want us and will do what they can to trick you so they can turn you back. You *must* study."

Mei Ling's heart constricted as she was reminded that the United States was not a friend to the Chinese, and she was surrendering her life to that place . . . and this man.

He continued, "This book contains the information the inspectors are looking for. It doesn't matter what is true. It only needs to match this. The Americans keep records on me each time I come and go. Each time my relatives came and went—they kept a report.

"If we explain to them that things have changed, that the temple has moved, that we no longer live in the village, they won't let me come back home, so we just tell them what they want to be true."

Home. A slight chill ran across her arms. California was her husband's home. Not China.

Kai Li placed another paper on the table. Two pictures in the upper left-hand corner stared up at her from a paper written in English. Kai Li's familiar face was on the right. A lovely young woman gazed out from the photograph on the left. Mei Ling's heart lurched.

"This is you now," her husband said. "Wong Lew She."

"Your wife?" Mei Ling asked. *First wife,* she corrected herself in her head. *My paper self.*

Kai Li nodded. He stared, lost in thought, then sighed.

"They will believe I am this woman?" Mei Ling said, doubt filling her voice.

"They have believed less credible exchanges," he replied.

"But she is so beautiful, and I am so plain," Mei Ling countered.

Kai Li stared at her. Shame flooded into her chest, and she felt heat in her cheeks. She hadn't meant to have this conversation.

"Not so plain," he answered. "They will easily believe *this* story—if you study."

"Will they ask me about her?" she asked.

"Yes."

"You will teach me? So I can tell them?"

He pointed. "The book will tell you what you need to say. Even about her."

Bo was suddenly by her side. He must have heard them talking. She looked at him as he stared at the image on the paper, his face blank.

"Mah-ma," he said in a small, quiet voice.

Mei Ling nodded, her heart twisting in compassion. He reached his hand out and stroked the picture with his small brown finger.

"This is your Mah-ma now," Kai Li said, not unkindly, but as a simple truth.

The little boy looked at Mei Ling, no expression on his face. She smiled just a little, hoping to reassure him. He blinked a few times and then looked away.

"We must be ready to leave. The cart will be here soon," Kai Li instructed.

Mei Ling nodded. She picked up her new identity and packed it into her trunk.

~

Mei Ling and Bo stood by the cart as Kai Li and the driver marched up and down the stairs, carrying the two trunks to the street. Bo didn't have one of his own, so his belongings were tucked in with Mei Ling's. A dusty black cushion sat on the wooden bed of the cart, but there were no curtains for privacy. Mei Ling reached her hands down, gesturing to Bo an offer to pick him up. The boy didn't raise his arms in response to her wordless invitation. She hesitated to pick him up if he wasn't comfortable with it. Before she took action, Kai Li grabbed the boy from behind and swung him into the wagon. Bo didn't react, but simply stood at the edge of the wagon staring forward.

Mei Ling looked for a stool or stairs but didn't see any way for her to join the boy. She looked at Kai Li, uncertain and afraid of appearing demanding.

"I am sorry." Her husband looked pained. Then he knelt on the ground with one leg bent forward. He gestured to his knee, encouraging her to use it as a step stool.

"I cannot," Mei Ling said.

Kai Li nodded emphatically. "Please."

Mei Ling was touched but also embarrassed. What type of man had she married? Her father would never have knelt down to offer his leg as a stool. But he was a scholar, not a merchant. Merchants were practical and resourceful.

Mei Ling nodded a shy consent and slipped off her shoe. She placed her bare foot on Kai Li's leg. She grabbed his outstretched hand and stepped up beside Bo. Kai Li gave her hand a little squeeze before he let go.

Her husband climbed to the front of the wagon with the driver, leaving her and Bo to make themselves as comfortable as possible on the thin cushions in the back. Before the upheaval caused by the warlords, she would have balked at traveling by donkey cart, but there was so much she did now that had been previously abhorrent.

They turned the corner and were surrounded by the usual cacophony and faces that filled the main road. Mei Ling spied a troop of acrobats in a public square. She tapped Bo and pointed, but he couldn't see over the edge of the wagon. She pulled him onto her lap and pointed again.

"Acrobats have come to wish us farewell," she told him.

He stared and then clapped in delight at the contortions. He twisted around to smile at her. She smiled back. Perhaps he was warming up to her. Traffic was so slow they had time to see a seven-person pyramid climb high over their heads before the acrobats disappeared from sight.

A pit formed in Mei Ling's belly as they drove through her old neighborhood. Her market, her temple, her streets were unchanged since they'd fled. She peered down her alleyway hoping for a glimpse of her former home, but she couldn't see it. Perhaps it had been burned and was gone forever. Perhaps it still stood and was occupied by another family.

Girls in school clothes, laughing and holding hands, walked by. In a dream from long ago, she was so carefree. Mei Ling had loved school and all that went with it: her teachers, friends, and learning. She hadn't appreciated it enough at the time, taking for granted that her life would always be so simple . . . and abundant.

Too soon they were at the southern gate, a border she'd been up to many times but had never passed through. Her heart lurched as they drove through, the wagon taking her away from her beloved Guangzhou. She squeezed the child on her lap, grateful for the comfort of companionship. A single tear slid down her cheek, but she didn't think anyone could see it, so she didn't wipe it away.

~

The multiday journey between home and the port city was tiring, though uneventful. Mei Ling grew stiff from the wagon and sore from sharing a strange bed. She passed the time learning details about her new husband from the book. Unfortunately it didn't answer her most burning question: What happened to Bo's first mother? She wouldn't solve the mystery in these pages, since her absence was not part of the official story. Mei Ling didn't ask, and Kai Li did not volunteer the information.

She and Kai Li hardly spoke to one another, but she didn't expect they would. They were finding a comfortable rhythm, each taking care of their own roles—just as her parents had.

Mei Ling missed Jah Jeh, her daily companion she shared her thoughts with. Each day she added to an ongoing letter to her sister, reporting the events of the journey but withholding the truth about her painful feelings. She was unwilling to burden her family with her fears—especially her sister who might be ill or angry, or both.

Hong Kong seemed similar to and yet very different from Guangzhou. The fight with the Nationalists had forced the Western corporations to move the center of their import and export activities south from Guangzhou to Hong Kong. The Western dominance in Hong Kong glared out of the architecture of new buildings and the smooth paved streets that made travel so easy. The streets were crowded but orderly, with people mostly dressed in Western clothing.

The wagon dropped them off at another windowless room near the harbor. Kai Li greeted the owner as if they were old friends. Mei Ling watched him chat about his journey to Guangzhou and was pleased that he introduced her and Bo to the man, though her heartbeat quickened to hear her false name. There was no kitchen to cook in or food service in this rooming house, so they walked to the harbor for their evening meal.

"It's beautiful," Mei Ling exclaimed when she saw the water.

Sampans, small boats, floated on the harbor; beyond them was the shifting open water. The cool breeze on her face felt like a blessing from the gods. She smiled at Bo, who was beaming, delighted by the seabirds darting through the air. Mei Ling could watch this scene for hours and never tire of its constant movement and shifting colors.

Kai Li pointed to a large ship in the port.

"Our ship, the *Persia Maru*, will be like that one, though ours will fly a Japanese flag."

Mei Ling studied the enormous vessel. It was larger than a building, holding more people than her entire village. Huge ropes secured it to the moorings, and men scurried on and off carrying goods in large baskets. Some baskets were so heavy that two men carried them suspended between two poles. In three days she would leave China in a floating city like that, a thought that was mostly terrifying but a little exciting too.

~

The next morning Kai Li brought them to a photography studio. He didn't give an explanation, but she could sense he felt some urgency to have a picture of the three of them together.

An assistant brought them to a room filled with ready-made clothes, the Western and Chinese outfits segregated from one another.

"Select what you like. Size is of no concern; we can make anything look like it fits," the little bald man said and then left them alone.

Mei Ling followed Kai Li to the Chinese side. He slid individual tunics across the pole one by one. They were clumped by style and color into five or six coordinated outfits in a large range of sizes. He stopped when he got to bright-red silk with embroidery and detailing exquisite enough for nobles. He looked at her, a question in his eyes. Did he want to buy these? She had never worn anything so beautiful in her life. She crossed to him, fingering the material, trying to read his mind.

"It is lovely," she said, offering hesitant consent for something she didn't know if he could afford.

Kai Li nodded and then crossed to the Western clothes. He slid through their complicated outfits until he came to a set that met his approval. Without asking her opinion, he returned to find the assistant.

The man removed the largest red silk tunic and assisted Kai Li into it right over his clothes. He adjusted the top using pins and the pants using rope until, from the front, it looked like it was tailored to Kai Li. Discomfort flooded through Mei Ling when the assistant turned his attention to her, obviously sizing her up with his eyes. While the matching red garment hung on the pole, he pinned and adjusted it. With a flourish he indicated that she should put it on. She was grateful he didn't attempt to touch her, but she felt self-conscious as the two men watched her button the long tunic. The assistant looked self-satisfied that it appeared to be a perfect fit from the front, despite the folds of extra fabric in the back.

Fitting Bo wasn't so easy. He screamed when the man tried to touch him. With a jerk of his head, Kai Li directed her to intervene.

She took the tunic and pants from the man and knelt down in front of Bo.

"You wear this and we will all match, see?" Mei Ling explained. Then she pulled his hands up and slid the small tunic over his head. He didn't resist. She turned him around, encircled him with her arms, and held out the pants. Using her to balance, he stepped into each long leg.

"Good boy," she whispered into his ear. The pant legs hung so long that she feared he would stumble if he tried to walk. Rather than risk more tears, she scooped him up. Kai Li nodded his approval, and they went into the room with the camera.

The photographer posed them in a row, but after looking through his lens, he had Bo stand on a stool. The boy perched between them, one hand clutching his little brown rabbit and the other resting on Mei Ling's arm for balance. The man bent behind the camera and directed them to hold still. Mei Ling steeled herself for a long wait, but the man straightened up almost immediately. The process had improved immensely in the five years since she had last posed for a photo.

The photographer removed a large glass plate and replaced it with another. After one more exposure in these outfits, they exchanged their clothes for the Western costumes Kai Li had picked out. This time they posed close to one another on a Western-style couch, with Bo sitting on his father's lap.

The man took one last shot of Bo's face by itself, and then they were finished.

"Return tomorrow," the man said. "After noon they will be ready." He quoted a price for one of each and indicated that a second of each would be at a much-reduced price.

Mei Ling watched Kai Li struggle with the decision.

"Would you like one for your family?" he asked.

"Yes, please," Mei Ling said. "They should be much relieved to see the face of their new son and grandson."

He nodded and held up two fingers to the salesman.

"Thank you!" she said, joy flooding into her heart, grateful to give her family this not-so-small connection. "And your family?" she asked.

"There is no one," Kai Li replied.

The book said otherwise, but Mei Ling didn't pry further. Perhaps she had misunderstood.

CHAPTER 5

Hong Kong
March 1923

Kai Li escorted them back to their room and then left without explanation. Mei Ling didn't demand he give her an account of his plans, but it was disconcerting. He returned a few hours later with bags of goods, one of which contained a woman's skirt, blouse, and hat in Western style as well as a boy's outfit of black knickers and a double-breasted striped shirt.

"Tomorrow we will go to the United States consulate for travel papers. I hope these will fit," Kai Li said.

Mei Ling held up the short dark skirt. It wasn't nearly so fine as the costume at the photographer's and had obviously been worn by some other woman. Had this been his first wife's? If not, where did he get it? Bo didn't register recognition at the skirt or the white cotton blouse with mother-of-pearl buttons. The clothes were large, perhaps made for a White woman originally, but she could alter them to fit her well enough.

She gestured to Bo to come close. He balked. Kai Li loudly tsked his disapproval.

"Was he like this before . . ." She stumbled over the question. "Before his mother died?"

"I don't know," Kai Li replied.

"Has it been some time since you've seen him?" Mei Ling asked.

"The day I met you was the same day I met him," he replied.

Mei Ling's heart lurched for Kai Li and for Bo. She kept her face composed and only nodded slowly.

"When did she . . . ?" Mei Ling couldn't find a respectful end to her question.

"March 23," Kai Li said without emotion.

"Last week? Or last year?"

"Last week."

Mei Ling sucked in her breath. The matchmaker had said his first wife had died recently, but she didn't realize it had only been a few days. Bo's reticence and Kai Li's rush to remarry were more understandable.

His face grew stony, signaling he was finished answering her questions. "Tomorrow, wear your hair as she did in the picture."

And then he left again, leaving Mei Ling alone with Bo. She pulled out the book to get answers. Her husband and Wong Lew She were married in October 1919; the bride was only sixteen years old. Kai Li had returned to California eight weeks after their marriage. Bo had been born months later, long after Kai Li had left China. Mei Ling committed the dates and locations of these events to her memory, aware that her future depended on memorizing these facts. There was so much that she had to learn . . . and pretend to be.

When Kai Li returned late in the night, he smelled of alcohol and cigarettes. She felt a measure of sympathy for him, imagining the confusion he felt from the sudden changes in his life, but nevertheless she was repulsed and disturbed by his condition. She pretended to be asleep when the near-stranger climbed into her bed.

~

Kai Li was obviously nervous as they prepared for the day. He washed himself carefully and put on the same Western suit and tie that he had worn for the wedding. He nodded his approval when she was dressed with her hair pulled back in a low bun like Wong Lew She's hair in the picture. Mei Ling felt self-conscious as they stepped outside. This short skirt showed too much of her legs to the world. Even with the stockings that American women were so fond of, she felt overly exposed.

First they stopped at the photography studio for the photos. They needed the one of Bo for his travel certificate from the US consulate.

"You look like real Americans," the photographer exclaimed, impressed by their Western clothing. Kai Li shook his hand rather than bowing when they departed for the consulate.

Mei Ling hoped she wouldn't need to speak while they were with the Americans. Her throat was so tight from nerves that she didn't believe she possibly could. The building on Ice House Street was intimidating from the outside with its columns and arches.

A young White woman with those strange blue eyes and straw-colored hair sat alone at a desk.

"--- - ---- ---?" she spoke in English.

"-- --- ---- -- --- - ---- --- --- ---, Bo," Kai Li replied. Stunned, Mei Ling stared at her husband. His English was perfect as far as she could tell. The book said he'd moved to the United States when he was sixteen. He must be very intelligent to learn so much in six years. She prayed she would do the same. Many Chinese never mastered English, even after years of living in California.

The woman looked at her and asked, "--- --- --------- - ---?"

Mei Ling stared at her in incomprehension.

"--- ---- ------ ---------," Kai Li said.

The woman asked again, "You are traveling too?"

Shocked at the flawless Cantonese to come out of this White woman's mouth, Mei Ling only managed to nod in answer.

The woman smiled at Mei Ling's surprise.

"I've lived here most of my life," the woman explained, offering unexpectedly personal information. Likely she was the child of missionaries or an exporter. In Guangzhou, Mei Ling had encountered people like her and had felt pity for them, knowing they didn't really belong in China. Now she was going to be one of them—a foreigner living in a new land.

The woman handed Kai Li a piece of paper, saying something to him in English. He walked to the chairs against the wall, sat down, and filled in the paper. She followed him with Bo in tow. She watched the pen move, recognized some of the alphabet, but couldn't make meaning out of anything he wrote except the numbers, which she'd learned from bank notes.

After he was finished they waited until a large White man with a red face and those strange light eyes came for them. Mei Ling's heart pounded hard in her chest as they entered his office.

She averted her gaze while the two men spoke back and forth in English. The application for Bo sat on the desk between them. Kai Li sounded meek as a mouse. The White man was like a growling dog.

"---- --- ---- --- ----, Wong Lew She," the impatient man said, anger in his voice.

He was speaking to her! Mei Ling startled to attention.

"I . . ." She was unable to stammer out any more.

"--- ---- ----- -------," Kai Li explained to him.

The man rose suddenly. He left and returned with the perky woman from the front desk.

"---- --- ---- --- ----," the man said.

"When was your son born?" the woman asked kindly.

Mei Ling froze. She looked at Bo, searching her mind for the answer.

"Bo?" she asked the woman.

"He is your son, correct?" the woman asked, then she whispered, "He likes to make people nervous."

"In Western dates?" Mei Ling asked, gaining herself some time. Her mind had gone blank; though she'd read his birth date just the night before, she could only remember that he was a Monkey.

The woman nodded. Slyly, Mei Ling glanced at the paper on the desk; a few dates jumped out at her. She recognized one.

"August 20, 1920."

Out of the corner of her eye she saw a slip of a smile tug up the edge of Kai Li's lips. The White man nodded. He said something and the woman left again. After a few more questions, the large man filled out an affidavit, attaching Bo's picture to it and squeezing it between an engraving stamp, and finally signing it with a silver fountain pen. He handed it to Kai Li, and they shook hands before they departed.

Once outside, Kai Li turned uphill. Mei Ling and Bo followed without question. He walked for ten minutes or so until he came to a lush green garden with a path to a wide stone staircase. Kai Li forged ahead; Mei Ling hesitated, afraid they were unwelcome on these grounds.

Pausing on the stairs when he realized he was alone, Kai Li explained, "This is a park. We may enter."

He continued, and she had no choice but to trail after him. There were so many stairs she had no breath by the time they came to a plateau with a giant fountain that shot water into the air. The liquid fell down to a large basin and then tumbled over the edge into an even larger basin of three interlocking circles. Bo skipped to the edge of the fountain and watched the excitement up close. Mei Ling joined him, going so far as to dip her hand in the cool water. She felt Kai Li's eyes on her. She turned to look at him. He pointed, and she stood to see what he wanted to show her.

She gasped at the spectacular view, unlike anything she had ever seen before. Perched high above the land she took in the bustling city and the busy harbor below. Past the harbor, the Pacific Ocean sparkled in the sun as far as she could see. It looked as if it went on forever, past the horizon. It was beautiful and terrifying.

Four weeks of sailing would bring them to San Francisco, the other side of the world. She was uncertain about being in the midst of the water with no land in sight for so long, but was also exhilarated to imagine how it might feel to be entirely surrounded by so much beauty.

She smiled at Kai Li, and for once he beamed back fully, not just a hint of a smile. As he looked straight at her with his dark eyes, she could imagine that he was pleased. She'd passed a big test today, not perfectly, but she'd put on the strange costume and found the answer to the question as if she were Kai Li's real wife and Bo's actual mother. She looked down at him, her new son. He watched a bird sail by and then turned back to splash in the water.

"San Francisco has hills and a bay. Perhaps you will enjoy it there too," Kai Li said.

Mei Ling felt her heart loosen. In that moment, she believed she might enjoy a life in San Francisco with this man and this boy. Kai Li was being kind, treating her like a genuine wife, not a paper one. She felt a little bit less like a fraud and had the beginnings of hope that they could become a harmonious family.

~

In their short time there, Mei Ling had grown fond of Hong Kong. The ocean breeze made everything feel fresh, and the birds were a constant source of entertainment. Eating at restaurants was an enjoyable activity that had been an extremely rare treat in her family, but without a kitchen she and her new family had eaten much of their food out in Hong Kong. Once again she was sorry to be leaving.

It had only been one week since she first opened the door to the matchmaker, but it felt like months had passed. Mei Ling stared at the two pictures on the small table in front of her, choosing which one to mail to the village before they left China. The faces of her new family stared at her. In one she was foreign; in the other Chinese. Would her family recognize her in these clothes? Mei Ling finally settled on sending the Western picture so her family could see what she hoped to become.

~

She felt slightly less self-conscious the second day of wearing the strange skirt in public. Two workers carrying their trunks followed them as they walked to the ship. On the way they stopped at the market for supplies for the long journey. Kai Li assured her there was plenty of food on the boat, but it was not always appetizing. She was glad that he was looking out for them.

The *Persia Maru* seemed large from a distance, and it felt unbelievably enormous as they approached it. Mei Ling felt like an ant waiting to join a colony as they stood in a long line to board. Afraid of losing Bo in all the activity, she held his hand tightly. Normally she would bind him to her body, but it didn't seem fitting in Western clothes. He pulled at her arm, wanting to get to the edge to see the water below. Kai Li picked him up and swung him onto his shoulders, a vantage point that pleased Bo.

Passengers hung over the railing, watching the activity below. Many kinds of faces peered down. Skin and hair went from light to dark, and the clothing was equally diverse. It was strange to see different kinds of people standing packed close together. In Guangzhou, Mei Ling had seen Americans, Hindoos, Russians, Mohammedans, and Filipinos, but they were each in their own communities and rarely mingled with one other. Once they were off the boat in San

Francisco, she expected all these different kinds of people would go their separate ways.

Her nerves were high as they got closer to the front of the line. A White man in a sailor uniform checked for tickets and identification for all of the passengers. Kai Li said he was confident that she looked enough like Wong Lew She to easily pass, but he seemed equally anxious, so she didn't believe his words.

As they inched their way closer to the front, an argument broke out ahead of them. A man yelled in Cantonese at the ticket taker. Mei Ling's heart sped up at the disturbance. Kai Li swung Bo off of his shoulders and handed him to her.

He walked to the front of the line and started speaking to the two men, speaking English as well as Cantonese. She couldn't understand them but watched the Chinese man find a paper in his bag and hand it to the ticket taker. The ticket taker looked it over, nodded, and then handed it back.

The Chinese man bowed to Kai Li, who bowed back.

The White man shook Kai Li's hand and said, "------ ----."

Kai Li returned to her side. When they got to the front of the line, the White man recognized Kai Li and waved aside their papers, taking only a portion of their tickets. He smiled at Bo and said, "---- --- ------, Wong Lew She."

Mei Ling bowed in thanks and boarded the ship, relieved that she'd made it past another guardian. Kai Li walked in the direction the man had pointed. At the back of the boat were two staircases; he stopped between them to show another attendant their tickets.

The man said, "--- --- -- --- ----; ----- -- --- -----."

Kai Li sighed heavily and looked pained when he translated, "Men are to the left and women and children to the right. We cannot stay together, but I will see you when we are allowed to walk on the deck."

His head was bent over in shame as he handed her two slips of paper. He bowed his goodbye and disappeared down the staircase, abandoning her with Bo.

Her Dragon woke up, furious. Her husband had been aware of their travel accommodations. Basic kindness would demand that he should have warned her about this separation.

Shocked and confused, she looked around as if she would find another path. The indifferent White official studied her, watching for a reaction. Mei Ling wasn't going to reveal her distress to this man. She took a deep breath, picked up Bo, and walked into the bowels of the *Persia Maru*.

CHAPTER 6

***The* Persia Maru**
April 1923

She stood at the doorway, wary and disgusted; nausea pressed at the back of her throat. She pressed her hand over her nose to block the stench. The hold was far worse than any place she had ever experienced. Dark, hot, and loud, the large room contained row upon row of wooden bunk beds. The stale air in this windowless space reeked. These seemed like quarters for peasants, not a merchant's family. She remembered the look of shame on Kai Li's face and understood this wasn't a mistake; she and Bo would be sleeping here for a month.

For now, she had no means to change her situation. Somehow she would survive these unpleasant conditions as they sailed across the ocean, but she was left with the unsettling suspicion that Kai Li was a less-successful merchant than the matchmaker had implied.

Loud laughter filled her ear and then bodies pushed roughly past.

"Water buffalo," one woman whispered loudly to her companion. More laughter as they headed into the rows of beds. Her cheeks went hot at the insult.

"They are not worthy of your calm," another woman shouted from her bed; then she motioned for Mei Ling to come to her.

The woman took the papers from Mei Ling's hands, read them, and then gestured. "Those your beds," she said, pointing to a top and bottom bunk that were thankfully against the wall. A measure of relief washed over Mei Ling when she spied her trunk on the floor.

She resisted the urge to collapse onto the filthy mattress and instead opened her luggage. Mei Ling made up a cozy nest on the lower bunk as best as she could with their bedding. Then she allowed herself to sink down onto the mattress and surrender to despair. Bo climbed up next to her. She patted his back, comforting both of them with that human connection. He was her only companion now.

Tears pushing against her eyes, she dug out her mother's jade Quan Yin. She unwrapped the precious goddess and rubbed her kind face. *Please watch over us and give me strength to make it through these unpleasant circumstances.*

~

She woke to the sound of children's laughter. *Bo!* Mei Ling bolted upright, her heart racing. How could she have let herself fall asleep while they were in this squalid place surrounded by strangers?

But he was on the bed right next to her, not only safe but giggling with a little Chinese girl. Mei Ling had never seen a grin on his face, let alone heard laughter emanating from his small body. She smiled.

"She's awake," the girl leaned over and whispered into Bo's ear. She looked to be about five years old, with sparkling eyes. Her brown hair, bobbed at her shoulders, poked around her head like a haystack; it hadn't been combed smooth in a very long time. The skin on her knees showed through holes of raggedy pants.

Bo's head whipped around; he looked at Mei Ling and patted her arm in greeting, then turned back to the little girl for more entertainment. The girl put her head down, then held still. Mei Ling feared she had ruined their game. She started to reassure the child it was all right to play when the girl suddenly raised her head and roared like a dragon. Bo smiled and nodded, encouraging the girl to continue. She bowed her head once again, froze, and then sprang another animal on Bo. He smiled and clapped as she made her way through the zodiac. The girl's monkey imitation elicited the greatest delight from Mei Ling's little Monkey. *Thank you.* Mei Ling silently sent appreciation to Quan Yin for sending this girl to them.

"That's his favorite!" the child said authoritatively. How long had they been playing?

"He is a Monkey!" Mei Ling explained.

"I'm a Dragon!" the girl said. Unless she was born in February, that made her six years old. "What about you?"

Dragon too! Mei Ling's mind yelled. Out loud she said, "Rabbit."

"Is that why he has that?" The girl pointed to the carved figure clutched in Bo's hand.

Mei Ling drew her lips up in a tight smile. She started to tell the little girl that it was from his first mother, but she remembered the need to hide their history and just gave a quick nod.

A sudden jolt startled the three of them.

"We're moving!" a woman's voice shouted.

Bodies streamed toward the door to the stairs. The little girl joined the crowd. Bo started to follow her, then turned back to look at Mei Ling. It was touching, and unsettling, to have a child looking to her for guidance.

Mui Mui's still face, after she had taken her last breath, flashed into Mei Ling's mind. She pushed it aside, unwilling to let herself be swallowed by sorrow.

Like this girl, when Mei Ling was young she had turned everything into a game for Dai Dai and Mui Mui. She and Jah Jeh had been responsible for them except when they were in school. She'd been so innocent back then, before she understood all that could go wrong in a life.

Mei Ling stood up and led Bo by the hand. When the crush of people became too much for his little body, she carried him in her arms.

They emerged to a night sky filled with stars. How long had she slept? There had been no sense of time passing in the darkened chamber. They walked until they found an opening by the railing. Mei Ling held Bo tight, afraid of losing him to the water. She felt a gentle hand on her leg. The little girl had found them again. She pointed to a bird and squawked. Bo leaned out of her arms to get to the girl. Mei Ling hesitated to put him down.

"I'll hold his hand," the girl said. She looked so earnest and hopeful that Mei Ling didn't want to disappoint her. She placed him on the ground with the admonition to stay close. True to her word, the little girl held fast to his hand.

Mei Ling looked for the girl's adult companion but saw no one who appeared to be watching over her. All eyes were on the glittering city they were sailing away from. Mei Ling's heart constricted. *Farewell, China.* She really was leaving her homeland, perhaps forever.

A partial moon, too small to show the Rabbit, hung over the city, invoking Ahma's parting words. Mei Ling wondered whether her grandmother could possibly be looking at this moon at this very moment. She sent a blessing to the bright orb. Knowing that it was shining down on the village made it more bittersweet.

Unless she was very ill, Jah Jeh was likely recovered by now. Was she relieved or dismayed to learn that Mei Ling had stolen her life? It would be weeks or even months until Mei Ling would know. She longed to read a letter from her sister with assurances of her well-being and forgiveness, but Mei Ling couldn't be certain that Jah Jeh would actually express her true feelings. Just as Mei Ling wanted to protect her family, Jah Jeh would want to shield her from unpleasantness.

"Bah-ba!" Bo's sweet voice broke into her self-indulgent thoughts. Kai Li had found them. He gave her a small nod and then looked out at the harbor, their son, and the little girl standing between them. Irritation at being abandoned simmered below her surface, but Mei Ling was glad he had sought them out to share this moment. She reminded herself that the fare was likely a large price to pay, even for a merchant. He must have saved for years for their passage, even in the dank quarters below.

~

When the harbor was out of sight, Mei Ling asked the little girl, "Where is your family?"

The girl pointed up to the second-class deck.

"My uncle is there," she said, waving toward the cluster of people at the railing overhead.

Mei Ling quickly scanned the group until she saw a man in a gray suit with a vest waving toward them.

"See him?" the girl asked.

Mei Ling did. "Is anyone with you downstairs?"

The little girl's face lost its animation. She shook her head, her loose hair swirling around her face. "He came alone to the orphanage."

Sympathy welled up in Mei Ling.

"Fuchan, Ahma, and my GiGi turned into ghosts in the winter. I didn't go with them, so Uncle is taking me to have a new life in America."

Typhoid, poverty, the plague, the flu, fires. There were so many ways that whole families perished and children became orphans.

"We are also going to America to have a new life," Mei Ling told her. "What's your name?"

"Siew," the girl replied.

Like Bo, one simple name for a child with a complicated story.

~

When the city was entirely out of sight, they returned below deck with Siew. Kai Li looked sorrowful as they parted at the top of the stairs.

"I hope to see you soon," he said.

Mei Ling smiled, touched at his words and yet still irritated that he hadn't warned her about the conditions on the boat.

Siew rejected Mei Ling's offer to sleep above them on the top bunk. Instead she returned to her own bed a few rows away. Like most orphans, the child was very independent and brave. So many children had to grow up too quickly.

It wasn't surprising that the bathroom facilities were cramped and unpleasant; Mei Ling got through with the reminder that *This is only temporary. In a few weeks I will be in our new home in San Francisco*. Without light by her bed she was unable to write to Jah Jeh, but she composed a letter in her heart and asked the gods to *Protect my family*. She wondered whether she would have difficulty falling asleep, but the motion of the boat was so soothing that soon she was dreaming with Bo cuddled up next to her.

A disturbing sound from the floor woke her in the night. She imagined a rat and shuddered to think of one so near. Mei Ling pulled up the covers, depriving the creature transportation to her bed, and looked over the edge. A petite arm protruded from underneath their bunk. Alarmed, Mei Ling cautiously stepped onto the floor and peered beneath the bunk. Siew was asleep under their bed.

This little girl needed their companionship, though she didn't know it herself. Mei Ling lifted the child into the warm spot next to Bo. She rummaged through her trunk, waking the woman in the nearest bunk. She bowed a silent apology. She spread out bedding on the top bunk and managed to climb up without waking anyone else. Being so high was an uncomfortable sensation. Mei Ling rested her back against the wall to save herself from a fall as she slept, then was lulled back to sleep by the rhythm of the ship.

She knew it was morning only because of the sounds of food being distributed. Women were queued up near the doorway to get bowls of rice with a few meager vegetables. Mei Ling joined the line, leaving the children asleep.

They were sitting up when she returned with their breakfast. The bean sauce and soy sauce that Kai Li had stowed in her bag made the food tolerable. She offered some sauce to the woman who had pointed her to her bed the day before.

"June Young." The small woman with a round face and lotus feet introduced herself after she accepted the offer. She spoke Cantonese with a strong accent. Maybe Min was her first language.

Mei Ling froze. This was the first time she would lie to a Chinese person about her name. "Wong Lew She," she said out loud, her heart pounding in resistance to her dishonesty.

"Is Wong your married name or original name?" June Young asked.

Mei Ling stared at her, not knowing how to answer the question.

Clarifying, June asked, "Is Wong your husband's family name?"

That was a question Mei Ling could answer. She shook her head.

"What's his family name?"

"Chinn," Mei Ling replied.

"Then in the US you will be Mrs. Chinn, Mrs. Lew She Chinn. It's the Western way, one family name. Go with it or you cause problems for yourself that you don't need."

"I will take your advice," Mei Ling said with a slight bow. "Thank you." Wong Lew She or Mrs. Lew She Chinn made little difference to her. Either one was something she wasn't.

"Like me, you are fortunate to have name that is good in English," the woman declared. It was hard to tell how old she was. Her cheeks were round from age and a good diet. Maybe ten or fifteen years older than Mei Ling—in her late twenties or early thirties.

She went on without a break. "I was Joon, and then I became June. You are Lew now. You can be Lou, and the Americans will understand and say your name right. With their alphabet we can be happy to them. The Americans like the familiar." The woman laughed at herself. "Maybe not just the Americans, eh?"

Mei Ling smiled as if she entirely understood what the woman was speaking about. It probably had something to do with the fact that English words had multiple meanings and representations, like Chinese characters.

"This your first travel across the ocean?" June asked.

"Yes."

"I moved there in 1909, a young mother like you. Our home is in Oakland, across the bay from San Francisco. Where will you live?"

"San Francisco," Mei Ling replied. "My husband is a merchant."

The woman's eyes narrowed, and she tugged up one side of her mouth. Mei Ling couldn't read her expression.

"This was my first visit back to see my Mah-ma. She is getting old. I beg and beg her to come with me, but she insists she must stay to tend to the graves of the ancestors." June clicked her tongue and shook her head to show her dismay. "The old ways die hard for some."

The woman continued, "San Francisco is busy, busy. We lived there for three years. Oakland is calm, calm. Many trees. More sunshine. And only a ferry away from the big city."

June was obviously a woman of strong opinions that she didn't hesitate to share. Mei Ling found it somewhat overwhelming but also refreshing. No one had ever spoken to her so plainly about adult matters. Maybe it was because she was married and being treated like a woman instead of a girl.

June leaned in conspiratorially and whispered, "Do you have a study book?"

Reluctant to reveal that private information to this acquaintance, Mei Ling furrowed her eyebrows as if she didn't know what the woman was talking about.

"It is okay. No shame in doing what you must to get in," June proclaimed, wagging her finger at Mei Ling. "I used one in 1909. I have another copy now. Who can remember the details from my husband's grandfather's village? The United States government is tricky. They write down what we say, but we Chinese are tricky too. We find their files and copy them down. We can study together."

June seemed to have no doubt that they were going to be confidantes or even friends. Mei Ling bristled at this bossy woman, but was glad to have a guide and companion on this journey.

"After breakfast we walk in the fresh air. Then we study the book. We take rests. Fresh air again. Dinner and then sleep. That is how we pass the time on this journey. We make the best of it, eh? That is how we succeed."

Mei Ling offered a weak smile as consent. June was like a windstorm . . . easiest to go in its direction, wise not to stay in it too long, and smart to know when you were about to be blown over by it.

CHAPTER 7

The Persia Maru
April 1923

Mei Ling was studying the book when the loud sound of the engines suddenly cut out, and the ship's vibration slowed. June toddled up to the deck on her lotus feet to learn the cause of this change.

"Nagasaki!" she exclaimed when she returned, as if Japan were not their enemy. "Come see."

Mei Ling's belly lurched at the thought of the treacherous country. Though it was far from Guangdong Province, all loyal Chinese people hated the Japanese for invading the Korean Peninsula and attempting to infringe on other Chinese territory. Nevertheless she followed June upstairs with the two children trailing behind, Bo clutching the fabric of her skirt and Siew holding his other hand. Like June, Siew had become a welcome companion on this journey, making their band a near-constant four.

Now it was Mei Ling's turn to be a face watching the shore from high above. The opposite vantage point from the one she'd had so recently. The sun on her skin and the cool breeze was a welcome contrast to the hot, dark hold below. And, despite the contempt in her heart, she could see that Nagasaki *was* striking, with its combination of Western and Japanese buildings and mountains rising up from the sea.

Mei Ling looked for Kai Li but didn't see his familiar face in the crowd. She sighed and took a deep breath. She admonished Siew to keep close and watch over Bo, but that wasn't actually necessary. The six-year-old girl hadn't willingly let either of them out of her sight since she joined their small family.

For Mei Ling, Siew's presence was a relief and a joy. Like an obedient and dutiful big sister, she entertained and watched over Bo, giving Mei Ling time to be lost in her own thoughts, study the book, and write to her family.

As they drew closer to the port, Mei Ling saw a long line of men on the wooden gangplank. Only a few women and even fewer children were waiting to board the *Persia Maru*.

"See them?" June pointed to a clump of ten or so women dressed in colorful kimonos who were boarding the boat close below them. Most were near Mei Ling's age but some looked younger, practically children. One older woman with graying hair, wearing plain clothing, moved between them. They were beautiful and full of life. Some were laughing and pointing, looking eager for an adventure. Others couldn't hide their despair. One young woman with bow lips and a round face stared back at shore, longing in her eyes. Mei Ling's heart swelled in empathy. She imagined that was how she must have looked as she was driven away from her village.

"Picture brides," June explained in her all-knowing voice. "She sells them to their future husbands in California. They must be watched over all the time because Japanese can't be trusted."

June's voice grew conspiratorial; she appeared to take great pleasure in making her point. "On the last trip, a Japanese girl left the boat in Hawaii with a Russian man that work on the ship. Oh, the chaperone was so mad! She lost her pay for that one."

Mei Ling furrowed her eyebrows at June, showing the skepticism in her mind.

"It's true," June insisted. "I hear it from a cook. He wouldn't lie to me; we are in the same clan."

June had made a point of speaking to all the Chinese people who shared the family name she used now and the one from her childhood. After a little conversation they would find a relative in common or seemingly in common—confirming the notion that they were family. She used this network to learn the news of the ship and gleefully reported it to Mei Ling. Mei Ling suspected she often exaggerated for effect, but it was possible that there was truth in this particular story.

"In America they cannot tell the difference between Japanese and Chinese," June whispered, obviously intending to shock Mei Ling. But instead this brought her to the edge of incredulity.

Mei Ling countered, "We are enemies, not the same at all."

"I promise, that is true. The Westerners don't know our clothes or our languages or our food or our religions. They only see our dark hair and dark eyes and think we are just the same."

"How can that be?"

June replied, "You don't believe me, but it is true! California is very different than China. We are separate but mixed up too. My children go to public school with German students, Filipinos . . . Japanese . . . and even a Negro."

"Public school?" Mei Ling asked.

"The government provides school for all children," June explained with a decisive nod.

That was even harder to believe than a Japanese woman fleeing with a Russian man. "Even coolies?"

"Everyone," June confirmed. "Of course, some schools are better than others. The Chinese are the best, so other kinds want to come to our school. Some say it should be more mixed up, but I don't think so. Everyone be nice to each other, sure, but stick with your own kind."

Mei Ling wasn't certain what she believed about being mixed up. She would wait to confirm the veracity of June's story when she got there herself. For the moment she would enjoy the fresh air and the sights below. It took hours for the boat to be unloaded with goods and people and then reloaded. But neither she nor the children tired of watching the exchange.

Before heading downstairs Mei Ling took a last look for Kai Li, but she didn't see her husband. It was unsettling. Was he busy? Ill? Indifferent? She could only make up a reason for his absence.

"You look for your husband, but he isn't here?" June asked a question that was a statement.

Mei Ling nodded.

"I will ask my cook clansman to find news of him," June declared. "That will make you happy again." June looked satisfied that she had solved her young friend's problem. Mei Ling appreciated the offer.

They returned to their bunks and Mei Ling opened up her book, ready to study again so that she would be fully prepared when the time came for her to disembark.

"What's a citizen?" Mei Ling asked June.

"It means you belong to that country. Let me see."

Mei Ling passed the book over, and June read the page.

"That is very good! Your husband is an American!"

"No, he's Chinese," Mei Ling said, surprised that June would think she married a White man.

"Some are both: Chinese and American," June replied. "See here." She pointed to a column of characters. "Your husband's grandfather was a coolie for building the railroad. His son, your husband's father, was born in America. So he is a United States citizen. It is the law there. If you are born there, you are a citizen and"—excitement filled her voice as she leaned in—"your children too!"

June continued, "Like I say, Americans are tricky, but Chinese trickier. A Chinese man named Wong Kim Ark argue that his father was born in America, so that makes him an American. The argument went all the way to the Supreme Court, and the highest judges agreed with him: born in America means you are an American. You are very fortunate. You made a good marriage for your children. Bo is an American too once you prove he is your husband's son."

Mei Ling still didn't understand how Kai Li could be Chinese and American, but she liked hearing that she had made a good marriage, even from June, who enjoyed stretching the truth for dramatic effect.

"Where do these books come from?" Mei Ling asked the question she'd been wondering since Kai Li gave the book to her.

"We paid a broker in Oakland Chinatown much, much money for mine. He sent the order to China. When I got to Guangzhou I picked it up," June explained. "For many people, it is their job. They arrange everything for paper sons and daughters and wives—they make these books, they make the documents, they buy the tickets . . ."

"How do you know the book will be good? Have the right information?" Mei Ling asked.

June shrugged. "That man has a good reputation, so we trust him. If this book were bad, we would tell everyone, and he would go out of business. Everybody knows everything in Oakland Chinatown," June said. Then she sighed and shook her head. "San Francisco is big, big. Too many people. Harder to trust there after the greedy, greedy immigration brokers took advantage of the big earthquake."

Mei Ling cocked her head and furrowed her eyebrows in a question.

June explained, "All the records burned up in the fire after the earthquake in 1906. Tricky Chinese say, 'My father born in America, so I am a citizen even though I was born in Guangdong. I have six children, two sons with me in America and two sons and two daughters in China with my family,' even though they only have four children. No one can check because all the records were gone. The two pretend children get papers that say they are Americans because their father is a citizen. Buy those documents and you become a paper son or paper daughter."

"Why does anyone choose to be a flimsy self?" Mei Ling asked, glad for the opportunity to learn about a term she'd heard of but not thought about in her past life. And now was.

"Why you want to go to America?"

I don't want to go to America, Mei Ling thought but didn't say.

"To have a better life, right?" June answered her own question. "Most don't choose. It happen to them when they are children. Poor parents think they are all going to starve. Being a servant in America is the best way for their child to live. Some people don't want daughters, so they sell them away. If you have no money to buy your own ticket, you agree to pay back your passage with labor."

June continued her explanation. "Big-money families make the investment hoping their second son will become rich in America to support them in their old age. Others go to be with their real family, but false papers are the only way in."

Like me, Mei Ling thought. She was married to Kai Li, and her false papers were her only way in for the Americans. But she was also deceiving her husband, telling him she was Yu Ling, her sister. The layers of her own false identity were confusing.

"So many people. So many reasons," June declared.

Mei Ling looked around the hold, wondering who else was in her same situation, building a life on a misleading foundation. She looked at June; perhaps she was presenting a false story built over generations.

"How many?" Mei Ling asked.

"Paper sons? Paper daughters? Paper wives?" June asked.

Mei Ling nodded.

"Who knows? Might be many. Might just be a few. No one says out loud." June shrugged and whispered, "Smart people keep it a secret."

Mei Ling's heart beat hard in her chest. If that was a warning, she didn't need it. She had no intention of telling anyone she was a paper wife.

~

After days on the boat, Mei Ling's travel garments were too filthy to continue wearing. She would have to figure out whether there was any means to wash them, but for today she changed into her black tunic and pants. She hated to have her precious coins away from her body but was relieved to be in more comfortable and practical clothes. She removed most of the items out of her trunk so she could squirrel away the gown with the coins at the bottom.

The silk bundle her mother had tucked in called her attention. Mei Ling opened it to find the four yellowing stalks. The plants were fading in this dark environment. Her heart sank. They might die before they reached the United States. Mei Ling rubbed the stems gently. *Find the strength to survive,* she encouraged the plants in her mind.

Siew looked over her shoulder and asked, "Should I get them some water?"

Mei Ling shook her head. "My Mah-ma said to leave them be until they can get in the sun. They just need to rest and survive on what they have in them."

Mei Ling looked at Siew, but the little girl was staring at the picture Mei Ling had placed on the bed.

"Is that your mother?" Siew asked, pointing to the picture.

"Yes," Mei Ling replied. "That is my family." *Was my family?* she thought to herself. It was confusing and painful to think of these people now—two were ghosts, and she might never see the other four again.

"He's cute! Like Bo," Siew said, pointing to Dai Dai.

"He's much older than that now. Older than you."

Bo's head looked around to see what they were looking at.

"Look, Bo," Siew said. "It's your family."

Mei Ling's throat tightened up. Siew had a certainty about her relationship to Bo that she wanted but didn't yet feel.

Bo pointed to Mui Mui and asked, "Siew?"

"No," Mei Ling replied, though she could see the resemblance between the two girls with their round faces and bright eyes.

Siew said, "That's not me, that's your . . . ?" The girl looked up at Mei Ling for an answer.

Mei Ling's heart swelled with sorrow. "Your aunt—my little sister," her choked-up voice managed to spit out. "She's a ghost now."

"Like my family," Siew said wistfully.

"Yes," Mei Ling said. *And Bo's first mother,* she thought.

"Manila!" June interrupted their poignant conversation. "Come, come."

Mei Ling smiled at Siew. The girl grabbed Bo's hand and led him away. Mei Ling savored the moment of quiet to pack up her treasures into the beat-up trunk. She kept the ongoing letter home so she could update her family while they were above deck.

She slid her trunk below the bed—all the way back against the wall. As she headed up to the deck, she realized that without any thought, she had trusted Siew to take care of Bo. They really had become a family, no matter how temporary.

Mei Ling inhaled the cool, fresh air at the top of the stairs. Blue sky sparkled in the bright sun. Hardly anyone had come out to see this harbor, so it was easy to find the others. Kai Li wasn't with them. She wished she could find out if he was ill or simply disinterested in them. Both explanations were troubling but raised very different fears in her heart.

June, oblivious to Mei Ling's concern, lectured about the Philippines. "They are an American colony. So they are Americans but not Americans. Like Korea is China but not China. Filipinos not tricky like Chinese to make the judges say they are real Americans. Big, big American military base is nearby," she whispered. "That is why America want the Philippines. They are afraid of Chinese strength, so they come all the way out here to show they are strong against China."

Mei Ling nodded, not particularly interested, but she just let June say her piece.

"After this stop we have long, long time until we reach Hawaii," the older woman said. "The most beautiful of all places. Paradise on earth. They grow so much sugar for America that it is cheap, cheap."

~

Three times a day, men who weren't Chinese came into their dank barracks with meals. As Kai Li had stated, the food was passable but not appetizing, which made Mei Ling all the more grateful for the sauces he'd provided for the journey. The brown faces, of many ages and backgrounds, grew familiar, but Mei Ling didn't interact with them, so it was surprising and disconcerting when one of them asked, "Are you Bo?"

Siew spoke up for her foster brother: "He is, and I'm Siew. Who are you?"

"Pasha," the dark-haired young man who was barely out of boyhood answered with a smile. Then he leaned close to Bo and said, "I have a message from your father."

Mei Ling perked up at the reference to her husband. Perhaps this man had the answer to June's inquiry about Kai Li's well-being.

The young man said, "He's too ill to get out of his bunk, but he hasn't forgotten you."

Relief and concern tussling in her, Mei Ling asked, "What's causing him to be confined to his bed?"

The young man raised his shoulders and replied, "I don't know, but I can ask."

It was only after they were out of the line that Mei Ling registered surprise that someone who wasn't Chinese was speaking Cantonese.

From then on, each morning as he served breakfast, Pasha would pass news between Kai Li and the women's quarters. Thankfully her husband didn't worsen but continued to be weak, with difficulty walking or keeping food down. Many of the women in their hold were also suffering and didn't get out of their beds except for running to the bathroom. Mei Ling was consoled by June's assessment that they would spend the journey crossing the Pacific Ocean miserable in their beds but recover as soon as they were on land. The sickness was caused by motion of the sea, nothing else.

Siew enjoyed her conversations with Pasha and didn't hesitate to pepper him with questions. Mei Ling considered it rude to ask personal information, but Pasha eagerly shared stories from his life, and Mei Ling was fascinated to learn about him. Pasha occasionally slipped Bo and Siew treats of pineapple or dried mango.

Pasha was from Honolulu on the island of Oahu in Hawaii. Growing up on a sugarcane plantation, he had watched the ships sail by on their way into and out of port. Two years before—when he turned twelve—he came on board with the dream of saving up enough money to purchase land of his own.

"How do you know Cantonese?" Mei Ling asked one day, adjusting to the custom of asking a personal question. She'd been curious for days about how a boy from Hawaii learned her language, and no one else asked him.

"On the sugar plantation I was the water boy. I ran around all the fields. I learned Chinese, Japanese, Okinawan, Korean . . . everything but English." He laughed. "No English speakers work the fields. The Americans will be gone soon, so English won't be important in Hawaii."

Days after they left Manila, Mei Ling experienced the seasickness for herself. In the morning she barely made it to a basin before emptying the contents of her stomach. June insisted plain rice followed by fresh air was the best remedy, so she forced down some food and made herself climb the stairs to the deck, leaving the children below and taking paper and pen.

June was right. The cool air and the expansive view restored her health. The sun sparkled in the sky, and waves sparkled in the sun. It was magical. There was nothing in sight, no birds, no land, nothing besides this boat in the midst of the enormous ocean.

She found a bench in a quiet spot to continue the letter to her family.

Fear is my constant companion, she thought but didn't write.

> Many on the boat are sick from the sea now that we are far across the Pacific *and so far from home*. My husband has taken to his bed in the Chinese men's quarters, so we haven't seen him in many days. *Weeks.* My traveling companion assures me that he will recover fully once we are on land *but I fear he is a weak man*. The expanse of the ocean is magnificent *and terrifying if I dwell on how alone and vulnerable we are*. The food *which was already horrid* has declined in quality because we cannot take on fresh supplies. We are managing to keep our spirits up, *though my appetite is lost, and I feel ill as well*.
>
> Two fellow travelers are welcome companions on our journey. June, a Chinese woman who returned home to Shekki to visit her mother after ten years, gives me hope that I will do the same one day. And Siew, a young orphan with an eager mind and kind heart like our Mui Mui, has adopted us for the

> journey. She keeps Bo occupied and all of us in good spirits. I spend hours each morning studying about my husband and his family so that I can pass the test on Angel Island. Otherwise we spend the time telling stories and folding paper animals.

Mei Ling left off there; she had many more days to speak of her travels before they landed in San Francisco.

~

The next day Mei Ling once again felt ill when she woke. She managed to keep hold of her stomach, forcing herself to eat and then sit in the fresh air until she felt better. The following morning Pasha handed her a small bag after he served her rice. She looked at him with a question in her eyes.

"From your husband," the boy said.

She opened the pouch; it contained crystalized ginger.

Pasha said, "He hopes the ginger will do more to settle your stomach than it has for his."

"Please pass my thanks on to him," Mei Ling replied. Regardless of how well it worked on her sea illness, her husband's thoughtful gift was a boost to her spirits.

A few days later, Pasha paused when it came time to serve Mei Ling her morning rice.

He stared intently at her, leaned in, and spoke so quietly that only she could hear: "The girl will bring you great joy."

Mei Ling was confused. "Siew?"

Pasha stared at Siew, his eyes glazed over. He closed his lids as if he were concentrating on something in his mind. When he opened them again, he had a sorrowful look on his face.

He replied, "Not Siew. I cannot see past the sorrow and an enormous challenge." He pointed at Mei Ling's belly and leaned in. "She will bring you great joy."

Mei Ling's hand went to her belly. Was she . . . ?

She asked, "I have a . . . daughter?"

Pasha nodded, his brown eyes clear again, calm and kind. Mei Ling staggered away with her rice. Was it possible? She considered how many weeks since her marriage night. Nearly four. Her monthly bleeding hadn't come when she expected it, but she had attributed that to the stress of the boat.

A baby. The thought added to her fear, but there was also excitement mixed in her spirit. She looked at Bo, the child she was already responsible for. She already cared for him so deeply. She touched her belly. This one would add love to her life as well—and joy too if Pasha was to be believed.

She remembered the names from her grandmother: Xinyi and Jingyi. She had a sudden urge to see the moon, so she could tell it her secret to pass along to her family. Mei Ling carried their grandchild.

CHAPTER 8

San Francisco Bay
May 1923

"Come, come!" June shook Mei Ling awake. "San Francisco. We are home!"

Home. Mei Ling didn't share June's excitement or sentiment, but it did give her hope. This wasn't home now, but in ten years she might feel that it was.

"Bring your book," June ordered.

Mei Ling roused the children. With the precious pages squirreled under her coat, she traipsed upstairs with the others. It was gray outside, and the air was moist with a heavy morning fog that hid the view of the city. Dread and fear built in Mei Ling. The boat wasn't nice, but she'd found a comfortable rhythm for herself and Bo. On Angel Island she would be judged and given entry to her new life or sent back in shame. And she would have to say goodbye to June and Siew, who'd come to feel like family.

"It is there, I promise. Soon you will see for yourself," June declared. "The most beautiful city on earth!"

Other people began joining them on the deck. Mei Ling scanned for Kai Li but was disappointed once again.

"There it is! See, see." June pointed to the land barely visible in the haze. "That way is Playland at the Beach; the other way is Marin. This is the Golden Gate."

She said it as if it were of great importance and had great meaning, but to Mei Ling it was a high cliff lost in fog.

When Mei Ling didn't respond appropriately, June declared, "The opening to San Francisco Bay!"

Just then she heard a familiar voice quietly say, "Hello, wife."

Her head jerked around. Kai Li was at her side. Relief washed over her. She smiled, so glad to see him, to know that she'd have his companionship for whatever came next.

Mei Ling took a good look at her husband. His hollowed-out cheeks and sunken eyes showed he'd lost much of his weight during the voyage. The Western suit hung off of his shoulders. Like her, he had attempted to clean up, but the grime from the journey couldn't be properly washed away on the ship. She felt tenderness rise in her. Soon they would be in their own home, where they could eat well and bathe properly.

"Thank you for the ginger to settle my stomach," she said.

He smiled shyly. "I hope it helped."

"It did." She considered telling him her suspicion that she was carrying his child, but something told her to wait. It was early yet. Spirits didn't always choose to stay. And, if Pasha's prediction was correct, Kai Li might not welcome the news that they were having a daughter.

"Now!" June whispered as she dropped her own book over the railing into the vast Pacific Ocean.

No! a voice screamed in Mei Ling's head. She might need it.

"Now!" June insisted. "Before anyone from the island can see you. It is still far away. Better this way. I know."

Mei Ling looked at Kai Li. She opened up the coat for him to see what she was hiding.

"Did you study?" he asked.

"Yes."

"You will be fine. Trust us. Your friend is right, let it go," he said. "It's safer that way."

She hung her arm down below the railing, the thick handwritten book dangling from her hand. How many hours had it taken to write down this information? How much money had it cost her husband? Fuchan had demanded that she treasure all writing, all knowledge, by caring for books. Her spirit cried no, but she apologized to the ancestors and opened her hand, sending the book flying down into the waves. She watched it hit without a splash. Slowly the salty brine soaked it up until it disappeared from sight below the surface.

"Oh, no!" Siew cried out.

"Not *oh, no*," June corrected the girl. "It is good—the right step for being the trickiest."

Mei Ling put her hand to her heart and took a deep breath. Destroying the book hurt, but she told herself she had done what was necessary. She wasn't the only one. As they passed through the Golden Gate, the two spits of land that framed the opening to the bay, she saw more books sail into the water. There were many paper companions—sons and daughters as well as wives—on this ship. Though if June was to be believed, even people who were not paper companions used the study books to get through immigration.

They traveled along the land on the right side of the bay. Strange shrubs edged in dark green grew along the sandy shore. A movement caught the corner of her eye. She looked down and saw a man on the outside of the railing. Adrenaline flooded her body. He needed rescue! Before she could yell for help, he made eye contact and shook his head.

She watched him inhale deeply and then let go. Her heart hammered hard as he fell into the water and disappeared under the wake of the ship. She stared at the spot where he entered the bay.

"Man fall in," Bo said in his sweet, high voice.

"Where?" Kai Li asked.

Mei Ling pointed.

"There he is, Bo," Kai Li said, pointing to a spot far away.

The man was swimming to the shore.

"Why?" Mei Ling asked, unable to form a whole question.

"No papers," Kai Li said with a shrug.

~

They sailed past many docks that poked into the bay. San Francisco was crammed with Western buildings packed against one another all the way up the steep hills that rose from the shore. A paved road ran along the waterfront with only motorcars rushing by. Mei Ling saw no hint of plants or animals.

"San Francisco!" June exclaimed. "The most beautiful city of all."

Mei Ling didn't share June's opinion. From the ship it was a disappointment compared to lush Hong Kong or Honolulu, and even elegant Nagasaki. This was a foreign land where she was going to be surrounded by many strangers, but it was her new home. She would find a way to appreciate it.

~

The boat shuddered to a stop after a painfully slow approach to a pier next to a lovely clock tower.

"Oakland, where I live." June pointed across the bay. Then she pointed to the left. "And Berkeley. See the towers? They match."

Mei Ling studied the land. In the midst of much green she saw two towers jutting into the sky. The three towers made a large triangle.

"I must go now." Kai Li interrupted the geography lesson.

"What?" Mei Ling was unable to keep the panic out of her voice.

"Citizens get off here. You will go to Angel Island for interrogation." He looked pained as he pointed to land in the middle of the bay. He leaned in with a whisper. "Remember only the details from the book. Don't say the truth, only the story from the book."

Her mind understood she had to lie, pretend to be Wong Lew She, but Mei Ling's heart resisted. Daughters with integrity didn't lie. Nor did wives. What if she wasn't clever enough to pull off the deceit? She would be sent back to China in shame, never to see her husband again. She looked at Bo. Would he be sent back with her or given permission to land? If they didn't believe her story, she doubted they would believe he was Kai Li's son.

Would his family take her in their village? Would hers? She shook her head to stop the thoughts.

"I will think of you every day until we are together again," Kai Li said. He rubbed Bo's head and patted Mei Ling's shoulder. He looked like he wanted to say or do something else, but he just turned and walked away. Her heart pounding hard, too soon she lost track of him in the crowd of dark heads.

They studied the gangplank from above. The line moved slowly as each person, mostly men, handed over documents. A second group of people were disembarking to the right: a line for White people. Mei Ling hadn't realized there were so many Europeans on this ship. Her angry Dragon rose when she saw that gangplank was soon empty while the Chinese, Japanese, Filipinos, and Hawaiians waited in a long line.

Bo pointed and bounced in excitement. "Look. Look."

He'd spied Kai Li. They watched him pass his papers to the official in a suit, his hand shaking. The official looked Kai Li up and down. The White man spoke; Kai Li responded. The man shook his head, returned the papers, and then Kai Li walked down the wooden board to the shore. He got to the end of the walkway and onto a patch of land by the edge of the water. He put down his suitcase and waved, a small, bittersweet smile on his face. They waved back. He stood there watching them from afar as the gangplank emptied. She was touched that he stayed.

Eventually the ship jerked away from the pier. Kai Li waved again. Mei Ling and Bo waved back until the boat turned away from the shore, leaving her husband out of sight.

CHAPTER 9

Angel Island
May 1923

The dock at Angel Island led to a lovely wooden walkway, lined by palm trees blowing in the breeze, which led to a two-story white building. A man sounded a large bell at the end of the pier, ringing out a loud welcome. Perhaps the name of this place would be fitting for the experience.

Their band returned to the hold for their trunks. Siew had a small sack she could carry on her back. The girl was young but strong and capable. With no one else to help them with their trunks, they made a caravan. Mei Ling held Bo's hand and one handle. Siew picked up the strap on one end of June's trunk with both of her hands, and June, in the middle, held on to both trunks.

They joined the line of Asian women and men disembarking. This time Mei Ling recognized the various nationalities: Japanese, of course, but also Hindoos, Sikhs, Mohammedans, and Filipinos. As they left the boat Mei Ling acknowledged the spirits: *Thank you for delivering us safely to this shore.*

She looked over to see the White line of mostly Russian Jews, the women in head scarfs. One White man in a cream-colored suit screamed at a customs officer, but she couldn't understand him.

June leaned over. "I cannot understand him, but the agent replied in English."

Before June could translate, a gruff officer barked orders to them: "---- ---- ----; ----- -- ---- ----!"

"We are on this side," June directed. "Men go over there."

Mei Ling stepped onto the earth on the other side of the world. She took a big breath to steady herself as she balanced the trunk and watched out to make certain Bo and Siew were near. The ground beneath suddenly shifted. She stumbled on the smooth dirt path, nearly dropping the trunk. Mei Ling stopped to get her bearings.

"You are dizzy from the boat," June said. "It won't last long. Maybe hours or days."

Mei Ling looked at June, confusion on her face.

"Just walk normal," June said. "The ground is good here, though it doesn't feel like it. Come!"

The man Siew had pointed out to them as her uncle, Suk Suk, walked up to them in the women's line. Without introduction he said, "Thank you for accepting my niece into your family for the journey. Come, Siew!" And then he walked off to join the men's line.

Siew stared at Mei Ling, begging her with her eyes for another option. Mei Ling's heart sank. As much as she and Bo had come to care for her, she had no right to ask that the girl stay with them.

Before Mei Ling could form a reply, Siew shrugged, put on a smile, and pushed a paper frog into Bo's hand. Then she ran after Suk Suk, waving as she went.

Bo ran after her.

"Come back," Mei Ling yelled. The boy stopped running, his head hung down in dejection, but he didn't return to her. Mei Ling went to him and brought him to their line. He looked as crestfallen as Mei Ling felt.

But there was no time to dwell on any sentimental feelings. June pointed to the front of the line; they had to leave their luggage behind in a shed. It had been wise to throw the book in the ocean. Women frantically dug through their belongings, retrieving only what they could carry.

"They say we will get it back, but I'll believe it when I see it," June said, laughing. "As the Americans say."

"How long will we be here?" Mei Ling asked.

Her friend shrugged.

"Last time, how long were you here?"

"No Angel Island before. In 1909 we go to San Francisco, to a house on the wharf. I was held for one week. They made Angel Island so they can keep us longer. Some even a year, I hear." June clicked her tongue in disapproval. Alarm rushed through Mei Ling. *A year!*

Mei Ling watched the women carefully balancing their belongings piled high as they walked into the white building. Everyone had bedding as well as clothing; some held frames and even food. Standing in the hot sun, she considered her options. She could tell Bo was tired and thirsty, but he didn't complain while they waited for their turn to leave their goods behind.

She opened her trunk and dug through it, overwhelmed by having to make a decision with so little information. She was glad she had changed back into the filthy skirt with the coins sewed in the hem. She pulled out a change of clothing for each of them, her family pictures, and the statue of Quan Yin. She looked at Bo. He could carry his own bedding, the crystalized ginger, and the bean paste. Mei Ling saw the fabric that wrapped the stalks. She looked around. This seemed an unlikely place for these to thrive, but if she was going to be here for weeks or even months, she wanted the stalks with her. She pulled them out. Then they left the rest of their belongings behind.

After checking in at the big white building, they were sent for a medical exam. The first room had women squatting like tree stumps. She was handed a pan and told to defecate into it. She was given no privacy besides what she could make with her own skirt.

June passed through this requirement quickly and was moved along despite her request that she stay with her "little sister." Mei Ling appreciated the older woman's desire to keep together, but she would have to get through this on her own. Bo stood at her side, strangers squatted around her, and shame burned through her soul. *I will do what I must,* she reminded herself. She closed her eyes and breathed in deeply to relax.

Eventually her body cooperated; not everyone was so fortunate. She walked past one old granny with tears pouring down her weathered face. The nurses weren't cruel, but they insisted that she would need to wait here until she met this humiliating requirement.

In the next room, with no regard for her modesty, a man gave Mei Ling a physical examination. She felt like cattle as he touched parts of her body, starting at her head, and spoke words to the nurse who wrote them down.

He touched her scalp. "-- ----."

He lifted her eyelids and studied her face. "---- --- ---- -----."

He spun her around and ran his finger down her spine. "-------- -----."

On and on it went, seemingly never-ending. Mei Ling felt her eyeballs burning; she bit her tongue hard enough to make it bleed, the shock of pain chasing away potential tears.

Bo stayed at her side, quiet and meek without Siew. Mei Ling's heart twisted at the thought of the little girl going through this humiliation on the other side. Was she being exposed to the men as they were examined? As much as she wanted to know, she didn't want to draw any attention to herself by asking about Siew. Her greatest desire was to get through this ordeal as quickly as possible. She did the one thing that was available to her—pray: *Quan Yin, please watch over her.*

It was nearly dark by the time Mei Ling and Bo were through the trial and pointed toward the women's dormitory. Her stomach growled as they climbed the wooden stairs. She thought of Pasha, offering food to the women in the hold of the ship. The boat was sailing back to Shanghai. Continuing the loop, though with fewer Chinese on the return to the United States if the immigration restrictions served their purpose.

The large dorm room was full of Chinese women of various ages. Large metal poles ran from floor to ceiling on two sides of the room. Three layers of mesh beds were attached on each side of the poles. A few were folded up like a butterfly's wing, but most were folded down and covered with personal belongings.

Narrow walkways passed between the bunks, and clotheslines were strung up between the poles, blocking the view. The last rays of the sun coming through the metal-covered windows confirmed her fear that this was a prison, not a guesthouse.

~

"Here, here." The sound of June's familiar, bossy voice sent a wave of relief shivering down Mei Ling's spine. She smiled at Bo, and they walked to the spot where the words had come from.

"No beds next to me, but I saved you these by the window. Good spot for you," June whispered close. "By the bathroom. Good for the baby, eh?"

"You know?"

"Of course." June beamed and pointed at herself. "Two children; I see the signs!"

Mei Ling stared at the cold metal beds. She pushed on the bare mesh that gave only a little—apparently they didn't deserve mattresses. She laid out their bedding and felt again; it was marginally better. The mesh was barely detectable, and it wasn't so cold through the material.

"Bo, you will sleep here." Mei Ling pointed to the bed on the right.

"With Siew?"

Mei Ling's heart lurched at the girl's name. She felt the same longing she heard in his young voice. She kept her reply cheerful. "No, with me. I'll be right next to you." She waved to the bed on the left side of the poles.

Bo's lip pushed out and started to quiver. Tears made his dark eyes shiny.

Mei Ling shook her head and tsked to show her disapproval for his outward expression of emotion. She shared his sorrow, but they weren't going to make a display of their pain, especially in front of these strangers.

She sat on the bed and patted the spot next to her. He climbed up beside her, the frog from Siew in one hand and his carved rabbit in the other. June sat on her other side without waiting for an invitation.

"I met everyone already," June declared and started in on the report. "All the ladies here are Chinese. Only women in this building. Non-Chinese are in other rooms. The men are in the other building—also separated Chinese and not-Chinese. See that one sleeping over there? She has been here more than one year!"

Mei Ling's stomach sank. One year! She hadn't imagined she'd be here for weeks, let alone months. A whole year—her daughter would be born by then. She looked around the horrid place—the walls were shiny white, clothes hung from the bed rails, and belongings were slid under the frames. The scent of humans and grease filled the air.

Distracted, Mei Ling missed what June was saying, but she tuned back in at the warning in her voice.

"Stay away. They are bad ladies, if you know what I mean. Only here for money."

Mei Ling didn't know what June meant. "Who?"

June pointed to the other corner of the room.

"I can tell by their fancy, fancy clothes they are no good," June insisted.

Mei Ling's confusion must have shown on her face, because June leaned in and whispered right into her ear, "Prostitutes."

A shiver of understanding shot through Mei Ling. She looked over but couldn't see the women through the sheets hanging between the beds. She looked back at her friend. June nodded, her eyes big.

Mei Ling stood up and casually looked over. The prostitutes were hardly more than children, maybe fourteen years old, dressed in nice silk gowns in bright red. They had red on their lips, which somehow made them look even younger.

The three girls were giggling on the bed. One of them looked right at Mei Ling, a challenge in her weary eyes. Embarrassed and uncomfortable, Mei Ling averted her gaze.

June pulled at her hand.

"We just leave them alone and they leave us alone, eh?" June directed.

"The Americans will let them in?" Mei Ling asked.

"Yes. If their papers and their story go together, and they are healthy, they let them in. The *tongs* arrange it—for the money. Too many come in this way and make bad feelings from the Americans for all the Chinese."

She changed the subject. "You missed dinner, but my clan are the cooks, so I bring you crackers. That is all they can give me to bring up here. You are lucky to have me. I will make sure you get good food at Angel Island."

Once again, Mei Ling was struck by the irony of the name. Maybe it was a mistranslation. Perhaps in English *angel* was an angry ghost, not a kindly spirit.

"Bo?!" Siew's familiar voice cut through the air.

Mei Ling's heart leaped, and Bo flew from the bed in the direction of that wonderful sound. He rushed back a moment later, holding Siew's hand, a huge grin on his round face.

"Look, Mah-ma. Siew!" Bo said.

Mei Ling nearly burst with joy. Siew was here, and Bo had called her Mah-ma! She waved Siew over and bowed.

"No girls allowed over there, so I can be with you again," Siew explained, bringing her shoulders up and scrunching her lips, as if she felt sheepish and uncertain.

Mei Ling pointed to the bed she was sitting on, hoping to dispel any fear that Siew wasn't welcome. "You sleep right here next to Bo." She didn't relish the idea of sleeping up high, especially if she was going to be here for months, growing larger and larger, but she was so happy to have Siew with them again that it didn't matter. The children could sleep on the side-by-side lower beds; she'd make do with the top bunk.

~

The next morning the sound of a bell woke Mei Ling before it was fully light outside. She looked over the edge of the bed where she had slept. The bunk below was empty. Bo was missing! In a panic she looked to see if Siew was still in her bunk. She was, and Bo was cuddled up next to the girl, fast asleep. He'd moved next to her in the night. Relief washed over Mei Ling.

"Men eat first," a bunkmate explained loudly to June. "Then us."

Mei Ling climbed down and woke the children. They walked to the cold tiled bathroom to wash up before breakfast. Siew flinched when she heard the loud sound of the toilet flushing, apparently for the first time. She was intrigued by that amenity and the running water in the faucet. It struck Mei Ling that she actually knew very little about the girl. She'd either been poor or lived in a rural village. From the looks of Suk Suk, her family wasn't poor, but a wealthy uncle in America didn't mean he took care of his family in China. Mei Ling vowed that whatever riches came to her in California, she would share with her family.

The dining room was packed with tables. A line formed for over-boiled rice and slimy vegetables. No tofu. No sauce. No tea. Even through her family's downfall, Mei Ling had always drunk something that passed for tea in the morning. This really was a prison.

Mei Ling attempted to eat the distasteful meal, but her stomach revolted. Her morning nausea wasn't chased away by this food. True to her word, June managed to get them something extra—a banana. Another first for Siew. She was wary, but Bo's excitement at seeing the yellow fruit was contagious, and she discovered that she loved it. Mei Ling's bite went a little way in quelling her nausea.

As they were leaving the dining hall, Mei Ling's eye was caught by characters carved into the wall. It was painted over, but she could still make it out as a poem.

It must have taken a very long time for this person to carve this poem into the wall. Would she be here so long? She looked around the dreary room. She placed her hand on her belly. Would this baby's spirit want to grow here? With a heavy heart she followed June outside.

"Do not think about that. We ignore the sad poems. Life in America is not perfect, but you can make a good one for you and for your children. I promise, promise," June lectured.

Mei Ling smiled, but her heart didn't ignore so easily.

They followed the line of women to a small metal cage lined with benches. A White lady sitting at one end welcomed the new women and introduced herself as Deaconess Katherine Maurer.

June leaned over and whispered, "She is the angel of Angel Island. Very famous lady."

Mei Ling wondered if she was a hungry ghost or a helpful spirit. It turned out she was a bit of both. As a missionary from the Methodist church, she worked to make the lives of the hopeful detainees somewhat more bearable. Most days she brought packages and mail from the mainland, taught them some English words, and reviewed basic skills for survival in their new home.

The three painted girls whispered to each other in one corner until the deaconess started calling out names. Then they listened attentively. The deaconess was delivering items from the mainland. A jolt of pleasure shot through Mei Ling when her name was among those that were called.

"Right here!" June pointed at Mei Ling.

"------- -- -------," the White woman said to Mei Ling. When Mei Ling stared in incomprehension, the woman gave a slight bow and offered a small bundle. Mei Ling unwrapped the bundle on the bench as Bo and Siew looked on with excitement. Tea!

Pleased but surprised, Mei Ling looked at June for an answer.

"From your husband," June declared. "He did not forget you."

A small satisfied smile crossed over Mei Ling's face as she read.

> Wife,
> I hope this tea will bring you some comfort during your stay. I await news of your release to your new home.
> Your husband

It was a short but welcome note. Mei Ling admired the strength and elegance of his characters.

When the White lady finished distributing the packages, there was no mistaking the disappointment in the eyes of one of the red-lipped girls. She hadn't received anything. She and her two companions rushed away from the cage. The red-lipped girl glared at Mei Ling as she stormed by.

The White lady others called Ma spoke out in English. "----. -- -- ---- -- ---- ---."

"She is teaching you English now," June said with a poke. "She said, 'Hello. It is nice to meet you,'" June translated. "She said 'repeat.'"

"-----," Katherine Maurer said.

The group repeated what she said.

"-----," the teacher chanted again.

The group repeated what she said; this time Bo and Siew joined in.

"-----," Deaconess Maurer chanted again.

The group chanted the word back. Mei Ling joined them in saying the word out loud, "Hello."

Bo, Siew, and June clapped for her.

"You know an English word now!" June exclaimed.

The lesson continued, quickly moving on to phrases that tripped up Mei Ling's tongue and mind, though Bo and Siew seemed to keep up easily. It was frustrating, but she concentrated and did her best to form the awkward words.

When the lesson was over, June asked Katherine Maurer when they would have their interviews, but the well-meaning White woman didn't have any information for them. Mei Ling would have to wait it out—not knowing if it would be days, weeks, or even months.

CHAPTER 10

Angel Island
June 1923

Days dragged by with few respites from the boredom and pervasive despair. Unappetizing food, the dull accent in each day, gave Mei Ling a sense of time passing but did little to soothe her queasy stomach. June tried to get her something appealing to eat at each meal, but it wasn't enough to keep her strong. Mei Ling's face grew thinner as her belly began to protrude.

Mei Ling feared that the information from the book would slip away before she met with the inspectors. She regularly reviewed the details, chanting under her breath the birth dates, lineage, and the layout of the village and their paper home. Siew had listened carefully enough on the boat that she chimed in when she heard a mistake.

One morning, as she was writing a paragraph to her family, the red-lipped girl walked up to Mei Ling.

"You can read?" she asked in perfect Cantonese.

Mei Ling confirmed no guard was nearby and then nodded. Looking wary, the girl held out a piece of paper.

"What does this say?" she demanded. As for most women, these characters probably held no meaning for her.

Mei Ling took the wrinkled paper and read out loud:

> Dangers await you in America!
>
> Beware of Fahn Quai: Donaldina Cameron, the White Devil. She lives in a brick mission house on top of a hill in Chinatown. Fahn Quai keeps Chinese girls locked in the basement. She will torture and poison you. The foreign devil women eat the organs of beautiful Chinese girls because they believe this will make them strong. Never go to the House on the Hill! Fahn Quai has placed Tien Wu under her spell. Do not trust either of them.

Mei Ling grimaced and looked at the girl. Her Dragon burned with outrage.

"Where did you get this?!" she asked the girl.

The red-lipped girl shrugged.

Mei Ling looked back at the note and studied the words, wanting to carve them into her memory so she could also heed their warning.

The girl held out her hand for the paper. A hard look on her face, she took the note and started to walk away. The girl turned back to give a slight bow to show gratitude. Mei Ling's Dragon rumbled in protection of the girl shuffling back to her friends.

Someone needed to help her find a path to an honorable life. Perhaps Ma Maurer had ideas for the girl.

Interrupting her musing, Bo asked, "Pee?"

Mei Ling took his hand and walked to the wretched bathroom. She could barely care for herself, Bo, and Siew in this place. What power did she have to protect the girls with the red lips?

~

When given the chance, Mei Ling went to sessions with Deaconess Maurer. One morning she was delighted to be offered a napkin, a needle, and colorful embroidery floss. Unlike some of the other women, Mei Ling was already skilled at needlework. Bringing an image to life stitch by stitch was a gratifying distraction from the dreary confinement. While she didn't earn any praise for her English, many of the women, including the deaconess, exclaimed over the beauty of her needlework.

After six days on the island, a White lady, one of the matrons who did the inspections with the doctors, offered the women in her dorm a walk around the island. Mei Ling's weak spirit rebelled at the idea of that much activity, but she could not deny the children the opportunity for some fresh air and exercise.

Only a small troop joined in the walk, while most of the women from the barracks were too emotionally or physically tired and chose to stay locked in the grungy room. Once she was away from the building, Mei Ling was glad she had mustered up the energy to be outside. The view was breathtaking in all directions. The waves sparkled in the sun as the small band walked north until they saw Tiburon just a short distance across the water. It was a green-and-brown gem growing up from the bay.

Forbidden from continuing around the island, they turned around and hiked south along a path past the hospital where the sick women were resting.

Siew and Bo held hands in front of Mei Ling as they marched on a path through scrubby trees. Siew spun a story into Bo's ear about the magical animals that lived in this land, her free hand gesturing as she spoke. Suddenly they passed out of the scrub, and the land across the sparkling bay popped into a stunning view. They stopped to look out.

June pointed and said, "See the Campanile—the tower at the university in Berkeley? Like we see from the boat."

Mei Ling followed June's finger. She nodded when she found the tall structure with a triangle on top jutting out at the bottom of the hills.

"We will go there together one day," she declared. Then she looked at Bo and Siew to make sure they were listening to her. "My children, Dorothy and Timothy, too. New friends for you!"

June missed it, but Mei Ling saw a flash of fear and sorrow cross Siew's face. Like Mei Ling, the little girl understood that this was a temporary arrangement.

"Maybe Suk Suk will let us have visits." Mei Ling dangled hope to the distressed child.

"Really?" Siew asked.

"I will ask. He seems like a very nice man," Mei Ling replied.

Siew's face went flat, and she shrugged. Mei Ling's chest constricted in sympathy. Losing her family, her home, and her country was difficult for Mei Ling at eighteen years old. It had to be even scarier for this six-year-old. She wanted to find the right words to soothe Siew's fears, as her grandmother had always been able to for her, but her mind was blank.

Instead she patted Siew's back like Fuchan used to do for her, suddenly understanding more of what those pats contained—a passionate desire to offer comfort when you had no actual power to change the situation.

~

When they returned to the barracks the red-lipped girl was pacing in front of her bed, yelling something in Min, a language foreign to Mei Ling. June seemed to be following the words.

The four of them observed the nearby drama from their small bunks just a few feet away.

June leaned in and whispered an explanation into Mei Ling's ear. "They discover she is having a baby, but she is not married." June tsked in disapproval. "She has to go back on the next boat. Like I say, she is no good."

In a flash the young woman marched over to them, fury burning in her dark eyes. Leaning in so close to June that her hair brushed against Mei Ling's cheek, she screamed in Cantonese, "You don't know me, you stupid *cow*!"

A furious and powerful demon had overtaken this young woman. She looked ready to kill June.

Mei Ling's heart beat hard and fast in her chest. She shielded Bo and Siew from the girl-woman's fury. Before she had time to do anything else, the girl-woman spun away. She returned to her bunk and collapsed. Deflated of her anger, she suddenly looked like a scared child instead of an evil spirit.

Her friends patted her shoulders. The other women in the barracks ignored her, probably afraid her fate might be contagious if they got too close. Soon a guard came to the door and called out, "Jui Lan." The girl-woman stood. She carried a small bundle of goods in her arms. Her friends bowed their goodbyes and watched her leave in silence. She stopped at the threshold and looked around. She caught Mei Ling watching her. Jui Lan's hard, sad eyes burned into Mei Ling's memory. How could someone fall so low?

~

The barracks was sober through the night and into the morning. They walked to breakfast with the nightmare of deportation as their companion. They all feared they would share a portion of Jui Lan's fate, even June, who acted as if her landing were guaranteed.

June returned to their table with four precious hard-boiled eggs from her clansman, but even that treat didn't remove the unsettling blanket over Mei Ling's soul.

"I hear sad, sad news of Jui Lan," June reported without the hint of glee that usually accompanied the setup that she was the bearer of interesting information.

Mei Ling looked at June, pain in her heart, sensing what was going to be shared.

"The cooks tell me she jump from the ship when they were far, far from shore." June shook her head side to side. "Nothing could be done. They watched her and waved a final goodbye."

Mei Ling took June's hand. She imagined Jui Lan's head bobbing in the water. Had her hard, sad eyes shown panic? Were her lips still red? Did she wave back? Was she resigned? Or furious? Mei Ling's heart pained for Jui Lan, but she was afraid for herself as well.

The girl-woman might have turned into an angry ghost, and June, Mei Ling, or the whole barracks might be the target of her fury. Mei Ling longed to burn incense and make a food offering.

Too upset to eat anything, not even a sip of tea, she squirreled her egg into the bodice of her tunic to give it to the hungry ghost. *Quan Yin, release Jui Lan's spirit so that she may be in peace,* Mei Ling prayed. Then she was flooded with remorse as she realized she had not thought to pray for the girl-woman before she was a ghost.

Mei Ling stood up from the table to leave. Suddenly her vision went blurry and her mind swirled downward until she was overcome by a dark shadow. She grabbed at the table and tried to sit back down, but it was no use. The last thing she saw before she lost consciousness was Siew's frightened face.

~

Disoriented when she came back to awareness, Mei Ling felt like she was moving forward. Her head was resting against someone. Two men carried her, making a chair with their arms. She jerked upright, but one of them shouted, "Stay still."

They rushed up a dirt path to a building she didn't recognize. The sounds of the waves against the shore told her she was still on the island. She slowly moved one hand to her chest; the egg was still there. She tried to reach the hem of her skirt, but it was too low to assure herself of the gold pieces.

Once she was in the building, urgent voices were soothed by bored responses, and she was deposited in a bed with clean white sheets and a soft mattress. The men who carried her left without a word.

She turned her head to look around the room, and pain exploded from behind her left ear. Feeling the spot, she found a huge lump on her head. An American woman in white nurse clothes, the color of death, came to Mei Ling's side.

"------ --- -----," the woman spoke.

Mei Ling stared at her.

"--- ---- ----- -------, -- --?"

Mei Ling could tell she'd been asked a question but didn't understand the specifics. She shrugged, hoping the gesture was universal.

"Are my children all right?" Mei Ling begged for information. "Bo and Siew?"

This time the woman shrugged at her. The nurse patted Mei Ling's arm and left. Mei Ling wished she could sit up, to look out the window to see where she was, but she feared she would collapse again. Without moving her head she looked around. It was another barracks, but there were fewer beds and they weren't bunked. No one was in the corner next to Mei Ling, but the others were all filled with women who were resting. Mei Ling realized she was in the hospital on the island.

The nurse returned to set a cup of water and a bowl of mush on the little metal table. The doctor, a White man, walked up to her and put his hands on her without introduction or permission. Mei Ling repressed her desire to slap his hands away or scream at him. She breathed in deeply to stop herself from flinching. Like in the exam when she first arrived, he touched her, saying something out loud to the nurse who wrote it down, and then moving to the next part of her body. He started at the top and worked his way down. Unlike a Chinese doctor he didn't look at her tongue or take her pulses. Her heart sped up when he pressed against her abdomen. She studied his face, but he didn't react. Then he violated her further by feeling her breasts.

Both White people left. Mei Ling took deep breaths to soothe herself. She still had no appetite, but she forced herself to drink the water and eat the bland American mush. Left alone, she rested in the quiet calm of this place. The view out the window was lovely but didn't distract her from her worries about the children and her uncertain situation.

"Are you a married lady?" another patient asked from two beds over.

Mei Ling nodded.

"Then you will be fine. He believes you are carrying a baby. He went to find your record, to make sure you are a good woman, so they don't have to send you back like that other one," the woman said.

Despite the stranger's assurances, Mei Ling was terrified. For hours she was left to wait in uncertainty.

The doctor returned just as the sun was setting.

"You --- -----——— --- ----- ----, ----- ---- ---- ---- --------. ------- --- --- --- --- --- --- ------ --- ---?" He spoke gibberish to her.

Mei Ling looked at him without comprehension and used some of her only English words: "So sorry. No much English."

Fury flitted across his face, raising fear in Mei Ling. He turned and rushed away. Again she was left alone with confusion and uncertainty.

Sooner this time, the doctor returned with a Chinese man.

The man bowed hello and said in Cantonese, "I am a translator. The doctor has requested my services. Do you prefer Sze Up, Sam Yup, Min, or Cantonese?"

"You speak all those?" Mei Ling replied in Cantonese, fascinated despite her anxiety.

He nodded and added, "And English, of course."

"Cantonese, please," Mei Ling requested.

The doctor, looking annoyed, said, "---- ---: You --- ------- --- --- --- ---- ----, ----- --- --- --- ---------. ------ --- --- --- --- --- --- ----- --- ---?"

Shame and anger flashed across the translator's face before he said, "He suspects you are pregnant—for the first time, though your file says you have a son. Perhaps you aren't who you are saying you are?"

Mei Ling's eyes widened, and her heart beat fiercely in her chest. Like Jui Lan, she would be sent back in disgrace. She wanted to protest her honor, tell this stranger she was a married woman, a good woman, but her mind froze, unable to form the right words. *Bo!* Would she ever see him again? Kai Li?

The doctor spoke his gibberish to the translator, then gave Mei Ling a look she couldn't read—his chin down and his eyebrows raised high.

The man translated, "No one else *needs* to know. Do you understand?"

Hope wiggled around Mei Ling, but she wasn't clear what the doctor was insinuating. Had the translator asked if she understood or did the American doctor say that and the translator repeated it?

"I don't," she said meekly.

The translator repeated her statement to the White man. He looked at her, disgust in his eyes. He raised his hand up. Mei Ling pulled back, fearing he was going to beat her, but instead of striking out at her, the doctor rubbed his fat thumb against his first two pale fingers. Then he spun around and walked away. The doctor wanted somcthing from her, but she still didn't know what. Mei Ling was left confused and frightened.

"A bribe," the translator explained. "For a payment he will keep your secret."

Understanding rushed in. Of course. The doctor was the same as any government agent.

Relief and alarm mixed in a peculiar combination. She wouldn't be deported immediately, but she had no American money.

"How much?" she asked.

"I suggest ten dollars," he replied.

Mei Ling sucked in her breath at the large amount. "How can I get that?" she asked.

"You can make promises or provide favors," he replied.

She stared at him, confused about what favors or promises she could provide and to whom. Her mind churned, and then a pit of nausea grew with the dawning of understanding: he was suggesting that she give sexual favors.

"Do I have time to ask my husband for the money?" she implored, though she didn't know if Kai Li had ten dollars.

The translator shrugged and shook his head. "It depends on the doctor's mood. Maybe he needs it tonight, so tomorrow will be too late."

Mei Ling nodded, her calm expression belying the emotion churning in her body.

"If you want to make a bargain, find Sun in the kitchen. He arranges such things. The cost is high, but maybe not as great as the alternative. Good luck."

Mei Ling was light-headed before, but now her mind was a misty cloud. She felt the eyes of the stranger in the next bed. Avoiding the woman, she rolled to her side, facing away from the room and toward the wall. She knew what she must do, though she felt ill at the thought of squandering her Ahma's hard-earned treasure. Mei Ling had no idea of the worth of a gold coin, but she fervently hoped it was enough to buy the doctor's silence.

Ever so slowly she inched up the hem of her skirt. When she could reach the pouch, she tried to wiggle her finger into the space between the top hem and her skirt, but it was sewed too tightly. She pressed the stitch between her thumbnail and her finger and rubbed back and forth. Her finger grew sore from the friction, so she switched to another one. Before that finger was in pain the thread was cut in two. She worked at the neighboring stitch, pulling it through the fabric until she could squeeze one coin out of the small space.

She curled into a ball, studying the gold coin for first time. Its ridged edge surrounded the head of an old woman: Victoria, the former queen of the United Kingdom; she faced sideways, her mature face covered with a crown and a veil. Mei Ling turned the coin over. Her heart sped up when she saw the image on the back: a man on horseback ready to slay a dragon. There were no numbers on the coin besides the date, so she had no idea of the worth in British pounds, let alone American dollars. She prayed it would be enough.

When the doctor returned, alone, she pressed the coin into his sweaty hand. His lips pulled up into a smile; a glimmer of excitement in his eyes left her with the impression that she had overpaid—perhaps by a lot.

Within minutes a man led her back to the barracks. The guard spoke no Cantonese and she spoke little English, so there was no way for her to get answers to the questions burning in her. She would simply have to wait to see if the doctor kept his end of the bargain.

CHAPTER 11

Angel Island
June 1923

Sleep that night was fleeting. An image of Jui Lan's head bobbing in the salty waves filled the dark of Mei Ling's mind each time she closed her eyes. Her heart raced in sympathy for what the girl-woman must have felt in her last moments on earth. Mei Ling sat up on her bunk and stared through the mesh-covered window. A small sliver of moon shone in the upper corner. Ahma, Mah-ma, Quan Yin. She longed for them.

Give me strength . . . and wisdom, she asked.

She looked at Bo and Siew, pressed closed to each other in one metal bunk. Would they send her back tomorrow—leaving them alone? The deportations happened very quickly, unless there was an appeal. And there was no appeal for a woman's immorality.

She had avoided thinking about it in the past, but at some point she was going to leave this island—and would leave Siew and maybe Bo behind.

Even if the doctor did not report her, she had her interview. Passing would mean she and Bo would be landed—leaving Siew, unless the girl had already passed through customs. Mei Ling forced herself to consider what would happen if she didn't pass. Bo might be sent back with her or sent to Kai Li . . . or left here alone.

She resolved to speak with the deaconess to find out what happened to children when a mother was returned to the boat. She had to plan for Bo . . . and for Siew.

In the morning, despite her exhaustion, Mei Ling put on a calm and cheerful front for the children. A server came to the long table where they were eating their *jook*—rice porridge.

"Doctor ordered extra food for the pregnant lady!" he declared as he ceremoniously placed a basket in front of Mei Ling. She looked inside to discover six boiled eggs, three bananas, and an orange!

The children and June clapped. Mei Ling's heart soared at the sight of the bounty. Perhaps she hadn't frittered away Ahma's money. The doctor was keeping his end of the bargain—and more. She wasn't being sent away, and she was getting extra nutrition. The spirit in her would grow strong with this sustenance.

In the middle of their time with Ma Maurer, a guard came and called out June's name. Mei Ling's heart hammered in sympathy. It was exciting—everyone was anxious to have their name called—but there was a risk, even for someone like June, who had every reason to be landed. Despite her outward nonchalance, Mei Ling saw fear in her friend's eyes.

Though there was nothing she could do for June, Mei Ling was unable to focus on the lesson. The interview reminded her that she had to make preparations for the children when her time came to be deported or landed.

When the session was over she spoke with the deaconess. The woman told her that Bo was too young to be left on the island alone. Should Mei Ling be sent back Bo would either be sent to Kai Li or returned to the boat with her, but the older woman couldn't say how each option was determined.

Ma Maurer confirmed Mei Ling's suspicion that Siew was considered old enough to be left on the island without an adult in the women's quarters. Mei Ling decided to ask one of the older ladies to watch over the girl should they be separated before the child was taken off the island. She thought through the faces of the women who had come to the island recently, since they would most likely be here until Siew was landed.

She would make friends with the kindest one and use some of the bounty from the doctor to entice her to watch out for Siew should they be parted. Mei Ling couldn't ensure the child's well-being far into the future, but she could hand her over to the care of another woman. And perhaps that woman would make arrangements for Siew's future.

They rushed upstairs when she finished speaking with the deaconess, but June wasn't back yet. It had only been an hour. Interrogations were rarely that fast.

Beaming when she returned a few hours later, June declared, "I passed. Like I say I would. I leave on the four o'clock boat."

Mei Ling forced a smile. Her throat was tight with emotion. She wanted June to go home, to see her children, but she was going to miss her friend.

In a rush as she packed, June commanded, "You write this down."

Mei Ling pulled out her writing paper.

"Chinese Presbyterian Church of Oakland at Sixth and Harrison. Every Sunday you can find me there. My home address is 911 Alice Street, Oakland. Like the lady's name. Very pretty. Only a few blocks from the ferry on Seventh Street. You come see me soon. Don't forget. Okay?" June ordered.

Mei Ling bowed, blinking back tears. "You promised Bo and Siew a trip to the tower at the university in Berkeley. I won't forget. Ever."

June bowed back and then opened her arms to hug Mei Ling close.

"Thank you," Mei Ling said, swallowing back embarrassing emotions. She rested her head against June's shoulder.

"We good ladies must stick together," June said. Her eyes were shiny too when the women bowed a final goodbye.

Mei Ling, Bo, and Siew went to the window to watch through the mesh. Eventually June walked outside. They saw her go into the shed to get her belongings and then board the boat. They waved to her as she sailed back to her real life.

~

Days later, a guard came to the door and yelled Mei Ling's name. Her heart sped up. This was it. Her test.

She took Bo's hand and waved at Siew. "Come."

"No child-en," the guard said in strangely accented Cantonese.

Mei Ling's stomach lurched. She hadn't left the children since June had departed. They would be alone.

"I will take good care of Bo!" Siew declared.

Mei Ling smiled at the little girl. "You are a good big sister. Thank you. Great Auntie is over there if you need anything."

Mei Ling pointed to the woman she had arranged to watch over Siew if she was landed soon. Siew smiled. Mei Ling patted the children's heads and left them.

With each step her legs and her confidence grew shakier. It was too long ago that she'd studied the book. She had reviewed the information in her mind, but she feared she didn't remember the details correctly or they were going to ask her a question that wasn't in the book.

The guard stopped in a doorway and pointed to a cold and dark room with no natural light. On one side of the metal table sat one White man, a Chinese man, and a White woman who had a machine in front of her.

"You may sit there." The interpreter pointed to a seat. "Your file says Cantonese. Is that your preferred language?"

Mei Ling nodded, extremely grateful that she and Wong Lew She shared a common first tongue. It probably wasn't a coincidence. The matchmaker had a reputation to uphold.

The White man opened the file on the table. He asked something in English. The woman typed into the machine, her fingers flying in all directions like a hummingbird.

The interpreter asked, "Applicant 3-23. Do you understand that you are under oath to speak the truth? If you are found to have perjured yourself, you may be deported or detained by immigration authorities in the United States."

Mei Ling nodded again.

The interpreter admonished, "You must speak so your answers may be recorded."

Mei Ling cleared her tight throat. "Yes."

"Do you understand that if you do not understand the interpreter you are required to immediately so state?" the interpreter asked.

Mei Ling started to nod but caught herself and said, "Yes."

"Applicant 3-24 is too young to be sworn in," the Chinese man said, speaking about Bo. Mei Ling started to answer, but the White man spoke again before she could formulate a reply.

The interpreter asked, "What are all your names?"

My only name is Mei Ling. She swallowed and said her first lie, "Wong Lew She. No others." Then she remembered: "I am told I will be Mrs. Chinn in the United States." Then she added with a bow, "If I meet with your approval."

She saw a flicker of a smile cross the inspector's face.

"Do you waive the right to have a representative of any kind—friend, relative, or lawyer—present during your testimony?" The interpreter repeated the question asked by the examiner.

I was never offered that kindness, Mei Ling thought, but said out loud, "Yes."

The interpreter asked, "Are there any persons in the United States besides your husband who may have seen you in China and know that you bear the relationship claimed by each of you?"

"No," Mei Ling replied.

"How old are you?"

Eighteen flashed in her mind. "Twenty years old."

"Do you intend to live here permanently if admitted?" he asked.

Mei Ling considered her answer. She hadn't yet stepped foot in America and she was expected to commit to it for her life—and her children. She looked at the inspector; his face was blank. Did he want a Chinese woman here permanently?

Hoping it was the answer he wanted to hear, she said, "Yes."

"Can you read and write?"

Yes, I'm an educated woman! Mei Ling replied, "No."

"Have you ever been excluded and deported or arrested and deported from the USA?"

Mei Ling was offended by the question but only said, "No."

Continuing with the insults, the interpreter asked, "Have you or either of your parents ever been inmates of an institution for the insane?"

Mei Ling looked directly at him and firmly stated, "No."

Looking satisfyingly uncomfortable, the interpreter asked, "Do you believe in the practice of polygamy?"

"No."

With a small shrug, as if to say that he was sorry, the interpreter asked, "Are you an anarchist?"

"No," she stated, glad for these offensive but easy-to-answer questions.

The interrogation continued with Mei Ling answering slowly and carefully, doing her best to recall the specific information from the book as the questions grew more detailed. After an hour or so, the door was opened by a young Chinese man. The current interpreter stood up and left without saying a word. The new man sat in the chair he left vacant.

The new translator asked, "Did you understand the previous interpreter?"

Mei Ling was surprised to be asked this again but simply answered, "Yes."

"How large is your husband's village where you have resided since your marriage?"

Mei Ling recalled the page and confidently answered, "A little over a hundred houses."

"In what direction does the village face?"

Mei Ling considered the question. She thought of the drawing of the village and answered, "West."

"How many houses in your row?"

"Ten houses," Mei Ling replied, keeping out the question in her voice.

"Counting from the head, where is your house?"

Mei Ling pictured the drawing and counted in her mind. She double-checked from the other direction. "Fifth house, ninth row, or from the north it's the fifth house, third row."

The inspector slid two pieces of paper and a graphite pencil across the table.

The translator said, "On one piece of paper draw a diagram of your home, labeling all rooms, and on the other paper draw the village, labeling the buildings, fields, and burial grounds."

Mei Ling's hand shook as she picked up the pencil. She adjusted her fingers to grip it as if she were uncomfortable holding a writing instrument. Slowly, aware that all eyes were on her, she drew what she recalled from the book. She started to label the buildings but remembered just in time that her false self couldn't write.

She said the name of each room and the translator wrote what she said in English. When she was finished, the inspector nodded but didn't give anything away by his expression. He asked another question in English.

The Chinese man interpreted, "Is the cooking stove in the kitchen portable or built in?"

A firecracker of fear exploded in Mei Ling's chest. That information wasn't in the book.

She made up an answer: "Portable."

The White woman typed in her answer without pausing. Mei Ling looked for assurance from the two men across from her, but neither affirmed or denied the credibility of her reply.

They asked more questions about the house: the number and position of the windows, information about who slept where, and construction techniques. After another grueling hour the inspector closed the folder and said something.

"We are through for this day," the Chinese man repeated with a nod.

Exhausted and ready for a rest, Mei Ling exhaled in relief. If they went on much longer she would make greater mistakes.

When she returned to the barracks, Siew was in the midst of regaling Bo with a story. He grinned up at Mei Ling and patted her leg when she joined them on the small bunk. A sweet, poignant relief washed over Mei Ling.

Gratitude for Siew welled up in her. The girl's bright spirit had made their time on the island bearable. Leaving Siew behind was going to be heart-wrenching for Bo and for her, and it would be made all the more painful because Mei Ling had no assurance of the girl's well-being.

To calm her anxious mind, Mei Ling pulled out the statue of Quan Yin. She placed her on the end of the bed and did some awkward but soothing kowtows. She focused her breath, inhaling love and exhaling peace. Then she did a loving kindness meditation for the girl. *May Siew be safe from all harm. May Siew be free from all suffering. May Siew know joy.* And then as her grandmother had taught her to do with anyone she felt angry with, she did the same for the interrogator: *May he be safe from all harm. May he be free from all suffering. May he know joy.* She took a final breath and opened her eyes.

Siew was standing by the bed staring at Mei Ling, her intense brown eyes welling up with tears. She blinked them back.

Siew whispered, "My Mah-ma used to do that." She looked down, hiding her intense emotions. Mei Ling's throat welled up in empathy, but she let the silence be. She touched the young girl's arm. Siew looked up. "She said she would show me, but she never did."

"I'm sure she would have. You were just so young . . ." Mei Ling's voice caught.

"Will you teach me?" Siew implored.

Mei Ling bit her lip and nodded. "Yes. I will."

That night Mei Ling repeated the instruction to Siew that her mother and grandmother taught her. *Bow low. Surrender to the ancestors, give them your troubles. Ask for equanimity for yourself, seek to be calm in all that you do. Bless others, especially those who make you angry. Breathe. Breathe. Breathe.*

"Thank you," Siew said when they were finished. She had an intense look in her eye like she wanted to say something but was fearful.

Mei Ling looked at her and nodded, encouraging her wordlessly.

Looking uncharacteristically shy, Siew stared at the bedding and spoke so quietly that Mei Ling barely heard her: "I wish you were my new Mah-ma."

Mei Ling's heart wrenched. Before she could get out a reply, Siew leaped off the bed and joined Bo playing on the ground.

Mei Ling studied the girl, glad she didn't have to respond. It was a touching and sweet plea—and impossible. Siew had a family she belonged with. Besides, Mei Ling's life wasn't settled: she was still becoming accustomed to being a mother to Bo, she had this spirit inside her to protect, and she had yet to learn if her husband was trustworthy.

But she was certain that no matter how unlikely and impractical, if it was offered to her, she would gladly take on the responsibility for Siew.

CHAPTER 12

Angel Island
June 1923

Mei Ling waited to be called back later that day, but no one came for her that afternoon. Each morning or afternoon she expected to hear her name, but three days passed and no one had come for her. A walk with a guard was a welcome distraction from the pain of waiting. They walked up the hill, heading into the large oak trees and low scrub. Angel Island was very dry and brown compared to the hills behind her village.

Revulsion swelled in her throat as they passed the hospital with the opportunistic doctor. She pushed her contempt away, determined to enjoy this moment of comparative freedom. Bo and Siew skipped ahead just a bit, cresting the hill before she did. When she reached them her breath caught at the stunning view of the water shimmering in the sunlight. Land rose up on the other side of the bay. Siew pointed to the tower in the distance, the Campanile at the university in Berkeley.

"That's where you are going to live soon!" she explained to Bo, certainty and excitement in her young voice. She must have remembered June's promise that they were going there someday, only turning it into home.

Mei Ling's heart sank. She didn't want to crush their hopes, but she didn't wish to have them believe a falsehood.

She took a middle ground. "We hope to visit someday, but no one lives there. It's only a clock. A very large clock."

The children seemed satisfied with her explanation and trotted on again. She followed along with just a few other women. Bo and Siew were the only children. Mei Ling didn't bother to make any conversation—she didn't need to become attached to anyone else. Her heart couldn't hold any more loss.

They walked around until the tall Tribune Tower in Oakland came into sight. Mei Ling sent out a silent greeting to June, who had mentioned that she often walked past it. The guard forced them to turn back before her future home came into view—San Francisco, where she hoped Kai Li was waiting for them.

Mei Ling drew strength and faith from a made-up image of her new home in San Francisco. She fashioned it after her house in Guangzhou, including a garden where she pictured the peony and chrysanthemum stalks blooming under her tender care, bringing beauty into a harmonious life. In her imagination she was a well-dressed wife of a merchant living in a warm and modern building with her two children and devoted husband. Perhaps Siew would live near enough that they could visit regularly—the children acting as cousins to one another in a land without clan. Her faith in a better future gave her the strength to keep her spirits up despite the dreary conditions she was currently in.

~

Weeks passed before a guard called her name from the doorway. Her heart sped up immediately. She could be landed or deported this very afternoon. One would mean leaving Siew; the other might mean leaving both children. She took a deep breath to calm herself, pinched her arm to chase away the sadness, and patted the children goodbye.

The guard gestured to the children, pointed at the door, and said, "--'- -- ---- -- ----."

Mei Ling pointed at Bo and Siew, and then pointed at the door, repeating his mime that the children should go with them. The guard nodded.

"You can come too," Mei Ling said, keeping her tone light.

"Come on, Bo!" Siew took his little hand. The children looked delighted at the prospect.

The guard's hand shot out, stopping Siew at the doorway. "--- ---. ---- the ---."

Siew's face, and Mei Ling's heart, fell.

"I'm sorry. We'll be back soon," Mei Ling said, but then caught herself. "Maybe not soon, but we will be back."

Siew blinked back tears, turned around, and walked slowly to the bunk, her hunched shoulders showing her hurt.

Mei Ling was torn, but she wasn't given time to explain or comfort. She was forced to immediately abandon the girl to keep up with the guard as he quickly walked away.

He led her to the same small room with the metal table. Eyes from three unfamiliar faces watched them take a seat on the other side. Bo had his own chair, but he could barely see over the table.

The inspector spoke in English and the translator said, "The inspector has familiarized himself with your case. Do you understand me?"

"Yes," Mei Ling replied.

"Do you understand that you are still under oath?" the man asked.

Mei Ling answered, "Yes."

"Your son is too young to take an oath, but we still need to ask him questions," the Chinese man said.

"Yes," Mei Ling answered though it wasn't a question.

"How old are you?" the man asked Bo.

Bo stared at the man.

"Does he speak?" the man asked.

Mei Ling didn't know how to answer that question. Bo hardly stopped talking when he was with Siew, but she doubted he would be forthcoming to this stranger. She wasn't going to encourage Bo to answer the man, because his answers might throw suspicion on their case. The little boy might claim Siew was his sister or mention his first Mah-ma. She just shook her head.

Then she remembered to say out loud, "No."

The interpreter spoke to the interrogator: "-- -- ----."

The interrogator shook his head and clicked his tongue. He asked the reporter, "-- ---- -- --- ------?"

"-- -- ----," she replied.

Anger burned in Mei Ling's cheeks. The specifics of what they were saying were lost to her, but the contempt and judgmental tones in their voices were pinpricks to her pride. She wanted to scream in Bo's defense; he was a little boy who'd lost so much. Who were they to judge him, or her?

The inspector asked a question in English and the interpreter turned back to Mei Ling, switching back to a neutrally respectful tone, as if she hadn't been able to understand that they were laughing at her and her son.

"Your husband says the stove in the kitchen is built in, which contradicts your testimony. What do you have to say about that?"

Mei Ling had answered wrong! She was going to be sent back. Her Dragon sent a flood of energy radiating out from her sternum. She'd sacrificed too much to lose everything now because of the status of a kitchen appliance.

"My husband spends no time in the kitchen," she replied, indignation hiding the fear in her voice. "How can you possibly expect him to know about our stove? It appears to be built in, but it's a deception. Only a ruse to make it appear something it's not."

She heard the click of the machine as the woman typed her answer. The inspector cleared his throat but gave no indication if he believed her reply. The questioning continued for hours on much of the same line as the previous interview. In fact many questions were repeated from before. She'd be bored if she weren't anxious about the outcome.

They ignored Bo, and eventually he put his head down on the table. She was afraid they would chastise him, so she gently took his arms and led him to lie down on her lap for a rest. He resisted at first, but then gave in to her tug.

Bo was still asleep when they stopped questioning her. The inspector stood up and left with her file in his hand. The silence of the room grew increasingly unsettling. Mei Ling listened to the waves hitting the shore and the occasional cry of a seabird. The White man returned after twenty minutes or so. He wrote something himself in the file and spoke out loud. The woman typed.

The inspector slid a piece of paper, covered in English writing, to her side of the table.

"Make your mark here," the translator commanded.

Mei Ling's fingers shook as she picked up the pen. She started to write her own name, but quickly caught her mistake and wrote a shaky *X* on the black line. The man snatched the paper back and carelessly put it in "her" file.

"You are done," the translator said and stood with a slight bow. "Good luck."

The *good luck* felt ominous. Confusion swirled inside Mei Ling's head and heart, but the translator was gone before she could ask about her status. She rose, lifting a sleeping Bo into her arms, bowed her respect, and left. If she was being deported, she wasn't going to let them see her despair.

No one was waiting to escort her back upstairs to the women's barracks. She'd have to make her way back by herself. She pleaded to Quan Yin, *Grant me equanimity for whatever is to come.* She felt the weight of

Bo's life as she carried his heavy body up the cold concrete stairs. Two months ago she was afraid of the burden of caring for him. Now she was terrified at the thought of being forced away from this dear boy.

~

Mei Ling sank onto the lower bunk. Bo, half asleep, crawled over to Siew on the adjacent bed. Siew cuddled him close, and he closed his eyes once again. Was he dreaming again or just dozing? Mei Ling stared at the window; the bright blue of the broken-up sky shone through the metal mesh, the constant reminder of her imprisonment. The fog had burned away while she was in that small room. It looked to be a beautiful day for those with the freedom to enjoy it.

Overwhelmed with the futility of her situation, she lay down. Siew reached a hand out and gave Mei Ling's arm a sweet pat. She sensed that Mei Ling was disturbed. Mei Ling smiled at the girl she'd be losing when they sent her back to China.

China. The thought of returning filled her with shame and dread. She and the baby would be a burden that her parents had thought they were free from. She wouldn't return to the village; instead she would make a life in Hong Kong. She'd look for a position as a servant.

Her heart started to race. She needed to carry out her plan for Bo and for Siew. She wanted to get the children to San Francisco, to Kai Li and Suk Suk, before they sent her away.

She sat up, got out her paper, and started a letter for Deaconess Maurer to deliver to Kai Li, not caring if they learned that she was literate. She had little to lose now.

Before she'd made a mark a guard arrived at the door. All eyes turned to him.

In Chinese he yelled, "*Dai Fow*: Law Bo Low, Wong Lew She, Jui Lum Shee. Chinn Bo."

Dai Fow. First City! She was on the list of people being landed.

She rushed to the guard. Pointing to her chest, she asked, "Dai Fow? Wong Lew She?"

The man nodded.

"Chinn Bo?" She pointed at Bo.

The man nodded.

"Siew?" Mei Ling practically begged.

The man tightened his lips in empathy, but he shook his head. Mei Ling closed her eyes tight, suppressing the urge to argue with the guard. She took a breath to calm her Dragon. And then nodded. The man held up both of his hands. In English he said, "--- -------."

Mei Ling held up all of her fingers. "Ten minutes? We have to leave in ten minutes?"

The man nodded and called out, "-- -- --- ---- -- --- -------."

Frantically she packed up their clothes and rolled up their bedding. Tears pushed against her eyes as Siew simply watched with a fully awake Bo at her side. She must have heard the conversation. Mei Ling got a piece of paper. She wrote her name, Kai Li's name, and the word *Presbyterian Church* on it.

She sat down close to Siew.

"Bo and I have to leave now, and they won't let you come with us," Mei Ling said gently, working to keep her voice calm.

"Great Auntie has promised to take care of you until you can be with Suk Suk." Mei Ling went over the arrangement again. Hopefully Siew would be landed before the older woman.

Mei Ling pressed the slip of paper into Siew's hand. "Don't lose this; use it to find us. You must be the one to look for me, because I don't know your uncle's family name or where he lives."

Siew nodded. Tears threatened to spill onto her cheeks.

"I will think of you every day. And Bo will too. You are his hero!"

Mei Ling bit the inside of her cheek. She sorted through her notebook until she found the page where Siew had drawn a picture of Quan Yin. She tore out the page and offered it with a trembling hand.

Mei Ling instructed, "You ask Quan Yin for strength. She will help you through anything. I will ask her too—for you."

What if this was it—her last time to impart wisdom to this child? She called up the words Mah-ma had drilled into her. The recipe for a good life: "Work hard, be kind, and be humble—and you will live a harmonious life."

Siew nodded, but it was too much for a six-year-old to take in.

"We love you," Mei Ling said, her Dragon roaring with sorrow and outrage.

"I love you," Siew replied.

"Soon you will be landed, and we will all go to the tower June told us about—and Angel Island will be our view instead of our prison." She spoke out loud in a quavering voice her most fervent desire, though she feared it was simply a dream.

Siew nodded. She leaned her body into Mei Ling, wrapped her arms around her waist, and squeezed tight. Mei Ling hugged the girl back, tears burning the back of her eyeballs. She didn't let go until Siew broke away. Siew patted Bo's cheek. She bent over him and rubbed her nose against his.

With a heavy heart Mei Ling slung their bag over one shoulder and took Bo's hand in one of hers. He held Siew's hand in his other. Mei Ling pulled him until his hand broke away.

"Come, Siew. Come," Bo's little voice called out as he beckoned her with his hand.

"Goodbye," Siew's small voice said. She lay on the metal cot, alone, watching them go, unshed tears in her glossy brown eyes.

Mei Ling felt ill at the betrayal of walking away from her.

CHAPTER 13

San Francisco
July 1923

Mei Ling waved to the barracks as they walked toward the dock but couldn't see if Siew waved back. She could barely make out the girl's face shrouded behind the mesh screen.

"Siew?" Bo asked.

Mei Ling pointed and then put a false cheer in her voice. "Siew is waving goodbye. Wave back to her before we get on our boat . . . for San Francisco. We're going to see your Bah-ba."

The news that he would be reunited with his father did nothing to change the look of dismay on Bo's face. They were leaving Siew behind. Mei Ling understood her son's feelings too well.

The guard directed Mei Ling to find the trunk she'd been required to store and told her to hurry. All those weeks of waiting and now she had to rush.

The trunk wasn't where she left it. Her heart raced at the thought of losing it. The guard commanded her to keep looking. They finally found it in a back corner. She wanted to confirm everything was still in it, but he didn't give her time. The young man yelled for a porter, who hoisted up their luggage and briskly walked toward the boat. Mei

Ling held Bo's hand and rushed along the long wooden walkway to keep up with the lanky man. He deposited the trunk on the deck for the short ride to San Francisco.

They were the last to board, and before she got her bearings, the boat pulled away from the island. They barely made it to the railing to wave at the building where she imagined Siew was watching them depart. Mei Ling didn't want the girl to think she'd been immediately forgotten. Mei Ling had known the day would come when she'd have to separate from Siew. But that knowledge didn't make it less painful. *Help us to find each other again,* Mei Ling asked Quan Yin.

They traveled along the east side of Angel Island, passing the parts she hadn't yet seen and then the penitentiary on Alcatraz Island. A young man, perhaps a prisoner, perhaps a guard, waved from the dock. She waved back.

Past the prison island San Francisco came into view. The long stretch of land ended at the Golden Gate, where the bay opened to the Pacific Ocean. Jui Lan had jumped into this water. An image of her head bobbing in the salty waves popped into Mei Ling's mind. She shook her head to clear it. She didn't have time to dwell on the girl-woman.

She looked forward where the port and the Ferry Building came into view.

"Look, Bo, that is our new home." Mei Ling pointed to the crush of buildings that covered the side of the hill rising from the bay. She inhaled deeply, taking in the moment.

"Mah-ma?" Bo asked. Was he asking about her or about his first mother? Mei Ling wondered.

She reassured him, "Yes. I will be living there with you."

He looked satisfied with that answer. "Siew?" he asked.

"Siew will be living with her uncle. She was only with us for a little while, but soon you will have a little sister to take care of," she told him, sounding more confident and satisfied with the situation than she felt. Bo looked confused but didn't ask any more questions.

In about twenty minutes they were pulling into the dock. Mei Ling searched the shore for Kai Li's familiar face but didn't see him. She hoped he'd been notified that they were on their way, but it all happened so fast that it was unlikely he was waiting for them.

A crowd of people rushed past them to disembark. They stood by their trunk, wishing for a porter, but none came. Worried the boat would leave with them on it, she decided they would have to move it as best as they could.

"Bo, you push and I will pull. It's time for us to get off," she instructed.

She bent over and Bo did as she asked. She took a deep breath and tugged. Slowly they managed to get their earthly belongings around to the gangplank. The crewman at the top of the ramp barked something in Japanese. Mei Ling shrugged at him. The man yelled, and a porter arrived and carried their trunk to shore. Annoyed by his attitude but glad to be relieved of the burden, Mei Ling and Bo followed close behind. Without ceremony or care he dropped it on the ground, spun around, and abandoned them in the crush of a large crowd.

Mei Ling grabbed Bo's hand before he was swept about by the swirl of people.

"Help me," she instructed the boy.

Together they pushed the trunk through the dirt to the edge of the crowd. Panting, she lowered herself onto the trunk and pulled Bo close next to her. She trusted that Kai Li would find them after he was finished with work for the day if they simply held still.

A stranger walked up to her, a Chinese man, and asked her in Cantonese, "Ride? Best ride in town. Very cheap!" He started to lift up the trunk even though they were still sitting on it.

"No. My husband will be here soon," she rebuffed him forcefully, hoping she sounded confident.

The man shrugged and walked away. Twice more, men offered them transportation, but she refused. Mei Ling and Bo sat, watching the boat load up with the goods and people that would soon be departing San Francisco. She thought about the cycle of the journey. For her it was an extraordinary experience, but for the crew it was their life. Eventually they were nearly alone on the large dock.

"Pee?" Bo said.

"You must be patient and wait until your Bah-ba comes," Mei Ling said, though her own patience was nearly gone.

Bo nodded.

"Thirsty," Bo declared.

"Me too. Bah-ba will be here soon. We can eat and use the bathroom then."

Bo nodded, but his eyebrows furrowed. Mei Ling patted his leg in reassurance, though she was wary too. With the clock tower declaring the time, she was fully aware that more than an hour had passed. What if Kai Li didn't know to come for them? She tried to remember the address she had given to her family. Brooklyn was the street, but Mei Ling could not recall her own address number, and the drivers had disappeared along with the crowd. Taking out a gold coin in public would be foolish. Waiting was still their best option for now, but if her husband hadn't arrived by the time the sun started to set, she would take a taxi ride to the church. Perhaps there would be assistance there.

"Peed," Bo said, his voice full of sorrow. Mei Ling looked him over. Sure enough, there was a damp spot between his legs.

Shame welled up in her. She bit her lip and took a breath.

"It's okay, Bo. We'll get you dry pants soon," she said, though she knew she was at the mercy of fate.

"I'm here." Kai Li was suddenly at her side. He had a sheepish grin on his face and bowed in greeting. Relief surged past Mei Ling's annoyance.

"Come." Kai Li picked up their trunk and led them to a waiting rickshaw.

~

They traveled for only a short time along the waterfront of the Embarcadero and then turned left onto a steep cobblestone street. Kai Li jumped out and helped push the rickshaw up the sloping hill. A few blocks from the shore Mei Ling felt as if she were in China again. The buildings rose up three and four stories, designed and painted just as they were in Guangzhou. Signs in Cantonese declared meat, produce, herbs, and fabric. Men roasted nuts and sold them to passersby. Merchants hawked goods. They turned too many times for Mei Ling to track the names of the streets and finally stopped halfway down a little alley.

Kai Li paid the driver and lifted the trunk. Mei Ling's hopes for her new home sank as they climbed up the dimly lit steps. The floor was covered with dirty, cracked tiles, and paint peeled on the walls. The building was so old that the damp smell made her nauseous. She breathed through her mouth to avoid the stench, but it was only marginally helpful.

On the fourth floor, Kai Li stopped at a beat-up wooden door. He opened it to reveal a space containing a bed, a table, and a kitchen—like their room in Hong Kong. This wasn't what she dreamed of. She felt him studying her reaction, but she was tired and hungry, too upset to put on a good face.

Mei Ling unpacked in a brooding silence. Tension built in the room until she felt like she might explode and reveal her Dragon nature. Bo watched without making any demands, not speaking to either her or Kai Li. Did he even remember this man? Was Kai Li going to say nothing to them about leaving them waiting for hours?

"Pee?" Bo asked meekly, breaking Mei Ling's ruminations.

She remembered that Bo needed a clean pair of pants. She pulled some out and gestured him over. He looked fearful as he walked toward her. Mei Ling closed her eyes and took a deep breath, searching for the calm stillness to tame her raging Dragon.

Food. Though she felt nauseous, she needed something to eat. She went to the tiny kitchenette and to her surprise, she found cooking for the first time in months soothing. By the time she put the food on the little table, she felt as if she had returned to equanimity.

Mei Ling served her husband, searching his face for a reaction. He smiled, but she was aware the food wasn't very tasty. She didn't know how to use the sauces in this well-stocked kitchen, though she hoped she might learn to eventually.

After they all ate but before they left the table, Kai Li finally spoke. "I'm glad you were landed. Did you have to wait for long?"

Wanting harmony in their meager home, Mei Ling considered what to say. "Not too long, thank you. We are glad to be here as well. Right, Bo?"

Bo nodded.

"I don't think he remembers me," Kai Li said, sounding resigned.

"It has been more than two months since he saw a glimpse of you. In time he will be asking you to tell him stories," she replied.

"Siew stories," Bo said.

The girl's name cut a painful slice into her heart. She replied, "You liked Siew's stories, didn't you?"

"The little girl from the boat?" Kai Li asked.

"She was with us in the barracks. She cared for Bo as a little brother. He misses her," Mei Ling said. Then she spoke as she would to her sister: "We both do."

Longing for news of her family welled up.

"Husband, have you retrieved any letters from my family?" she asked.

Kai Li's eyes widened in alarm. A sudden, nauseating realization flooded Mei Ling.

"You cannot read, can you?" she asked.

Kai Li shook his head.

"Nor write?"

He shook his head again.

"You paid someone to pen the notes you sent me on the island?" she questioned, trying to keep the accusation out of her voice but not succeeding.

He nodded.

Her Dragon woke up, causing her to blurt out her accusation: "You aren't a merchant, are you?!"

Humiliation and fear covering his face, he bowed his head in shame.

Her Dragon roared so fiercely she had difficulty remaining in her seat. All those weeks on the boat and the island she got strength from imagining a beautiful home, not a dingy hovel.

"Husband, may I take a walk outside? By myself?" she asked through a tight jaw.

He looked up at her, fear in his eyes, maybe a hint of anger. Then he gave one sharp nod in agreement.

Mei Ling stormed out of the room, working to hide her overwhelming feelings of sorrow and anger. She made her way down the stairs to the alleyway. There wasn't anything growing. The crush of buildings closed in on her. She studied the signs at the corner of Stockton and Sacramento Streets, committing the names to her memory so she could find her way back. Turning onto Stockton, she walked up a steep hill, searching for greenery and open space. Did no one grow anything in this city? At the crest she looked through the crowded buildings and caught a glimpse of the bay, the same body of water that had imprisoned her on Angel Island.

She longed with a ferocious desire to be back in the barracks with Siew. At least there she still had the dream of a beautiful home waiting for her to give her strength and hope. But now she was awake in this reality.

She was living in a small tenement room with two, and soon three, people. Her husband was illiterate, probably a laborer, as she and her children would now be too. Her parents' investment in her future had come to nothing.

Mei Ling leaned against a brick wall. People rushed by, ignoring her. She sank into a squat, the still-warm brick radiating heat against her back, tears pushing out of the corners of her eyes. She bit her lip, but it did nothing to chase away her sorrow. Alone for the first time in months, she released her pent-up emotion in this public place. The tears flowed and flowed.

When her eyes ran dry, she stood up. A sliver of a new moon was cresting over the building to the east. Was it coming from China or going there? Both, she realized.

She felt a blessing from her Ahma radiating down in the moonlight. She breathed it in. Then she sent her blessing back up to the moon to shine down on her family when it traveled around to the other side of the world. She felt the grace of connection across the miles and months.

Mei Ling inhaled deeply, feeling the moist fog enter into her lungs. *I will be strong. I will create harmony.* She wiped her eyes and released her jaw, putting on a serene face before she walked back to the miserable dwelling that was her only home.

CHAPTER 14

San Francisco
July 1923

When she returned she didn't demand an explanation, but Kai Li was ready to give her one. He invited her to sit across from him at the rickety table in their one-room home.

His expression fluctuating between shame and self-righteousness, Kai Li confessed, "Wife, as you have realized, I'm not a merchant. I work as a domestic servant in a grand house on Nob Hill."

Mei Ling forced herself to look calm and nod slowly, encouraging him to reveal more.

Kai Li continued, "For generations, Gam Saan Haak labored in the United States and only visited family in China. But the US government is making that arrangement impossible.

"The laws here are growing ever tighter. Before the gate closed all together, I paid one thousand dollars for papers that say I'm owner of the Western Produce Company in Oakland. Posing as a merchant was the only way for me to secure a visa for Wong Lew She and for Bo."

He looked at her. "For you."

Kai Li looked back at the ground and explained, "I did not have one thousand dollars, or all of the money for our tickets, so

I borrowed the balance before it was too late. The funeral and the matchmaker have increased our obligation. We will not always live in such conditions. The debt will be paid off in four or five years, and we will move to a larger home."

Our obligation. Mei Ling kept her face calm as she listened. She nodded as if she understood while her chest exploded in outrage, and she swallowed back a rising nausea.

All the facts from the matchmaker could be lies. She didn't know what was true about the man her life depended upon. She wanted to know more but didn't want to open the door that would invite him to question her and cause her to lie to her husband, further eroding her own integrity.

He wasn't the only deceitful partner in this marriage. At the matchmaker's advice Mei Ling had lied to him. Kai Li professed to be a merchant in order to get a visa and appear as a suitable match for Jah Jeh. Mei Ling was presenting herself to him as Jah Jeh, a Rabbit, and as a Christian.

She was hiding her Dragon and her faith. They had each acted in bad character, and as a consequence she had a life without integrity.

She'd been foolishly naïve to believe the story she'd been told. Bo might not even be his son, but a paper son Kai Li was paid to bring over. This man's name might not even be Kai Li. They were a good match, not because they were an Ox and a Rabbit, but because they were both deceitful.

He was a paper merchant and she was a paper wife. Her family willingly gave up Confucian teachings about living an honorable life to secure her future. It hadn't been her decision to marry this man. Duty required that she respect her parents and go along with their wishes for her, but she feared they were foolish to surrender her to these circumstances.

Mei Ling had been hesitant to tell Kai Li about the child growing within her. Now she understood why: she didn't trust him. She knew that Pasha had spoken the truth—this baby would be born a girl. Too many men didn't greet their daughters with joy, and Kai Li might be one of them. Mei Ling had to prepare an escape in case her husband demanded that they end the girl's life, or if he abandoned her once their daughter was born.

She tapped the coins from her grandmother against her leg. They felt like a talisman of safety. Just as one of them got her through Angel Island, she hoped they would help her to find a safe place to be away from this man if he proved to be entirely untrustworthy. She didn't know how far the money would go to keep her and Bo safe, and the daughter who was on the way, but the coins gave her a sense of security.

Mei Ling took a calming breath and told Kai Li what she thought he wanted to hear: "Husband, we must do what we must to survive in these difficult times. I understand."

He sighed and smiled at her, looking much relieved, but Mei Ling knew better than to trust how he looked or what he said.

~

That night Siew visited Mei Ling in a dream. Siew's little face pressed against a mesh screen like the ones on the windows in the Angel Island barracks, but somehow large prison bars too. The girl pushed her arms all the way through the gaps, up to her shoulders, reaching for Mei Ling, but an invisible veil separated them. Sorrow filled Mei Ling's sleeping heart. Slowly Siew's face grew more and more desperate until it utterly transformed. Her bright eyes hardened until they were dark stones in her sockets. Then Siew's fingers grew sharp bear claws. She slashed at the invisible veil but couldn't remove it. Fear joined the sorrow, and Mei Ling startled awake. Her heart trotting like a goat, she looked around the still-dark, still-dank room.

Her husband, that virtual stranger, lay on her right side. Bo dozed on her left. A trickle ran down her cheek. Slowly, carefully she slid from the bed. She dug out the picture of her family and her statue of Quan Yin. Desperate to find strength and faith she made an altar in the corner of the room, despite her husband's devotion to Christ. She kowtowed to Quan Yin and her family, surrendering her fear and sorrow, doing loving kindness meditations for Siew and Kai Li, and asking for strength for herself and harmony in her new family.

~

When Kai Li rose, Mei Ling prepared him tea and rice. She would fulfill her duty toward him. Perhaps he would do his duty as well. Time would reveal if this was a real marriage.

His eyes took in the altar in the corner without comment, his expression flat. She was relieved, as she had no need to speak of it.

"Chinatown is small, only a few blocks. There are some bad places very nearby, not suitable for an honorable wife," Kai Li explained. "The streets are fine, but stay away from the alleys besides this one . . . especially Bartlett Alley. It has only bad women."

Mei Ling understood his meaning. She nodded.

"And the post office. Do you know where that is?" she asked. "I wish to mail a letter to my family."

His cheeks burned red, in shame or anger she didn't know. He told her the directions to the post office, advised her on the best market, and left her some coins.

"Tomorrow I will go to the produce market in Oakland," he said. "I rise when it's still dark, and you don't need to wake so early. I'll shop for you when I do the shopping for my employer."

Mei Ling nodded. Then Kai Li left for nearby Nob Hill, where he worked six days a week as a houseboy in a mansion. Her husband was only just above a lowly laborer in social standing.

~

When Bo was awake and ready to go out for the day, Mei Ling tied him to her back. They were going to explore this foreign land together. She would learn about their new city, looking for Siew as she went. And try to discover how she might survive here should Kai Li prove to be an unreliable husband.

She followed Kai Li's directions to the post office. A long line of Chinese people held packages and envelopes, waiting for their turn to speak with a clerk. Mei Ling watched carefully so she would know what to do when she made it to the front. Both clerks spoke Cantonese, so she was able to follow their interactions. So far no one had asked for any letters; they either left their mail or bought stamps. She rehearsed what she was going to say.

When her turn came she told the lady at the counter, "I'd like to mail this letter to my ancestral village near Guangzhou. Please."

"You only want the one stamp?" the woman asked without looking at Mei Ling.

"Do I need more than one?" Mei Ling asked.

The woman replied, "Do you want to mail more than one letter?"

"No. Just the one. To let my family know I'm here, safe." Mei Ling's voice broke. She cleared her throat.

The Chinese woman looked up and studied Mei Ling. "Is this your first day?"

Mei Ling nodded, feeling self-conscious.

"Welcome. It's good here; don't let anyone get you down," the woman advised; then she said, "Six cents. For the letter. It will take two months to get there."

Mei Ling nodded. Two months. So much time and so much money. But that was all she had to stay connected to her family, besides her meditations.

"Is there any mail for me? Wong Lew She," she asked, her heart quickening with desire and her tongue tripping over the false name.

The woman shook her head, but she had not even looked for a letter.

She explained, "The mail will be brought to your house. Did you give your family the street and number?"

Mei Ling nodded.

"It will be left there soon after it arrives here," the woman said.

Mei Ling must have looked confused, because the woman laughed.

"There are many surprises here. The first year is the hardest, but it gets better after that. I know—I talk to people just off the boat every day."

Mei Ling slid a few coins and the envelope to the woman. "Thank you," she said. "For your kindness and for the information."

The woman smiled with a nod and beckoned the next customer forward.

Mei Ling walked up a steep hill toward the shop where her husband suggested she buy produce. Along the way she pointed out the colorful lanterns and buildings to Bo. She found the store but kept walking. Before they shopped, they were going to the Ferry Building in case Siew was on the morning boat. Perhaps Suk Suk would be waiting for the girl and they could plan a visit.

They came upon a short street with tall, dramatic buildings painted in bright colors. They had porches and banners waving from them. A temple dedicated to Tin How was bustling with petitioners coming and going. Mei Ling vowed to return after shopping to leave an offering of oranges to thank the sea goddess for their safe arrival to this land. Some buildings had words carved into their façades. She read *Wong Family, Hip Sing Tong.* They must be the benevolent associations that provided assistance to the people in those clans.

Mei Ling walked up Grant, a thriving commercial street with bright-red lanterns hanging overhead, and turned toward the bay on Jackson. The contrasts in this small neighborhood were dramatic. A few steps later she was stopped short by what she saw. Bartlett Alley, the one Kai Li had warned her about, was a short block away from Grant but another world entirely. She stared down the dark and muddy lane. Women's faces peered through bar-covered windows. One girl-woman caught Mei Ling's eye. Her slender fingers were pushed through the mesh screen and her dark-brown eyes were devoid of hope. She gave a little wave with her pointer finger. Mei Ling sucked in her breath. She rushed away, but the girl-woman's face hung in her mind's eye.

Her legs were shaky, making it difficult to navigate down the steep hill with Bo on her back. She breathed a sigh when she got to the Embarcadero. A White man growled something as he passed her, causing her heart to speed up again. She didn't understand his English, but his tone was clearly threatening. She sped up until she reached the spot where she and Bo had waited for Kai Li the day before. It was nearly deserted. She was the only woman in sight.

She untied Bo and led him to the rocks by the edge of the water. He climbed up a boulder and squawked at the seagulls.

A different White man walked up to them and sneered, "--- --- ------- --- - ------?" Then he laughed and walked away.

You are not welcome here. The message was loud and clear even without a shared language. On the deserted landing, she was vulnerable to this unwanted attention and disdain. She took in a shaky breath and pushed aside her fears. Looking out at the bay she thought of Siew on Angel Island. She imagined what she might be doing. Mei Ling's improbable hope was that Siew was boarding the boat after her interview. She imagined the surprise and delight on the little girl's face to find her and Bo waiting to welcome her to San Francisco. If not that unlikely situation, perhaps she and Great Auntie were meeting with Ma Maurer for English lessons.

Mei Ling felt someone's eyes on her. She turned just a little to see a group of White men glaring at them. Adrenaline rushed through her body. They weren't safe here.

"Come, Bo!" she yelled to her son. She scooped him up and rushed away, not bothering to bind him to her back.

Relief flooded through her when they crossed the border into Chinatown. She wanted to greet Siew as she landed, but not if it meant risking Bo's safety. The girl would have to find her at church, or they might see each other on the street. Chinatown wasn't very large. It wouldn't take too long for them to cross paths.

~

Mei Ling and Bo explored Chinatown for several days. She looked for an open field or empty lot with children playing but didn't find any space where Bo could run freely. All of the ground in Chinatown was covered with pavement and buildings. In China, even a big city like Guangzhou had such a place.

Mei Ling found clay pots for the three living stalks from Mah-ma. One of the peonies had died during the journey, but the other three plants were holding on to life. She considered using one of her own coins for the purchase, but she didn't want Kai Li to know she had her own money. Instead she asked Kai Li's permission to use some of the grocery funds. He agreed that it would be a good use of their food funds, since the plants would bring them soothing and healthy tea when they took root and flourished.

Mei Ling kept a constant watch for Siew. Each time she spied a girl with dark hair in a bob, her heart pounded in hope it might be her, but every face was a disappointment.

One day Mei Ling wandered the other direction on Stockton Street and found great entertainment for Bo. The street ended with a wide tunnel that electric cars and the occasional auto drove through. Pedestrians would walk on the sides or go to the top of the tunnel to an elegant balcony that was curiously out of place. Just a block past the staircase was the cable line on California Street. Mei Ling found a curb to sit on and they watched the cars drive by. Bo waved at the conductors and was occasionally rewarded with the sound of a bell.

They explored farther down the steep hill until they came to Union Square, a fancy shopping district with a public plaza in the middle. She hoped this might be a nice place for Bo to run freely; the looks and comments they received let her know that they were out of place. They would return to California Street to watch the cable cars go by, but that would be their boundary.

Mei Ling had never been so companionless. She had no one to speak with besides the young boy. There were no school friends, no villagers, no family to share her life with.

Kai Li was tender and kind—to the point that her heart and mind started to believe he might be a faithful husband despite his initial deception. Each night he returned home exhausted, but he always asked about her satisfaction with the day. She found herself looking forward to his companionship, but she reminded herself to remain cautious and watchful.

Mei Ling wrote faithfully to her family but didn't share the full truth of her living situation. There was no need to cause them concern or regret. Each day she looked in the basket in the entryway, hoping for a letter in return, but she had yet to hear from them. Her greatest comfort came each morning and night when she kowtowed to her altar, asking the ancestors and Quan Yin for strength and guidance.

When she began to feel anger or sorrow for her life circumstances, she reminded herself that Mah-ma had lost so much—her home and two of her children—yet managed to keep her equanimity. Mei Ling desired to do no less.

She'd placed the picture of the three of them, Kai Li, Bo, and herself, next to the picture of her family in China. She took comfort in the thought that her mother, sister, and grandmother looked at the same picture so many miles away. Until she got a letter from them, that thought was her best solace.

Mei Ling made dinner each night, but none of them enjoyed her meals. Many times Kai Li ate hardly any of the food she put on his plate, and she could tell that he was forcing himself to eat the little that he did. It was demoralizing, but she agreed. She tried to prepare tasty meals, but her food was as bad as the offerings on Angel Island and the steamer. The baby inside her didn't add to the strength of her appetite.

~

On Sunday her loneliness was assuaged a bit. Kai Li stayed home, and she looked forward to an entire day together. He dressed in his suit for church and suggested she wear Western clothes as well. She shouldn't have been surprised, but she hadn't considered all that it would mean to be in a Christian family.

Mei Ling nodded. She was nervous to go to church. If she acted improperly in the foreign place, one of her lies might be revealed to Kai Li. But she also hoped that Siew would be there since she had written the name of this church on the paper that she had given to Siew. If she was no longer on the island, Suk Suk might bring her there. And perhaps Mei Ling would make an acquaintance, or even a friend, in a Christian church.

Her palms were slippery from nerves as they walked through the doors of the building. They walked upstairs to the second floor. She studied those around her and followed Kai Li's lead closely. Bo was awed into silence by the large public space. Perhaps he had never been to a Christian worship before either.

The sanctuary was cool and dark in a comforting way, though there were no candles to light and no altar with gods. They slid onto a wooden bench with a back. They faced a metal sculpture with a cross in the middle surrounded by metal vines that curved out ending in candleholders shaped like pretend flames. When the music stopped a White man wearing a robe stood up. He spoke for a long time in Cantonese. His words were difficult to follow and provided no comfort. She stopped struggling to listen to him and looked around the room, examining the little girls who might be Siew. Suddenly, the crowd stood up in unison and the organ started to play. She leaped up, pulling Bo to stand as well.

Kai Li picked up a bound book and turned it to a specific page. He held it up for her to see. He must have had the words memorized, because he sang out in a lovely voice. A sweet tingle ran down her back.

She looked at the people surrounding her—strangers, singing together. A gray-haired woman in the row ahead slid her arm through the crook of the old man she stood beside. Mei Ling felt her heart open a bit. Perhaps she would be so familiar with her husband someday. Mei Ling looked back at the book and followed the printed words. Soon she dared to add her own voice to the singers.

The song ended too soon and they sat once again. The minister spoke, and she drifted into her own thoughts until two familiar names caught her attention: Donaldina Cameron and Tien Wu.

She recognized them from the paper Jui Lan had asked her to read on the island. The flier had said they tortured Chinese girls, but this minister praised them for serving the Chinese community. He said they assisted girls and women escaping from forced prostitution or facing abandonment by their husbands. He asked that they bring donations to the nearby Presbyterian Mission House.

Abandoned by their husbands. The phrase jarred Mei Ling back to reality. She looked at Kai Li as he stared ahead at the minister. She rubbed her belly and greeted the little one growing in her. Mei Ling had to stay wary and alert, not be lulled by her hopes that Kai Li would be a devoted and reliable husband and father. She'd keep walking the double path of creating a harmonious marriage while finding a means of surviving without him. This week she'd bring an offering to the Mission House to pave the way should she need to escape there when this daughter was born.

Eventually the service ended. Kai Li led them away before she had a chance to speak with anyone, dashing her hope that she might meet a few Chinese ladies for companionship. She stopped at the doorway for a last scan for Siew but didn't see the girl.

~

Finally, on August 10, weeks and weeks after she'd left her family in China, Mei Ling's chest exploded in excitement when she saw Jah Jeh's precise characters on an envelope addressed to Wong Lew She. Rushing up the stairs, she hardly noticed whether Bo was keeping up with her. She forced herself to open the envelope carefully lest she tear the precious letter. Her hands shook as she read.

April 15, 1923

Treasured sister,
Your family thanks you for sharing news of your life with us. The photo with your handsome husband and healthy son has a place of honor in our home. Your words brought Hong Kong to life. We feel as if we have been there ourselves. You have had an amazing adventure.

Village life hasn't changed. We are cultivating our own rice now and may have extra to sell at the markets. The sweet potatoes, peanuts, and lychee have been planted, so we are hopeful for plenty to harvest soon. Please don't laugh at your sister, but you would hardly recognize me in my straw hat and peasant clothes. I have found that I don't mind working in the sun.

Mah-ma used a few precious coins to buy a mandarin tree. We are hopeful that it will bear us lucky fruit by the New Year.

We look forward to news of your life.

Forever and always,

Your loving sister

Tears streamed down Mei Ling's cheeks. Her sister's calm and kind voice pierced her heart. Mei Ling missed Jah Jeh, and the others, with a fierce physical longing.

The letter ended too quickly. She longed to read more details of their lives but was grateful for the mostly reassuring news. Her sister had recovered and no one else had fallen ill. Most important, Jah Jeh expressed a measure of forgiveness: *I have found that I don't mind working in the sun.*

April 15. Four months ago her sister touched this paper. Mei Ling smelled it, hoping for the scent of home, but she was disappointed. The crops Jah Jeh told of were no longer starts. They had already matured and been harvested, their remains turned under to enrich the soil.

Her relationship with her family was out of time. She wouldn't hear about changes in their lives as they were happening, but only long after. Nor would they know hers. At this moment Jah Jeh might be married and living with her husband's family far from their ancestral village. In fact it was most likely that Mah-ma had worked quickly to find a replacement match before Jah Jeh was too old.

Mei Ling read the note again, slowly this time, uncovering more meaning. Investing in a mandarin tree meant they expected to stay in the village, giving up hope of returning to Guangzhou. She wasn't surprised, but nevertheless she felt sorrow for her family. She pictured Jah Jeh working in the fields under a large conical hat, looking like all the others under the open sky. Another indication that they weren't planning to return to city life. Last year, despite their offers of help, she and Jah Jeh hadn't been allowed to touch the dirt when the family planted with Mah-ma, insisting that they preserve their hands to make the most fortuitous marriages possible.

Jah Jeh's hands, no longer unsullied, would mark her as a laborer. There was no going back for her. Mei Ling looked down at her own clean and neat fingers. She sighed and took in a deep breath. *That was supposed to be me,* Mei Ling thought.

You cannot change her fate. Ahma's words echoed back to her across the miles and months.

Mei Ling took in another deep breath and chanted:

May she be safe from all harm. May she be free from all suffering. May she know joy.

May they all be safe from all harm. May they all be free from all suffering. May they all know joy.

CHAPTER 15

San Francisco
September 1923

As the baby became larger, her energy grew smaller. Each day she was more tired and lethargic than the one before. Her condition was obvious for all to see, but still she didn't speak of it.

One night after she climbed into bed, Kai Li asked in a timid voice, "Perhaps we will have another son someday?"

"Very soon, husband, I believe we will," she replied.

He smiled that sweet smile again, his dark-brown eyes bright. She nearly believed they would share a life path, but the word *son* cut away that hope. Kai Li patted her arm affectionately. To her disappointment he rolled over rather than turning toward her. She didn't entirely trust him, but she'd come to look forward to his touch.

~

She meant to take Bo out each day, but some afternoons the sun was setting and they hadn't yet been out. Her mood changed along with the season. The chill from the fog made it cold inside and out. Wrapping up in many blankets was the only way to stay warm. The stalks on the kitchen window hardly got a nourishing ray of sun. Her meager care wasn't enough to keep them from withering away. She feared that Kai Li would chastise her for her poor cooking and housekeeping, but when he came home to warmed rice and dried fish, he seemed more concerned than angry.

One day he brought food with him when he walked through the door.

He looked sheepish as he said, "Wife, my household sent me with this." He raised a bag. "May I add it to our dinner?"

Mei Ling nodded.

He opened a container and a delicious scent poured out. Kai Li ladled fish-tail soup with lily bulbs and carrots into bowls. The familiar smell brought tears to her eyes. He bowed a little and they sat together to eat. She felt his eyes on her as she spooned the traditional autumn soup into her mouth. It was delicious and comforting, and she felt her muscles loosen as she warmed up inside.

She smiled and said, "It's flavorful. Please tell your cook thank you from me."

He looked very pleased with her praise. She furrowed her eyebrows at him. She hadn't meant to, but he was behaving suspiciously.

"It's my cooking," he confessed.

A husband who cooked! Mei Ling was stunned and pleased. Though as a house servant he probably was able to do all kinds of traditional women's work.

"I'm a fortunate wife, then," she declared. "You are a very good cook."

He acknowledged her praise with a shy nod.

After that he brought something nutritious and delicious each night to supplement her simple offering. Despite his concern about having enough money to feed them and keep them housed, he also spent precious coins on ginger to soothe her nausea and raspberry leaf and red-clover tea to support strong *qi*. She appreciated the food and Kai Li's care; however, his attention didn't entirely assuage her loneliness and skepticism. She continued planning for two futures: one with Kai Li and one where she would walk a path on her own. She was touched that he was attending so thoughtfully to her needs, but she wouldn't trust their marriage until she saw his reaction to their daughter.

~

Kai Li expressed his hope the baby would come on Jesus's birthday, but Mei Ling thought that would be too soon. By her estimation she would deliver sometime after the Western New Year.

The Christian celebration of the birth of a baby was a sweet novelty to her. At church on Sunday the minister spoke about the challenge of the advent—the time of waiting. Mei Ling didn't usually find solace in the Christian messages, but that week it felt like the minister was speaking directly to her, offering her comfort in the face of the unknown. He reminded her that with faith all things were possible. She didn't share his belief that Jesus would provide her with all that she needed, but his message gave her hope nevertheless.

Once again the minister asked the congregation to be generous to the Presbyterian Mission House.

More than once she'd brought a donation of rice to the building at the corner of Sacramento Street and Joice Street. She'd determined that it could be a temporary refuge for her and the children should Kai Li transform from a seemingly gentle soul into a monster after their daughter was born. If need be, she'd gather her strength after the birth to go to that building and then find June in Oakland. That was as far as her plan went, but it would serve her in the immediate future.

Mei Ling was confident her friend would have ideas for how a woman like her could survive in this land without a husband. She'd likely have to become a seamstress or house servant. It would be a lonely, unfortunate life. She didn't want to be abandoned, but if Kai Li forced her to flee, she had a plan. They had somewhere to go.

~

A warm trickle down her leg woke her up. She pushed the material from her gown between her thighs and walked out of their room and down the hallway to the shared bathroom, utterly ashamed at having wet herself.

On the toilet, an enormous contraction built in her belly until she nearly cried out in pain. Slowly the muscles began to release. She sat, breathing in and shaking, until it subsided all together and her stomach went soft. *She's coming!* Fear and excitement in equal measure surged in Mei Ling's heart. Mei Ling had never been to a birth, but she had heard the first one could take a long time and was the most uncomfortable. Her mother and grandmother told her and Jah Jeh that it was nothing to dread and the reward was well worth the struggle.

Kai Li might be right. If this took many days, their child might be born on the anniversary of Jesus's birth. Mei Ling rubbed her belly and telegraphed a message to her daughter: *You'll be in my arms soon. I promise to take care of you, no matter what.*

Siew's face flashed in Mei Ling's mind. *I hope you are well, little one. When this daughter is old enough, I will look harder for you.*

~

In the dark, Mei Ling laid a towel on the bed and climbed back into its warmth. She snuggled into her husband, her back pressing against Kai Li. In his sleep he wrapped an arm over her hip and cradled her belly with his hand. He had no idea their life was about to change dramatically.

The uncertainty that had been her constant companion was about to be resolved. She wanted to have this life with Kai Li as her husband. Mei Ling prayed to Quan Yin, *Please have him be as devoted to this daughter as he is to Bo*.

She slept fitfully, dozing between mild contractions. Sometime while she was sleeping Kai Li left for work, and she found herself alone with Bo when she woke. Except for that first one, the labor pains were mild enough to hide. She went about her day as best as she could, pausing to breathe and stretch when a cramp required her full attention.

Mei Ling had little experience with birth but trusted that it would progress as necessary—and that she could manage it. She'd heard it was wise to have a sharp knife close at hand for cutting the cord, and she left a basin of water by the bed as well.

By late afternoon, she was unable to do anything besides attend to the labor. She paced until a pain consumed her body, then she would kneel at the side of the bed, resting her arms and head on the flat surface, and letting her belly hang low. Bo patted her back gently.

"Mah-ma will be all right," she explained to him. "The baby is coming to join us." She tried to smile reassuringly, but she imagined it appeared as a grimace as another pain came. It must be confusing to the boy. She regretted that she hadn't told Kai Li the baby was coming. He might have been able to stay home to care for Bo, and perhaps give her some comfort too, though men didn't belong in a birth room. More than ever she missed Jah Jeh, Ahma, and Mah-ma.

The surges started coming one after another, barely allowing her breath to return to normal before another one came. She was exhausted by the intensity and starting to fear something might be wrong. Why wasn't this baby born yet? This was so much harder than she anticipated.

"Uh-oh!" Bo's voice cut through her stupor.

She lifted her head from the bed. He pointed to the floor. She looked between her legs. *Blood!* A stream of red ran down her bare thigh. When had she exposed herself by removing her clothes? She started to shake so hard she couldn't stop herself. With the next surge, the sounds of a wild animal filled her head. Was that sound coming from her? From Bo?

Someone was by her side.

"Mah-ma," Mei Ling called, though her mother was far, far away.

She opened her eyes. It was Kai Li. He brushed the hair back from her face. He pulled at her arms, but she resisted. She couldn't leave the floor. Another surge hit. The sound repeated. Her limbs shook.

Mei Ling grabbed at her husband; desperate, she looked him straight in the eye and begged. "Help," she cried. "Help me."

Kai Li's dark-brown eyes grew round and large with panic. When the pain subsided, she released him and collapsed back over the bed. He backed away from her. Through the haze, she watched him take Bo and leave through the door. She reached out an arm, wanting to cry out in protest, but she had no strength.

Tears ran down her cheeks as sobs racked her body. Her fear had come true, but even worse: Kai Li had abandoned her *and* taken her Bo. She was going to die alone in this room.

Wave after wave came, too many to track. The door opened. A slight woman walked through and came right to her side.

Mei Ling grabbed at the stranger. "Help me," she begged.

The woman replied, calm in her voice, "I'm here just for that purpose: your husband sent me to be with you."

A shiver of relief surged through Mei Ling. She wouldn't die alone.

"I'm going to touch you. Don't be ashamed, for it is our natural state."

Mei Ling rested her head against the bed, exhaling deeply, and surrendered herself to this auntie's care. Cool cloths cleaned between her legs. Warm tea passed her lips. Strong arms pushed on her back. Hours passed until with a sudden force she had to go to the bathroom. She struggled to stand up.

"It is the baby, ready to see the world," the woman said. "No need to find a toilet. Push him out in this room."

"My baby is a girl," Mei Ling replied.

"Then she will take her first breath right here," the woman said lightly.

Mei Ling teared up. "He wants a son. What if he doesn't accept her?"

The woman sighed and shook her head.

"What do I do?" Mei Ling implored.

"You will do what needs to be done. Like mothers before you," the woman said. "But don't concern yourself with that right now. You just get this baby out."

The urge built up until it barreled through her like a galloping horse. She could think of nothing besides the desperate need to get this baby out. Then it subsided.

Again and again the fierce desire overcame her, forcing her to bear down with all her might. Then it released her. Between the compulsions, Auntie patted her arm, offered her tea, and wiped her brow with cool cloths. Mei Ling was unable to move from the side of the bed, so the woman knelt next to her, attending to her needs on the firm wooden floor.

"I see the hair!" The woman beamed at Mei Ling. "Good girl. You are doing so well. You are a good mother."

Mei Ling reached between her legs, feeling for the bulge. The woman guided her hand until . . . she touched her baby for the first time. Mei Ling's heart swelled. Her daughter was nearly here!

With the next surge the baby's head came through her legs.

"One more!" Auntie encouraged.

But the force was gone.

"Push," the woman shouted. "All on you now. Push!"

Mei Ling bore down, and she felt the rest of the baby's body slip out. A huge surge of relief rushed through her.

With a newfound focus she turned around, lifting a leg over the cord that still bound her to her child. Sitting on the floor, up against the bed, on top of all sorts of cloths and mats, she reached for her child. A girl. Just as Pasha predicted. A perfect, beautiful daughter.

She cradled the baby on her chest as the little one panted, lifting her head up and down a little. Mei Ling rubbed her sticky back, unbothered by the mixture of red, white, and clear birth fluids.

"It's okay. I'm here," Mei Ling cooed to her daughter. "You're safe."

The little girl coughed and sputtered, attending to her first responsibility: breathing. Mei Ling wondered at the glory of this precious child while the woman attended to the afterbirth and tied off the cord. Her daughter wiggled toward Mei Ling's breast. The baby's head bobbed up and down, her mouth wide open, until her lips landed around the knob of nipple. Then she sucked hard, startling Mei Ling and causing her uterus to contract. The intensity waned after a few sucks, and Mei Ling felt her whole body surrender to joy.

Joy! Mei Ling looked at her daughter. So much love bubbled up in her chest that it hurt beautifully. Her grandmother had chosen well—Jingyi was the perfect name for her daughter. Mei Ling had Joy right here.

~

The baby suckled while the woman cleaned and packed Mei Ling with herbs to stem the bleeding. After they were finished, Mei Ling climbed into bed. The woman washed Joy and wrapped her in swaddling cloths. Then she left to tell her family it was over. Mei Ling was staring at the precious new life in her arms when Kai Li and Bo returned to their room.

Kai Li stood at the doorway, his face hard to read. He mostly looked afraid, but perhaps there was relief there too. He walked forward and bowed. At his side, Bo mimicked his father, and then climbed onto the bed with Mei Ling.

"Baby?" Bo asked.

Mei Ling's heart beat anxiously in her chest. "Yes. This is your sister?" She meant to state it definitively, but it came out as more of a question. She smiled at Bo. He reached out a little finger and rubbed it ever so gently across Joy's cheek.

Mei Ling smiled at his tenderness. She looked up at Kai Li. Tears streamed down his face. He was displeased. Her heart sank and her throat swelled. All happiness fled from her heart. She swallowed hard and bit her own lip to prevent herself from crying.

"A daughter?" Kai Li asked.

Mei Ling nodded, her face as tight as her heart. Protective fury built in her.

Steely-voiced, she whispered, "You are disappointed not to have a son, husband."

"No," Kai Li replied in a whisper, shaking his head slowly. "We have a son." He looked at her, not bothering to wipe away his tears. "Now we have a precious lotus flower too. She is beautiful. Thank you, wife."

Mei Ling's heart cracked open wide. She put her hand to her mouth to squelch a sob. Her shoulders quivered as she wept in relief. She wouldn't need to escape Kai Li to protect her daughter; she could keep walking this path with him. Bo wiped at her cheek.

"Mah-ma sad?" he asked.

She shook her head slowly. "No. Mah-ma is happy. So very happy."

She smiled at Kai Li, feeling for the first time that they might become a strong and honorable family despite the deceptions that started their marriage.

She gestured to Kai Li, raising up their daughter, offering the small package to her father. His eyes grew wide.

"Come, sit. Hold your daughter," she directed her husband.

Cautiously he lowered himself. She placed the infant in his arms. Kai Li stared in wonder at their Joy.

Finally he spoke, his voice hoarse with emotion. "I didn't get to see my son when he was born. I missed too much. With this one I won't miss anything."

Bo leaned against Mei Ling and patted the precious baby in Kai Li's arms. Mei Ling squeezed his small body and kissed the top of his head. She smiled at her husband, holding little Joy, her heart exploding with happiness.

CHAPTER 16

San Francisco
December 1923

Mrs. Woo, the birthing companion, returned the next day with soups and herbs. Kai Li hired the woman for the traditional month of rest. Mei Ling would mostly stay in bed to regain her strength so she could make rich milk. Many men invested in the confinement month only for sons, but Kai Li wanted strong milk for his Joy. Mrs. Woo even took Bo out each day, giving Mei Ling time to rest and enjoy her miraculous newborn.

Kai Li left in the dark and returned after sunset. He worked even longer hours to pay for the expense of Joy's birth. Every night Kai Li brought home his delicious cooking to nourish her body and lift her spirits. Mei Ling was so grateful for his efforts and wished she could do more to relieve him of the financial burdens of their home.

She asked Mrs. Woo, "How can a wife fulfill her domestic duties and help with the expenses?"

"Many women sew at home," Mrs. Woo explained. "Most do simple seams by hand or they lease a machine, but I have another idea for you. This needlework is exquisite. I know a store that would pay well for it."

"For this?" Mei Ling pointed at a flower on Joy's blanket. Embroidery was something that every woman did. She couldn't imagine someone would pay her for it.

"Yes. Many men in America have no wives. And some Westerners want to buy what we Chinese make." The woman shrugged. "We women must take what advantages we can find, right?"

"Yes we must," Mei Ling agreed.

"I'll arrange it for you," the woman said. She pointed to the runner on the table. "Can I take this to show him the quality of your work? I will negotiate top dollar for you."

Mrs. Woo returned a few days later with good news. She pulled out some plain runners in green silk trimmed with black. "My connection says he will give you two dollars for each one you finish."

Mei Ling gasped. She could embroider a table runner in three days. She might be able to add five dollars a week to their household! Minus the cost of the embroidery floss, which she could purchase with one of Ahma's coins. Her skills and Ahma's generosity would add to her family's well-being. She decided to keep this news private from Kai Li until she was certain of a successful outcome.

~

When the month was over, Mei Ling journeyed out with Joy and Bo on her own. She fed the girl, wrapped a new napkin around her bottom, and then tied Joy onto her chest. It was a sweet feeling to hold her so close, almost like she was inside her once again.

She grabbed the letter for her family with the news that they had a new granddaughter and set out holding Bo's hand. The air was still damp and gray. She wouldn't keep Joy outside for long, but it felt good to be in these somewhat-familiar streets. Bo trotted by her side, happy to be in his mother and sister's company.

Mei Ling still scanned young faces, hoping to see the child who filled her dreams, but she no longer expected that she would simply run into Siew one day. The girl most likely didn't live in San Francisco's Chinatown. She'd learned that California was very large, bigger even than Guangdong Province. Siew might be hundreds of miles away.

First they walked up the steep hill to the post office, then to Mei Ling's favorite produce market. The women at the market fussed over the three of them—giving them garlic and papaya for the new mother and a stick candy for the new brother. Lastly she went to the meat market for pig's feet.

She didn't cook dinner many nights, since Kai Li brought delicious food home. However, she wanted a soup to keep their livers warm and the baby strong in the winter. By the time she returned to their one-room apartment she was ready for a nap, but she was proud of herself. She'd navigated the streets of San Francisco with two children.

~

Mrs. Woo stopped coming over each day, but once a week she returned to collect Mei Ling's meticulously finished caps and runners and supply Mei Ling with plain ones.

"The boss man likes your work," the woman said as she handed over two silver dollars in exchange for four caps. Mei Ling delighted at the compliment. She'd worked hard on each one, wanting to make certain her work was high enough quality to keep it coming.

The woman went on, "But you don't have to make them so nice."

Mei Ling stared at her, confused.

"Go faster. Make more. He keeps selling them all." The woman laughed.

"I will." Mei Ling agreed to pick up the pace and lower the quality.

Kai Li would be happy, and relieved, to hear the news of her success. She'd started sharing her earnings after a few weeks of sales. Remembering her Ahma's words, she kept a portion of her pay secret to add to the coins from her grandmother, but most of it went toward their debt.

At the rate they were paying, they had about two years before the immigration costs for her and Bo were settled. Kai Li's income covered their basic expenses: food, clothes, and housing. They had just enough money so long as they stayed healthy and continued living in these crowded quarters, a single room for four people.

~

"Wife," Kai Li spoke up at dinner. The formality in his voice raised concern in her heart. "I have been given a fortuitous opportunity." He sounded disappointed, contradicting his words with his affect.

She stared at him, keeping her face calm, not letting her mind travel too far into fear.

"The Johnson Produce Market has invited me to be a peddler on Alameda Island. The current one is moving to the Delta to work for his uncle. I can earn nearly double my current wages, and our children will no longer have a father who is a servant."

Mei Ling waited to hear the problem behind this seemingly good opportunity. Kai Li studied her face, looking for her reaction.

"That sounds like wonderful news, husband," Mei Ling replied. She went on, probing gently, "Though I sense concern in your spirit."

"I will have to leave very early every day except for Sunday to take the ferry to Oakland," Kai Li said. "And I will return late, late."

"You won't see us when we are awake?"

"I wanted to miss nothing of her young life. Now I will miss everything." He shook his head and sighed. He looked right at Mei Ling, his eyes telegraphing his confusion. "I'm sorry to burden you with my foolish desires. This opportunity is a blessing to our family, and I must be grateful."

"Husband, it isn't foolish to want to know your own children." Mei Ling was so very glad that he did. Hoping to cheer him up, she asked, "You will be home all day on Sundays?"

"Yes."

"Well, that will be a day for family. A holiday once a week. Bo and Joy will have you then; that is more than so many fathers and children have." Mei Ling thought of all the children in China whose fathers were living in the United States, only to be seen every few years, if at all.

He pursed his lips, conflicting emotion on his face. They sat in silence, absorbing the bittersweet news.

~

The new position meant that Kai Li left before the sun was shining and returned in utter darkness. He saw Joy when she woke in the night to feed, but Bo was asleep the entire time Kai Li was home—except on Sundays. Mei Ling hadn't realized how helpful Kai Li was with the children until he was no longer around. They all missed his delicious and satisfying meals. He had occupied the children when she washed up in the communal bathroom down the hall. It had been a welcome time of solitude. But now it was one of the most stressful parts of her day—juggling the three of them in a small, damp space.

She was lonely and exhausted; a soup of anger simmered below her surface. She regretted her childish feelings but couldn't seem to overcome them. Kai Li was also exhausted and tense. Their savings grew but their spirits didn't.

On Sundays Kai Li slept, growling at the children if they disturbed his quiet. He didn't even attend worship. He grew thin and weak. After several weeks, Mei Ling couldn't keep her concern to herself.

"Husband," she said to him one Saturday evening after he returned late, "you work hard to keep our family strong. Thank you. But we can't be strong if our head is weak."

Kai Li glared at her. She'd never seen that look on his face.

"Wife, you don't know your place!" Kai Li scowled.

Mei Ling replied, "I only have your well-being in my heart."

Kai Li sucked on his teeth with his tongue, making the clicking sound reserved for contempt. Then he walked out into the late night, leaving her alone with the sleeping children.

Anger and worry burned in her. She hadn't handled this delicate situation well. Rather than being a comfort or support to her husband, she had driven him away. Now he was furious with her. And she was lonelier than ever.

Hours later, well into the early morning, the door opened. Mei Ling pretended to be asleep, curled up in protection. He came to her bedside and hovered over her. When the smell of alcohol hit her nostrils, her heart sank and her throat swelled. She felt his fingers tap at her shoulder. Her heart sped up. More taps. Still she didn't move. Kai Li's hand wrapped around her upper arm and shook her, not hard, but insistent. She could no longer pretend to be asleep. She opened her eyes, steeled for his anger.

"Wife. I'm sorry for my emotional outburst," he said. Mei Ling's shoulders dropped and she exhaled.

He truly looked remorseful. She sat up slowly. He sank to the bed.

"I must work," he implored. "But I'm too tired to be a kind husband and father."

"Husband," Mei Ling whispered and took his hand. "You sacrifice too much. Can we move close to your work?"

His head jerked up, his eyebrows raised in surprise. He looked as if she were making a lovely but impossible suggestion, like flying to the moon. His eyes moved from side to side as he considered the idea.

"We have a lease," he finally replied.

"When does it end?" she asked.

"Next year," he replied. "We can move then."

"What is the penalty?"

"Too much," he replied. "One month's rent."

"Husband, surely your health is worth one month's rent."

He looked doubtful.

She asked, "What will you save on the ferry?"

"Ten cents a day," he replied.

That was a start, but not the equivalent of a month's rent. "Perhaps rent is less in Oakland or Alameda?" she suggested.

He looked like he was considering that idea.

"Please, husband, will you find out?"

"I will try," he agreed, though he did not look confident. She smiled at him and touched his arm gently. He leaned in for an embrace. She wrapped her arms around him and held him against her body, glad to be past their conflict.

CHAPTER 17

San Francisco
May 1924

Only a few days later Kai Li came home before the sun had set. Clearly excited, he carried a pink box and placed it on the table with a flourish. He nodded to Bo, encouraging him to open it.

"Cookies!" Bo exclaimed when he saw the small, white Western cookies and the sesame balls with red bean paste.

"Wife," Kai Li proclaimed like an excited child. "You are wise and kind."

Mei Ling laughed at the praise. Her husband's joy was contagious.

"I have found us a new home in Oakland. As you suggested it will cost less each month. Even with the penalty we will come out ahead," Kai Li explained. "Even better, it's only three blocks from the produce market."

"Oh, husband! That is wonderful news. I'm happy for you." She beamed at him. "For us."

Though he didn't fully understand their conversation, Bo picked up on their happiness. He clapped his hands and jumped up and down in pleasure.

On Sunday morning movers put all of their belongings on a rickshaw. It was unnerving to trust their belongings to these strangers, but Kai Li had confidence in these men. But Mei Ling kept her most precious treasures with her: the items from her altar. She considered keeping the pots with the anemic peony and chrysanthemum stalks, but realized she was more likely to break them along the journey than the movers. Mei Ling also left a note in the mailbox with their new address, hoping that letters from China would find their way to her.

They walked to the Ferry Building, Joy tied tight on Mei Ling and Bo holding her hand. The May air was perfect on her skin and the sun shone down on them. It was bitter to leave the room where Joy had been born, but oh so sweet to be heading to a new home. Mei Ling had already looked through her papers to find the note with June's information. She would finally seek out her friend.

They boarded the ferry to Oakland. Standing at the rail, they watched the bustle below. *Goodbye, San Francisco.* Mei Ling was surprised she had fond feelings for the place. She was going to miss her first American home.

Once they sailed past Yerba Buena Island, Angel Island came into view to the left and her heart constricted. Siew's sweet face popped into her mind, and her heart filled with yearning to confirm she was well. Once they were settled she vowed she would put greater effort into finding out what happened to the girl. Perhaps June would have ideas for how to find her.

"Bo, there is Angel Island, where we . . ." *were held captive,* she thought, but said out loud, "stayed."

She looked across the bay. "And there is the tower. The Campanile. Remember?"

Bo shook his head. Of course he didn't remember. It was nearly a year since they had left the island.

"Someday we are going to take a ride high up to the top of that tower. With our friends Siew and June," she explained.

Bo's brows pulled inward; he was trying to remember. Then he shrugged and pointed to a seagull flying high above them. Mei Ling smiled and nodded.

They landed at a long wooden dock that jutted far into the water. This side of the bay had hills like San Francisco, but they were farther in the distance and covered with trees, not buildings. The sun shone in a bright, cloudless sky. Mei Ling savored the noticeably warmer air.

Kai Li led the family to a Key System train. It was filled with all kinds of people. She steeled herself for hostile or curious glances, but they didn't draw any special attention. When Bo dropped his wooden rabbit, a Negro man in a dark-blue uniform handed it back with a smile as if it were totally ordinary for them all to be on the train together.

They rode past the edge of a downtown with a few large buildings. Oakland felt like a city, but it was much less dense than San Francisco. As June had said, there were more trees and less people over here. They got off at Sixth and Webster Streets.

This Chinatown had streets built wide to accommodate cars. The two- and three-story modern buildings had businesses at the street level with signs in English and Chinese, and apartments on the upper floors.

Kai Li's hand shook as he put the key in the lock at the front door. Mei Ling wondered if he was nervous or excited. Probably both. She vowed to act pleased no matter their new living conditions. They walked through a polished oak door up the stairs to the second floor. Mei Ling wouldn't miss walking up four floors. He opened another door to reveal their apartment. A large room furnished with a simple brown couch and two stuffed chairs on one side, and a large table with six light wooden chairs on the other. Past the table she saw a kitchen through an archway. Mei Ling was confused.

"There is no bed?" she asked, concern filling her voice though she'd meant to stay positive.

Kai Li crossed through the living room and opened another door with a flourish. A room with two beds and a dresser.

"A separate bedroom!" Mei Ling exclaimed in true delight.

Kai Li nodded and said, "And look."

He walked to another door.

Mei Ling gasped and a chill went down her back. Dumbfounded, she looked at Kai Li with wide eyes.

"Our own bathroom!" she exclaimed. "Husband, can we really afford this?"

Kai Li looked so proud as he answered, "Yes, wife, we can."

"Mah-ma, look!" Bo's voice came from the back of the bedroom.

Mei Ling rushed to his side. He pointed out the window to a small backyard. She could plant a garden! The peony and chrysanthemum could come out of their pots and really take root. Mei Ling hadn't felt so happy since the day of Joy's birth.

"Husband, you have found us a wonderful home."

Kai Li beamed.

~

After they unpacked, they went out into their new neighborhood. Mei Ling's heart sang in the lovely May day. It was sunny and warm with a slight breeze. They strolled down Webster Street across the railroad tracks to the produce district. The air was filled with the smell of rotten fruits and vegetables, even though the businesses were closed for their day of rest. Kai Li stopped in front of Johnson Produce.

"This is where I select the best vegetables and fruits for my customers. Then I take my cart to Alameda." He pointed down Webster Street. They walked three blocks to the water.

An unusual bridge crossed the estuary between Oakland and Alameda. Two wide wooden docks on each shore were connected by a metal span.

Cars and horse-drawn carts traveled in both directions down the middle of the bridge. Pedestrians crossed the span on the outer edges.

Kai Li pointed. "It's very crowded during the week. The metal section in the middle turns to allow the boats through. When it's turned I must wait with the crowd until the boats pass and the bridge is complete again. Then we all rush to get to where we are going."

They strolled along the right side of the wooden dock. Bo let go of Mei Ling's hand and ran toward the open edge. Fearing he would tumble into the water and be swept away by the tide, she rushed after Bo. Kai Li reached him first.

"You must be very careful," Kai Li chastised Bo.

Kai Li kneeled by their son and pointed over the edge. He held Bo's body steady while the little boy looked down at the murky water far below.

"If you fell off you would float out the Golden Gate to the Pacific Ocean, and we would lose you forever."

Bo's eyes went wide and he backed away. Kai Li stood up and swung Bo onto his shoulder.

"We'll cross this bridge some other time," he said. "Today, let's see Oakland's Chinatown."

They walked back toward their apartment, past their street, and turned right on Seventh Street.

Mei Ling gasped. One block past their new apartment was a park. It was plain, but it was green and there were trees. Children, Chinese children, played on the grass. They found a bench to rest on. Bo watched tentatively, but Kai Li took his hand and walked with him to the edge of the children.

Mei Ling watched him crouch down to Bo's level. He whispered something in Bo's ear. Their son nodded and then took off in a run. Kai Li chased after him in a big circle.

Mei Ling laughed. She'd never seen either of them run so freely. Bo ran toward her and threw himself over her lap, breathing hard.

She rubbed between his shoulders. Joy tilted sideways to peer around from Mei Ling's back. Bo kept his face hidden in her skirt and then popped up with a *boo* at his sister. Joy laughed and kicked her legs. No one could make Joy laugh like Bo.

Kai Li joined them on the bench, slightly out of breath. Mei Ling welcomed him with a pat on the hand. They smiled at each other, Kai Li looking as happy as she felt.

"Our new church isn't far from here," Kai Li said. "I went to the minister for assistance and he arranged for our apartment."

"We're fortunate to be Presbyterians," Mei Ling said, for once feeling grateful for the church. "My friend June attends that church."

Kai Li looked confused.

"From the island," Mei Ling reminded him.

"Oh, yes," he replied. "We can go next Sunday. Perhaps you will see her then."

Mei Ling wasn't going to wait a week to find June. She'd go to that address tomorrow.

"They have English classes at the church, if you wish to attend," Kai Li said.

"Speak English, me?" Mei Ling asked.

"Why not?" he replied. "It will make them proud."

Who? Mei Ling started to ask, but then she followed his gaze. The children. Bo and Joy would be fluent English speakers.

"There is the school that Bo can go to when he is five," Kai Li said. "Right over there."

Mei Ling looked where he was pointing. Across the street was a squat building with a playground surrounding it. She looked at Bo, playing *boo* with Joy, as she and Kai Li spoke.

"Will we really have the money to send him to school?" she questioned, wanting to confirm June's assertion that school was for everyone.

"The government pays. Even for Chinese schools," he replied. Then he corrected himself, "Not Chinese-language schools. Those are private, like the Kuomintang schools. But the government pays for schools for learning reading, writing, and math, even for the Chinese living here."

"For girls too?" she asked, her heart beating hard in hope. She wanted her daughter to be educated.

Kai Li smiled. "Yes, for Joy too. Boys and girls attend that school."

Satisfied, Mei Ling nodded. Her husband was a peddler, but perhaps here her children would rise higher.

They left the bench and walked to the markets. Kai Li chose vegetables, tofu, and a chicken to celebrate their new home.

Mei Ling embroidered in their living room while Kai Li cooked them a feast. Tantalizing scents filled their living space.

Mei Ling spoke out in a serious voice. "Husband, it isn't fair."

"What?" Kai Li asked, concern in his voice.

"I'm the only one who gets to eat your delicious meals," she teased.

He smiled. He started to speak and then stopped himself.

"What?" she asked.

"I'm silly," he said, looking chagrined.

"What?" she asked again, wanting to know his heart.

"I used to wish for my own restaurant," Kai Li said with a small smile.

Surprised, Mei Ling asked, "Truly?"

He nodded. "As I said, it's silly."

"That isn't silly, husband," she replied. "I think it's a grand plan."

Kai Li shook his head. "It isn't a plan. Only the silly dream of a foolish child."

Her heart went out to him. Mei Ling thought of all the dreams she'd spun for herself during hard times. Most recently she stood on Angel Island, dreaming of being landed and visiting this place where she was right now. Without that she might not have had the will to wake up each morning.

"Husband, it's never foolish to have a dream. Even if it never comes to be. It can give you the hope you need to keep going."

He shrugged. He looked resigned and a little angry.

"Perhaps you will be a cook in a famous restaurant someday," she said.

He shook his head.

She looked at him, confused. Why was he so doubtful?

"I have tried to get a job in a restaurant," he explained. "I don't have the right connections because I'm not in a clan."

"Why aren't you part of the Chinn clan?" she asked.

"It's expensive and complicated to join the association. They say they help every Chinn, but some benefit more than others. The church is enough. We don't need a clan," he insisted.

"Maybe it will be different now that we are in Oakland," she suggested.

He shrugged. Then his voice changed tone, becoming upbeat. "Wife, tonight is a celebration of what we do have. Let's not let my childish dream take away from our first night in our new home."

Mei Ling smiled and nodded. But she wouldn't forget his desire.

~

In the morning, Kai Li left for the produce market and Mei Ling did her morning devotional before the children woke. Wordlessly, she and Kai Li had come to an understanding. She went to church as he expected, and she kept her family's spiritual traditions in their house. She sipped her tea and soaked up the wonder of this new home.

Mei Ling dug through her trunk until she found the note where she had written down June's information: *911 Alice St, Oakland.* This morning they would find her friend.

They walked the few short blocks under a bright-blue sky. Mei Ling buzzed in excitement and a little fear. Would June be as excited to see her as Mei Ling was to see June?

Mei Ling knocked at the two-story building. Her heart beat hard and fast as she waited for someone to come to the door. An old, white-haired woman with deep wrinkles opened the door.

After bowing her respect, Mei Ling asked, "Does June live here?"

The woman shrugged. She looked Chinese, but she didn't seem to understand Mei Ling. Mei Ling tried to think of another way to say June's name but was at a loss. She traced the character on the palm of her hand, but the old woman shook her head and said something in what sounded like Min. Mei Ling was so disappointed. She hadn't brought paper to leave a note, but she could come back later to do that.

Tears pushing at the back of her eyes, Mei Ling bowed goodbye to the old woman. She took Bo's hand and walked down the stairs. She considered her options as they traveled the street. June said the church would always know where she was. Perhaps the office was open today. They would walk over there before she went home.

"Yu Ling?!" A voice interrupted her thoughts.

Mei Ling spun around. June was standing two feet away from her. Happy energy surged through Mei Ling's chest.

"Bo!" June cried out. She rushed forward and scooped them up in a hug. She looked just the same as on the boat.

"I have been waiting, waiting for you," June scolded. "Why haven't you come to see me!"

Mei Ling laughed. She was the same June in Oakland as she was on the boat and the island.

"Is this the baby? Born already? Time goes fast, eh?"

"This is Joy," Mei Ling said. "She's five months old."

"A girl, eh?" Her voice got quiet. "How he take it?"

"Kai Li loves Joy very much," Mei Ling replied.

"Hooray! You do have a good husband. Come, come." June took Mei Ling's hand and led her into the backyard.

Now that she was with June, she regretted she hadn't sought her out before. When she was in San Francisco, it felt too overwhelming and too expensive to cross the bay. And she'd harbored doubts that June would be glad to see her, but all her insecurity faded in the presence of her friend.

"The Ahma who answered the door in the front didn't recognize your name," Mei Ling explained.

"Did I forget to say go to the back?" June asked.

"Yes."

"Sorry. Sorry. But all good now. We are back together." June smiled. Mei Ling hugged her old friend, so grateful to see her again.

June brought them up to her home, a small apartment in the back of a well-kept fourplex. She introduced Mei Ling to her mother-in-law, who lived with them. The small, gray-haired woman delighted in the baby and offered to take Joy and Bo to play in the yard.

When the older woman was out of earshot, June whispered, "She scolds me for not giving her more grandchildren, but smart Chinese ladies take the herbs to keep their families small. One son. One daughter. That is enough."

Mei Ling laughed. "You will have to teach me. Where is the rest of your family?"

"Dorothy and Timothy are at school. My husband is at work at the cannery in Emeryville."

June made tea and served it in delicate blue-and-white porcelain cups. They sat at a wooden table in the kitchen to catch up on their lives.

June's first question was, "Have you seen Siew?"

Mei Ling shook her head, her heart twisting at the sound of the girl's name. She prayed for Siew every day, and Siew often visited Mei

Ling's dreams, but she was too busy with Bo and Joy, embroidering, cooking, and cleaning, to seek out the girl.

June tsked. "So sad. She is a lovely girl," June said. "I hope she is safe, though I suppose we will never know."

Mei Ling felt ill at the thought of never knowing what happened to Siew.

"Do you know how I could find her?" Mei Ling asked.

"What is her uncle's name? Everyone knows everyone. I can ask around."

Mei Ling shook her head. "She did not know any name for him other than Suk Suk."

Her friend squealed in delight when she heard that Mei Ling now lived only a few blocks away. She insisted on showing Mei Ling around Chinatown, introducing her to the market owners and sharing the local gossip. They parted with a promise to meet at Lincoln Square Park that afternoon so their children could play with each other.

As she walked home, Mei Ling's heart sang. She had a friend to meet at a park where the children could play. There were trees, not many, and not very big, but still trees along the street. Her husband would be home in time for them to eat dinner together. They had their own bathroom with a flushing toilet and a yard to plant a garden. She looked forward to writing home. At last she had great news about her new life.

~

"Your sleep was disturbed by dreams again last night," Kai Li mentioned. He kept his voice casual, but Mei Ling could tell that he was upset. Her nightmares were interrupting her husband's much-needed sleep.

Mei Ling replied, "I'm sorry. Joy and I will sleep in the living room so you can get your rest."

"I'm not worried about my well-being," Kai Li said. "I'm concerned that you aren't happy."

"I'm very satisfied in our new home," Mei Ling protested. She didn't want him to believe that she was ungrateful.

"Wife, please tell me. What troubles your sleep? Why do your dreams turn to nightmares each night?"

"Every night?" Mei Ling asked.

He nodded.

Shame seeped into her chest. She thought she had been successful in keeping her unwarranted and foolish concern for Siew to herself. She looked at her husband; she measured her own trust and decided to tell him the truth.

She confessed, "I dream of Siew. She visits me in my sleep, and she is very troubled. In the day I tell myself she is fine. But every night she returns to tell me otherwise." Mei Ling teared up. "I'm sorry, husband. She isn't your concern, and she's disturbing your sleep."

Kai Li's face flashed relief, then empathy. He said, "I'll try to find out where she is, to confirm that she's well . . . and we can both sleep better." He smiled.

She wanted to reassure him that it would be worth his efforts. "If I'm confident that she is being cared for in a nice home, then I will sleep well."

"You have a tender heart, wife," Kai Li said.

Mei Ling nodded, uncertain whether her husband had complimented or insulted her.

To explain the strength of her emotions, Mei Ling revealed more about her past. "Siew reminds me of my sister. When I imagine her alone and scared, or sick, I . . . Mui Mui was only six when she died of cholera. We nursed her, but in only three days she grew too weak until . . ." Mei Ling sighed. "It was terrible, but she wasn't alone. What if Siew is alone?"

"You don't trust her uncle?" Kai Li asked.

"He didn't seem to understand the needs of a little girl. He'd made no arrangements for her, on the boat or on the island. Perhaps he means well, but he doesn't know how to care for a child."

"Does he have a wife?" Kai Li asked.

Mei Ling shrugged.

Kai Li took her hand. She was embarrassed to be so disturbed by the needs of a little girl she'd only known for a few weeks. There was so much suffering in the world that she couldn't possibly stay all of it. If she were wise she would focus on her own family and trust that wherever she was, Siew was being cared for, but Mei Ling seemed to be foolish when it came to that little girl.

"Thank you," Mei Ling said, relieved that she might find peace and grateful her husband respected her deep feelings.

"Compassion is nothing to be ashamed of," her husband said gently.

CHAPTER 18

Oakland
July 1924

Mei Ling looked at her sleeping children. Joy slept on her back, one arm thrown above her head. Bits of fine black hair stuck to the moisture on her face. Bo lay on his side, one arm over his sister. His eyes moved back and forth; then the corners of his mouth tugged up in a slight smile. Mei Ling's heart nearly burst with love. In less than a month, Oakland had begun to feel like home.

It had been one year since she walked off that island. One year since she sat for hours on that dock, uncertain about Kai Li's devotion to them. One year since she realized she was married to a worker, not a merchant. She wished she could fly back to that time and whisper to herself, *You will all be all right.*

Because she was—more than all right. She had no way of knowing then that she could be so satisfied with this life: being married to Kai Li, a man who had lied to her and to whom she still hadn't told her real name. And loving these children, one of whom didn't even come from her body, but she didn't care. Taking care of this house that didn't have a field in sight but was home nevertheless. With a flushing toilet of their own! And she earned money for her family with her embroidery.

She was constantly mindful that it was a fragile life. If the children got sick, if Kai Li were injured, if their apartment burned down, if he learned the truth about her and no longer trusted her. If . . . if . . . if. She had to remind herself not to focus on all the ways their life could fall apart. There were too many. For now she was satisfied, and that was so much more than she had dreamed of last year.

True to his promise, Kai Li made inquiries about Suk Suk and Siew. They had little information to begin with, so it would take many steps, like a treasure hunt or a puzzle. After a few dead ends, Kai Li found someone with access to the passenger records from the boat. Fortunately there were only two male Chinese passengers who boarded with a single female child. One man was a Wong and the other a Lee. They would go to the Wong and Lee family buildings in San Francisco hoping to learn where they lived.

Next Sunday, after worship, the whole family took the train to the Seventh Street pier, where they boarded a ferry to San Francisco. The journey stirred much emotion in her heart. It hadn't been so many weeks since she had arrived on this side of the bay, uncertain and anxious. She was returning to San Francisco hopeful for answers that would calm her heart, and she was afraid she might not get them. In the distance she saw the hateful island. She telegraphed a message: *You didn't destroy me.*

The Wong building on Waverly was bustling with activity. They waited on hardback chairs for someone to come out to provide them with information. This entire association was dedicated to tracking and supporting those in the Wong family who had migrated to the United States. There were chapters in many cities where any Wong could go if they were in need of a loan, housing, a job, or help settling a dispute. Some family associations were rumored to have ties to less-respectable businesses, but mostly they were a means for the Chinese community to band together for mutual support in a new nation that didn't serve them.

Mei Ling still wondered if they would benefit from a connection with the Chinn family association. Most Chinese, even those connected to Christian churches, kept ties with a family tong. But Kai Li insisted that the church was enough.

A man came out from an office holding a large leather-bound book. He sat by them and skimmed through the pages until he found the man they had asked about. He wrote down Mr. Wong's address on a piece of paper and handed it to them. He lived on Twelfth Street and Harrison in Oakland. Mr. Jack Wong was practically their neighbor. They would have to wait to seek him out, but it would be simple to do so from home.

At the Lee building they were made to wait longer but came out with the same information: a slip of paper with an address. Mr. Lee lived on Washington Street not far from there. Mei Ling's body pounded with nerves as they walked up a steep hill to the address. Kai Li knocked on the door. Mei Ling stood back with the children. She gripped Bo's hand tight.

A teenager opened the door.

Kai Li asked, "Is Mr. Lee home?"

The boy shook his head.

Kai Li looked back at Mei Ling. "Ask about Siew!" she whispered.

"Does Lee Puey You live here?" Kai Li used the legal name from the boat.

The boy shook his head.

Mei Ling burst out, "Siew? Does Siew live here?"

The boy's face contracted in pity that bordered on contempt. "No. There is no Puey You who lives here. And no Siew either."

Mei Ling's heart sank. She sighed. "Thank you for your trouble," she said.

The boy closed the door on her hope. She walked away, deflated.

~

They stopped at their old apartment to look for a letter from Mei Ling's family. It tugged at her heart to enter the building that Joy was born in, but she was glad to be out of this damp and crowded building. The basket in the entryway disappointed her by having nothing with her name. She'd left a note with her new address at the post office and one in the basket. Perhaps a letter from her family was on its way to her in Oakland.

Before walking downhill to the ferry they visited Golden Imports, the shop that sold Mei Ling's embroidered table runners and caps. She'd never been there, but now that Mei Ling was in Oakland, Mrs. Woo was unable to act as the delivery person. Mei Ling looked forward to finally meeting the owner. Mei Ling was surprised and happy to see one of her runners displayed in the window. She remembered the challenge of getting the tail feathers on those pheasants twisted around each other just right.

"So much money!" Kai Li gasped.

Mei Ling looked at the dangling tag. Her heart shot up through her head. Could that be right?

"I'm paid nearly a tenth of that amount," she whispered. She looked at Kai Li, incredulity covering her face.

"Are you certain this is your work?" he asked.

She nodded decisively.

"Let's approach with caution," he said. "Like gentle rabbits." He smiled tenderly, causing her heart to do a flip. He believed he was speaking of her, but that was her sister. She felt shame that she was lying to him, and then wondered whether he was still deceiving her as well. She inhaled slowly to calm herself and covered her emotion with a tight smile.

The store was crammed with treasures. Statues of Buddha and Quan Yin in various sizes and many materials filled the shelves to the left. On the right they passed through aisles of goods for the kitchen:

beautiful and plain bowls, plates, chopsticks, and knives. Mei Ling scooped up Bo and handed him to Kai Li. She didn't want him breaking objects they didn't have the means to pay for.

A kind-looking older gentleman approached them. "I have only the finest goods in the store. You can be assured you are purchasing quality when you buy here. What can I help you find?" He spoke in perfect Cantonese, but Mei Ling detected an American accent. He'd been born in the States.

"My wife, the seamstress who embroiders some of your goods," Kai Li replied, "wanted to meet you."

The man looked at Mei Ling, his eyebrows pulled up in doubt. "You must be mistaken. I personally select all of my embroidered goods. We have never met."

"This one," Mei Ling burst out. "I made this one."

"No. No." The man shook his head. "Mrs. Woo brought that to me. She is most skilled. Whatever she brings me sells very, very quickly."

"Mrs. Woo told you it is her work?" Mei Ling challenged, her heart clenching like a Dragon's claw.

"It's her work," the man insisted.

Mei Ling took two runners and three caps from her bag.

"Oh," the man exclaimed. "I see." There was no doubting it. Mei Ling's unique style proved what she was saying.

"I am happy to buy from you directly," the man said. "Mrs. Woo can be forgiven for keeping her discovery to herself. We each do what we must to survive, but I have no need for a middle person."

The man gave a hearty chuckle. Obviously he found this amusing, but Mei Ling was outraged and embarrassed that she had allowed herself to be used like that. She'd misplaced her trust in that old woman, believing that she was looking out for Mei Ling's well-being when in fact she was using Mei Ling for her own purposes.

The man disappeared behind the curtain, returning with American money in his hand.

"Three caps, two runners?" he asked, looking directly at her, which confirmed her suspicion that he was American born.

She held his gaze and nodded. He handed her a ten-dollar bill and four silver dollars—four times what Mrs. Woo had been paying her. She could always earn this rate—if she was willing to take the ferry to San Francisco. She waited a beat, expecting him to give her plain caps or runners as Mrs. Woo had, but he didn't. He just stared at her. She would have to sew them herself. But even with the cost of silk and the ferry, she would come out ahead.

"Anything else?" he asked.

She started to shake her head, but then asked, "Would you like me to make anything special for you?"

The man looked at her, his eyes moving back and forth in consideration. He pulled down his brows and nodded.

"I would be most grateful for a wedding gown for my daughter. The ceremony is September 14," he replied.

"It will be my honor," Mei Ling replied with a smile, quickly planning in her head. "American style or traditional Chinese?" she asked.

The man sighed. "My wife will want Chinese. My daughter, American."

"Ask each of them what is most important to them. I can combine both," Mei Ling said. "I will strike the perfect balance. Your wife *and* your daughter will be happy. I promise. Then you will be happy."

He nodded and smiled. "So I will be seeing more of you directly?" he asked.

"You will," she confirmed.

She walked away, glowing in satisfaction. They had an address in Oakland that she sensed would lead to Siew, and she was going to earn even more money to support her family. She had earned enough today that she would send five dollars in her next letter to China and was optimistic they could spare more after she was paid for the gown. Feeling in harmony with life and with her husband, she smiled at Kai Li and he beamed back.

CHAPTER 19

Oakland
July 1924

By the time they got home it was far too late to knock on a stranger's door. She burned with impatience, but Mei Ling would have to wait until the next day to discover whether Siew lived just blocks away from them.

The next morning Kai Li went for his produce at the usual time. But instead of walking across the bridge to peddle the goods in Alameda, he returned home.

He pushed the cart laden with colorful fruits and vegetables into their backyard. Mei Ling feared his employer would be angry, but Kai Li assured her that he had that much autonomy. As soon as it was fully light outside, their family walked to Harrison Street.

The house was lovely. Freshly painted in bright colors, red-and-yellow paint showed off the architectural details of the ornate Victorian trim. This was the house of a well-off family. Mei Ling felt a warm relief. Siew would be well cared for in this home.

Anticipation walked with her up the twelve stairs to the narrow front door. Kai Li knocked. In a short time the door swung open. Her heart leaped in excitement when Suk Suk's large face peered out at her. Then it sank as confusion drew his thick, dark eyebrows together. Eventually he placed her, and his eyes went wide in alarm, his face flushing red. In embarrassment? Anger? She couldn't tell.

He rushed out onto the porch and slammed the door behind him. Glaring at Mei Ling, he asked, "What business do you have here?"

Kai Li spoke up. "My wife would like to assure herself that your niece, Siew, is well."

"She is," Suk Suk barked at her. "I will send your regards."

"May we see her?" Mei Ling implored, pushing past her fear. "Bo is so fond of her and misses her." Mei Ling's voice caught. *Me too,* she thought.

"No." The man opened the door and vanished as quickly as he had appeared.

Mei Ling blinked at the red door. She wanted to pound on it, to yell for Siew, but suppressed that urge.

Bo looked at her longingly and his little voice asked, "Siew?"

Enraged and heartbroken, Mei Ling took a shaky breath. Kai Li placed a gentle hand on her arm.

"We can try again another day, wife."

She nodded, blinking back tears. They were painfully close, and yet too far away from finding the answer she needed to sleep well.

They trudged back to their home, Mei Ling's heart so heavy she couldn't speak. Kai Li walked into the backyard for his cart. Mei Ling, Bo, and Joy stood on the sidewalk waiting for him. Mei Ling watched a bird fly into a nest, its beak full of black mush. Three baby birds, their feathers all in, chirped at the parent.

Kai Li maneuvered the bulky cart past the side of their building. Stacks of colorful vegetables and fruits filled the bed. Kai Li picked up Bo and pointed to the produce: greens, lettuce, onions, tomatoes, lemons, limes, and even bananas.

Kai Li picked up a small bright-red fruit and handed it to Bo. "Try this. It's delicious."

Tentatively Bo nibbled at it. Then his eyes shone in delight. He shoved the rest in his mouth.

Kai Li laughed. "Not the stem, the green part. We don't eat that."

Bo pulled it back out. Her husband handed one of the little fruits to Mei Ling with a smile. His tenderness nearly caused her tears to spill over. He saw that her heart was heavy.

She bit into the small fruit. Her taste buds delighted in the sweet, tangy flavor.

"Strawberry," Kai Li explained with a grin. "It's called a strawberry."

"Awberry!" Bo repeated. "Yum."

Kai Li offered Mei Ling the basket of fruit with a slight bow. Mei Ling accepted it gratefully. He put Bo back on the ground, kissed Joy, and squeezed Mei Ling's arm in affection. He grabbed the handles of his wooden cart and wheeled it down the street. She watched him walk away with a strong mixture of emotions in her heart. Perhaps she loved this man, the mysterious peddler with a kind heart. There was so much she didn't know about him, and so much he didn't know about her, but she was certain about his concern for her and the children.

~

At the park that afternoon, Mei Ling told June about her morning. She worked on a cap, enjoying the afternoon sun and fresh air while their children played. Joy crawled around her feet, going three arm lengths away before she scampered back toward them.

"Where is the house?" June asked.

"Harrison at Twelfth," Mei Ling explained.

"On the corner? The big yellow with red. Fancy, fancy house?"

Mei Ling nodded.

"Ah, that is Jack Wong's home," June said.

"Yes!" Mei Ling replied. "Suk Suk is Jack Wong."

"He is not a good man." June leaned in and whispered in that tone she reserved for prostitutes on the island. "He gamble, gamble all the time. His wife is scared, scared."

"How do you know this?"

June pointed to her ear. "June listen, always listen to learn. His children go to Lincoln School too. We mothers talk, talk all the time, but his wife never join us."

Mei Ling asked, "Have you ever seen Siew at Lincoln School?"

"No. I would have said so, right?" June replied with a tsk. "I would not ask you about Siew—but tell you about her."

"If she lives with them she can go to Lincoln School, right?"

"Yes," June replied, reservation in her voice.

Mei Ling stared at her friend, encouraging her to continue speaking.

"She is young," June explained. "Maybe too young for school and they send her later or . . ."

Mei Ling nodded, her heart constricted, waiting for June to continue.

"Or . . . maybe they never send her to school. Maybe they bring her to be a servant and just say she is a niece for the Americans."

Mei Ling sighed. June was right. Stories from the boat weren't to be trusted. Siew might very well be a paper niece.

"It looks like a nice home for Siew, even if she is a servant, but seeing her would be a relief," Mei Ling said.

"Some people like to pretend they have no past," June replied. "It may be for a good reason, but he is not a very nice man."

Mei Ling teared up.

"Siew is a good girl," June declared. "I will find out if she is happy."

Mei Ling smiled at her friend. "Thank you. Very much."

~

Two days later, June had news. "I asked his wife about the little girl that was with him. I mention that we were bunk neighbors on the boat and on the island. I say she is a very nice girl. It must be nice to have her working in your home."

Mei Ling perked up in hope. "What did she say?"

"She says she does not know who I am talking about."

"What?"

With her mouth in a frown and her head shaking from side to side, June replied, "Siew does not live with them; the wife knows nothing about her."

Mei Ling's throat was so tight she could hardly breathe.

"I do not think she is lying to me, but I can tell she was angry, angry at the question," June said. "Even though I ask nice."

June patted Mei Ling's leg in sympathy, but it didn't help assuage her feelings. Instead of alleviating her concern, this information added to it. If he had ensured an honorable future for Siew, Jack Wong would be willing to share her location. Her Dragon was roaring and burning with desire to learn the truth.

The next morning she returned to the corner in front of Suk Suk's house. She was going to come to this corner and stand there with her children until he told her where Siew was. He owed her that after she cared for Siew for all those weeks.

She stared up at the house with Joy tied to her back. Bo played peekaboo with his sister. Mei Ling's legs grew tired, so she paced back and forth. The street was quiet, though a few people passed by. After an hour she felt foolish. He probably wasn't aware that she was there. Perhaps this was futile, but she couldn't just let Siew go.

Just as her stomach was telling her it was time for lunch, the door opened. Her body went on alert. A middle-aged woman came out. She stared at Mei Ling, but didn't say anything as she passed by.

Mei Ling stayed for as long as she could manage it, but Bo needed a nap and they all needed to eat. She led them back home but vowed to Siew, *We will keep looking for you.*

They returned the next day. And the next. Mei Ling didn't tell Kai Li about their mornings because she didn't want him to chastise her for her foolishness. Also, if he didn't know, he couldn't forbid her from pursuing information about Siew the only way she knew how.

On the fifth day, the door opened. Suk Suk's angry face glared at her. Perhaps he had been aware of her vigil for some time. He marched down the stairs, Mei Ling's pulse quickening with each step. Afraid of him and yet excited she might get her answer, she took a calming breath, not that it succeeded in slowing her heartbeat. He marched uncomfortably close to her, a threat in his carriage.

"What are you doing here?" he challenged.

"Tell me where she is, and I will leave you alone," Mei Ling replied, unable to keep the quaver out of her voice.

"She isn't your concern," he yelled.

Anger welled in her. She yelled back, "You don't dictate who I'm concerned about. I will stand here every day until you tell me where she is." She glared at him, looking him straight in the eyes. Slower, she articulated, "I must see that she is all right."

"She is fine. She's just a girl." Contempt filled his voice. "An orphan girl who would have died of starvation on the streets of Guangzhou if I hadn't brought her here."

Rather than dissuade her, his words and attitude strengthened her resolve. "The address," she demanded.

"I assure you, she is a servant in a good home." He switched tactics in the face of Mei Ling's stare. "It's more than she would be had she stayed in China. I rescued her from a life of depravity."

"The address," she declared again. "I won't let you be until I see her."

He took a measure of Mei Ling. She let her Dragon build up inside her, showing him the power of it. The tension was physically painful, but she refused to look away or even blink. While she glowered at him she pictured Siew's face, forcing herself to keep fighting for her.

Bo rested his hand against her leg, but she didn't let that distract her; rather she drew strength from his touch. He needed to see Siew as much as she did.

Suk Suk sighed. She'd won.

"672 Eleventh Street in Oakland. Use the back door if you go there." He shook his head. "You are wasting your energy on her."

"She isn't a waste . . . of my energy or anything else."

She spun around and walked away. Her anger made her so shaky she feared her knees might give out, but she stepped forward steadily until she was confident she was out of his sight. Only then did she stop to lean against a pole and take in a deep breath.

She looked down at Bo. "We did it! I have her address. When your Bah-ba comes home, we can find your Siew."

"Siew," he repeated sweetly, sounding like he longed for her, though Mei Ling still doubted he could possibly remember his temporary big sister.

~

It was less than a mile from their apartment to the address, but the four of them passed through many different worlds on their way. First they walked through Chinatown. The wooden Edwardian and Victorian multistory buildings were packed tight with commercial spaces on the first floors and apartments on the upper floors. Merchandise was on display out on the sidewalks to entice customers to come inside. When they reached Broadway, the main street of Oakland, Kai Li paused to point out some landmarks among the art deco skyscrapers: the *Tribune* building and city hall. They were modern and elegant, reminding Mei Ling of the newest buildings in Guangzhou. A few blocks past Broadway, businesses gave way to a residential district full of beautiful Victorians with large yards on the sides, front, and back.

They came to a magnificent house at 672 Eleventh Street—the nicest home she had ever seen in the United States, three stories high with ornate gold trim. This was the residence of a very wealthy, very prestigious family. Relieved and somewhat intimidated, she followed Kai Li around the side of the building and up the porch stairs. There were two doors. He looked at them, shrugged, and chose the one on the left.

"Please say nothing," Kai Li instructed.

She bristled at his direction, but he was right. Her charged demeanor wouldn't serve them in this situation. She needed to act like a meek Rabbit and let his Ox plow the way forward.

Her heart pounded hard as he knocked gently on the door. When it swung open, he held out their offering, six bright and round oranges.

A middle-aged White woman with bright-blue eyes and dark hair stood in the doorway. Mei Ling's heart sank. How would they communicate?

But then, surprising her, Kai Li spoke: "---- -------."

She had forgotten he spoke English so well. He had a whole life separate from her, communicating with his employers and customers every day.

The woman replied, "---- -------. --- I ---- ---?"

He offered the oranges, with a bow. The woman looked confused, then amused. She took them.

"-- ---- ----- ------- ----- --- ------ ------," he said. "-- ----- --- --- ---- ---. Siew?"

"Yes, -- ---- - Siew ---- ---- ----."

"--- -- ---- --- ----- -- ------- ---- ---?"

Yes. Siew. She was in there!

The woman looked him up and down. Then she looked at Mei Ling, who smiled, trying to win the woman over.

"Siew?" Bo's voice called out.

Mei Ling started to shush him, but the woman smiled at the boy.

"-- ------," she said. Then she half closed the door.

"Well?" Mei Ling demanded.

"She said 'Of course,' which usually means yes. I believe she is getting Siew."

"Siew?" Bo said again.

Did he really remember her, or was he just remembering Mei Ling's stories about the boat and the island? Mei Ling quivered in anticipation. She stared through the gap into the house, yearning to get a glance of Siew, but all she saw through the slit was a small slice of shelving on a storage porch.

The door swung open to reveal Siew, standing directly in front of the White woman. Mei Ling's heart leaped in joy. She looked just as Mei Ling remembered, only a little taller. She wore a plaid Western dress and her dark, shiny hair was brushed flat. She looked healthier than she had on the boat, but Mei Ling detected a bit of sadness in her eyes. Siew stared at them, looking between Mei Ling and Bo. Mei Ling's heart sank.

Siew didn't seem to remember them or care to see them. The child loomed large in Mei Ling's spirit, but they hadn't known each other for very long. In the intervening year Siew might have forgotten about them or made new attachments.

Suddenly the girl's face split wide in a grin. "Bo!" Siew squealed. "It really is you!" The girl rushed to Bo, giving him an enormous hug, lifting him off the ground though he was nearly her same height.

Siew then wrapped her arms around Mei Ling's legs. Staring up at her, sheer delight on her face, she exclaimed, "You found me! Like you said you would!"

Mei Ling smiled at the girl, relief and joy bursting through her cells. They'd done it. Found Siew!

Siew said, "I wanted to find you, but I lost the paper. I'm sorry."

The girl looked so earnest and pained that Mei Ling regretted placing that burden on her.

"It's not your fault. We both did the best we could to see one another again. And now we are!" Mei Ling said, reassuring herself as much as the child.

Mei Ling knelt down and pulled Siew into a full embrace. The girl stiffened at first and then melted against Mei Ling, wrapping her arms tight around her in a giant hug.

The White woman spoke up, "--- ---'- --- ---- - ----- -- --- ------. ---- ---- ----."

The unintelligible English words frightened Mei Ling. Was the woman sending them away so soon? She looked at Kai Li, wanting to know what had been said.

He gestured with his head. "She says we can have a visit in the garden."

Mei Ling rose and bowed her gratitude to the woman, her eyes wet with emotion. The woman smiled, her eyes also moist, and nodded back at her. Siew grabbed Bo's hand and ran ahead.

Questions swirled in Mei Ling's head. She wanted to learn about Siew's year. Had she been treated well? How long had she lived here? Had she lived anywhere else?

But she didn't interrupt the reunion between Bo and Siew. The adults observed from a white-washed wooden bench while the children ran around on the grass, returning to Mei Ling to include Joy in their game. Siew looked good, clean, with enough meat on her bones.

"She is very sweet, like you said," Kai Li observed as they watched the children play. "Bo is so happy to see her."

Mei Ling nodded.

"You are still worried, wife?" he asked.

Mei Ling's chest constricted. She didn't want to appear ungrateful. Her heart was much at ease, but something was wrong.

She shrugged.

She managed a hoarse whisper, "She doesn't belong here."

"It's better than many children have," Kai Li stated matter-of-factly.

Before she could reply, Siew ran back to the bench and collapsed on it, out of breath. Bo followed right behind.

"It's Siew, Mah-ma." Bo grinned as he patted the girl's back.

"Yes, Siew." Mei Ling beamed back at him. "You remember her, don't you?"

His little head nodded up and down vigorously.

"You live here, Siew?" Mei Ling asked.

"Yes," the girl answered.

"For how long?"

The girl shrugged.

"Who takes care of you?"

Siew's shoulders dropped. "I take care of myself."

Mei Ling's heart twisted. "What do you do here?"

"Whatever the cook says," Siew answered. "Some days I polish. That's my favorite 'cause I get to sit for a long time and pretend."

"What other work do you do?" Kai Li asked.

"You're Bo's daddy! We met once on the ship," Siew declared.

Kai Li nodded.

"Joy is very cute!" Siew announced.

Kai Li smiled. "I agree."

"Now I have a sister and a brother!" Siew said with a smile, but there was a challenge in her voice. An edge of anger too.

Bo roared in Siew's face. She laughed. He ran. She followed.

Mei Ling's heart and mind swirled in confusion. She was glad to see Siew so healthy. But a servant? In this fancy house with White people? Was that all the fates had in store for the girl?

All too soon the door swung open again. The White woman stood on the porch staring at them, signaling their visit was over.

Mei Ling's soul protested, but her mouth kept silent. This woman stood between her and Siew. If she wanted to visit the girl again, this housekeeper would have to agree. Mei Ling wasn't going to act argumentative or unappreciative.

Mei Ling looked at the children. Siew was tickling Bo on the grass while he giggled and wiggled in pleasure. Siew stopped suddenly when she saw the housekeeper.

"Bye, Bo. Be good," Siew said, and she hugged him tight. She stood up, walked up to Kai Li, and bowed.

"Thank you for bringing Bo to visit with me," she said politely.

She walked to Mei Ling, wrapped her arms around her waist, and squeezed. Mei Ling patted her silky brown hair. Without letting go, Siew whispered up to Mei Ling, "I like being with you and Bo better." She squeezed again and then let go.

Tears pushed at the back of Mei Ling's eyeballs. She longed to assure the child that they would be back, and that they could visit often, but she wasn't going to make up a tale. Siew was a servant in a fine home. The White family wasn't going to allow her to have visits very often—especially with people who weren't even her real family. Her heart beat hard, and her throat swelled up.

She wanted to yell, *I love you. I won't forget you*, but she buried the words. Bo slipped his hand into hers.

"Bye, Siew," his sad, high voice yelled across the distance.

They shuffled home in a bittersweet silence. Mei Ling chanted a loving kindness meditation for Siew: *May she be safe from all harm. May she be free from all suffering. May she know joy.*

CHAPTER 20

Oakland
July 1924

Mei Ling's extreme agitation was calmed by the visit with Siew, but her heart wasn't at peace. While she wasn't being actively harmed—she was warm and well fed—the little girl had to be lonely. Mei Ling needed to find a way to have regular visits with Siew in order to quiet her chattering mind.

Ruminating on her dilemma in the middle of the night as her family slept around her, church popped into her head. The Americans took great pleasure when Chinese became Christian; perhaps the housekeeper would allow Siew to spend Sundays with them. And a gift of an embroidered runner might facilitate her agreement.

In the morning she told Kai Li her idea. He heard the longing in her voice and agreed to ask Miss Haw, the housekeeper. Mei Ling quickly finished a runner, stitching into the final blue-and-purple butterfly a prayer: *Quan Yin, offer your compassion and mercy to Siew. Persuade Miss Haw to let her fly to us.* She wrapped it carefully and sent it with Kai Li. After work he would present her gift and make their plea.

Through the day Mei Ling fluctuated between anxiety and excitement. She distracted herself by gardening and working on the wedding gown for Mr. Young . . . and imagining Siew walking into church with them on Sunday.

Kai Li returned late, after dinner was cold, but his sharp nod and sweet smile told her that he was successful. They would see Siew again on Sunday. Mei Ling breathed a sigh of relief.

"Thank you, husband," she said.

"You're welcome," he replied. "Miss Haw was very agreeable. I can tell that she feels affection for Siew. I hope that knowledge eases your heart."

Mei Ling nodded, for once her Dragon purring at the knowledge they would see Siew once a week.

~

"Ah!" June leaped up and screamed when she saw their family walk into church, drawing the attention of the people in the nearby pews. Mei Ling beamed as June fussed over Siew.

"You remember Auntie June, right? I helped your Mah-ma to find you! She worry, worry so much. But I say to her, Quan Yin wants you to be a family. And I am right!"

Mah-ma. The word cut through Mei Ling. She didn't share June's certainty about her relationship to Siew. Good mothers didn't allow their children to live in as servants—not when they were as young as Siew.

"Dorothy and Timothy, come here," June called to her children. "This is your new friend, Siew. I told you about her before. From the boat."

"Hi," Dorothy said.

"She doesn't speak English," June chastised.

"Hello," Siew replied to June's daughter. "I -- ----- -------."

"----'- --- ------. ------- -------!" June said.

Mei Ling watched the conversation, conflicting emotions surging through her. She was proud that Siew could already speak the language of this land, and yet felt left out because she didn't understand most of what they were saying to one another. Siew and Bo filled in the seats by June's children. The three older children chatted in English. Soon enough Bo and then Joy would share this language with Kai Li and June.

"I must learn more English," Mei Ling declared to June.

"Yes. Yes. You must if you want to be a real American. It took me a long, long time. But now I understand most of what I hear, and I am not too afraid to speak. I learn right here at church. You can too."

Mei Ling nodded. She wasn't going to let herself be left entirely behind.

~

Weeks later, the five of them once again sat in the pews at the Presbyterian Church in Oakland. Sundays had become the day when Mei Ling felt the most peace. Spending the day in the company of Kai Li *and* Siew was a treat that made her heart sing.

Partway through the service the minister introduced two guests with familiar names: Donaldina Cameron and Tien Wu. The women led the Presbyterian home where Mei Ling had planned to escape had Kai Li rejected Joy for the failure of being born female. Her anxiety from last winter seemed foolish now because nothing brought Kai Li more delight than his daughter, but that wouldn't have been true for all men.

As Miss Cameron spoke in English, Mei Ling's mind drifted.

Then she listened to Tien Wu's translation: "Our program for Chinese girls is expanding to the East Bay. We have purchased land near Mills College and need your assistance to create a sanctuary where young ladies rescued from a wretched life can be safe. Please listen to this testimonial to know the truth of what we are saying."

A young woman stood up and spoke in a slow, quiet voice, forcing Mei Ling to lean in to hear her words.

"I was very young when I came on the boat with an auntie I had never met. My parents sold me to her because they had no money for food for a fourth daughter. She promised them I would work in a nice home, and then she would arrange a good marriage when I became a woman.

"I was a servant for many years, but when the time came for marriage, a husband was not found for me. I was dressed like a bride, but I was not to be for one man."

The girl's voice dropped even lower. Her face flushed red with shame. Mei Ling's throat closed tight. She looked at Siew, who was staring intently at the young woman, paying close attention to the story too similar to her own.

"I will not say in a church what happened to me, but I am ashamed, and very grateful that Tien Wu and Lo Mo, Deaconess Cameron, rescued me from that life. Many girls need to be saved from that fate. Thank you."

Deaconess Cameron spoke up again in English. Mei Ling shook with impatience to know what she was saying. Finally Tien Wu translated, "We need your help to build a lovely home for these girls in east Oakland: the Ming Quong Home for Chinese Girls. There they will be free to learn and grow in Christ's love."

By the time they had finished speaking, Mei Ling's Dragon was roaring in panic. Siew was going to share that fate if they did nothing. She looked at Kai Li, her wide eyes signaling her outrage. He nodded with a sigh; he shared her concern.

Mei Ling leaned over and whispered to him in the pew. "We must speak to her. Ask her to rescue Siew!"

"Of course, wife."

When worship ended they stayed until the room cleared out. Before they approached Miss Cameron, Mei Ling told Siew to play with Bo in the corner so she wouldn't hear their conversation. After introductions, Kai Li explained their situation in English. Mei Ling watched, feeling ineffectual and angry, as the two of them conversed.

Miss Cameron pointed to Tien Wu and said something else in English.

Together Mei Ling and Kai Li spoke with the Chinese woman, giving her details about Siew.

Mei Ling pointed to the girl and implored, "She is a very good girl. Respectful, helpful, obedient. Nothing bad should ever happen to her."

"I can see that she is lovely," Tien Wu replied. "From what you say she is in no current danger. We have many, many that we must get out of immediate harm. But I will keep her name and learn what we can do to be of assistance."

Mei Ling left the conversation dissatisfied and frustrated. She couldn't tell if they were going to help Siew. Did she and Kai Li need to pay a bribe? Kai Li confirmed that Miss Cameron had asked for a donation.

The following week she brought one of her precious gold coins to church. As she offered it to the minister she thought, *May this keep Siew from all harm.* The minister took it. He expressed his gratitude that it would add substantially to their congregation's contribution.

"We are hoping Miss Cameron and Tien Wu can help our . . ." Mei Ling stopped speaking in the middle of her sentence, uncertain what Siew was to her. She wanted him to take their request seriously, so she said, "Foster daughter."

"I'm sorry you know someone directly affected by this horrible practice," the pastor said. "What is her name?"

Her voice full of emotion, Mei Ling said, "Siew."

"I will pray for her. What is her last name?"

Mei Ling's heart constricted. It felt like a betrayal that she didn't know Siew's real family name. Siew felt like family, but Mei Ling knew so little about her. She shook her head.

Kai Li said earnestly, "We plan to be of support however we can."

Mei Ling looked at her husband, so grateful for him and his kind heart.

~

Concern for Siew overshadowed all the good in Mei Ling's life. The girl was constantly on her mind. The girl's desperate voice intruded upon her day: *Save me, please. There's no one else.* Unless Mei Ling was speaking or listening to another person, those words filled her ears. All too often an image from her dreams would pop unbidden into her mind's eye in the middle of the day. The woman from Bartlett Alley, but with Siew's face, staring through the mesh screen.

A desperate ghost was haunting Mei Ling, but Siew was alive. Perhaps Siew's mother had found them across the Pacific Ocean to badger Mei Ling into keeping her daughter safe. Mei Ling was certain the ghost was distraught, not angry.

Mei Ling took her children to the backyard. She told Bo to find a smooth rock. They poked around the bushes until they found the perfect one. Mei Ling noted one last cheerful peony bloom on her mother's stalk. Yellow blossoms were getting ready to burst out on the chrysanthemum stalks. The plants had made it.

Taking the rock upstairs, she wrote the character for "protection" on it. She readied the children for an outing, cut the last pink peony bloom in the yard, and then walked to the mansion where Siew lived. No one paid any attention to her as they traveled through the downtown. She felt almost invisible, a welcome contrast to the hostility in San Francisco, though still strange.

A large bush sat by the sidewalk in front of the grand house. She parted the green foliage to place the stone, the peony, and the paper frog Siew had made so long ago for Bo. It was a simple altar, but it would provide some protection for the girl. *Watch over her,* she begged Quan Yin. There was no need to ask for an ancestor's intervention; the ghost was the one demanding that Mei Ling remove Siew from peril.

Then they walked to the park. Mei Ling wanted to talk to June to get her advice about the spirit.

When the children were out of earshot, Mei Ling asked her friend, "Have you had any experiences with ghosts?"

"No!" June's voice drew out and her eyebrows furrowed. "Have you?"

"I worry about Siew too much. Images of her in bad places come into my mind," Mei Ling said. "I suspect a ghost is placing the thoughts there."

"Does it stop when Siew is with you?" June asked. "On Sundays?"

Mei Ling nodded.

"Then it is a ghost!" June declared, certainty filling her voice. "Her first mother. She probably push Siew to you on the boat."

"How do I make her leave me?" Mei Ling asked.

"You give the ghost what she wants: save her daughter. She will help you. You make a good team, right? Just because you die, you don't stop taking care of your children. She is a good mother, watching out for her daughter even after she is a ghost."

Mei Ling told no one else about the spirit, but she had found a way to quiet the voice of the ghost during the day. In the morning she and the children walked almost a mile to the house where Siew worked to leave an offering of a flower or food at the altar and ask Quan Yin to protect the girl.

Then the frightening images would stay away until the night when there were no distractions to chase away the voice and the images. Mei Ling assured the spirit that she wouldn't forget Siew, but still it haunted her sleep. Again and again she was startled awake by the image of Siew's sweet face riddled with pain as she peered out from a metal cage, waiting for a stranger to claim her body for his pleasure.

Her obsession was harming her health. Pervasive nausea was her constant companion. Fear was a shawl wrapped tight around her shoulders. She had no appetite and was exhausted. She forced herself to stay in bed all night in spite of the anxiety, and then she struggled to get out of bed in the morning to make tea for Kai Li before he went to work.

She hoped to hide her nerves from Kai Li and the children, but she feared it was affecting her family's harmony.

She looked to the moon to connect with her grandmother, but that ritual and her prayers to Quan Yin didn't work their usual soothing magic. For Bo and Joy she strove to seem calm, but even their cheerful spirits did little to assuage her undying panic. Her mood improved when Kai Li was home in the evenings, and she almost felt normal when Siew was with them on Sundays. But as soon as they parted from her, the fear and sorrow clawed at Mei Ling.

She repeatedly assured herself they had time—Siew was only seven years old. But she feared that one day the girl would be traded away, like merchandise, without a trace. If Siew disappeared, Mei Ling would be haunted for the remainder of her life. They had to do something to assure her safety.

One night she asked her husband, "Can you please go to the police?"

Kai Li sighed. He knew what she was speaking about without asking. He came to her on the couch, sitting close, and shook his head. He was refusing her request. Her Dragon fire started to build.

"Wife," he said gently, "I don't believe that will help the situation. The Oakland police have no concern for Chinese girls who might be harmed—someday."

Mei Ling's fire simmered.

He continued, "They won't ask the Pardee family for Siew."

"Who?"

"The man who owns the home where she lives is very powerful; he was the governor of California."

Mei Ling argued, "Prostitution is illegal; the newspaper rages against it constantly."

"Prostitution, yes, but she is only working in their home. The police aren't concerned with what might happen to a little girl years from now," he replied to her, kindly but firmly. "Even if I go to the police, and they agree to remove Siew from the Pardee home, do you believe they will simply bring her to us?"

That *is* what Mei Ling imagined, but in the face of his question she was embarrassed to admit it. She shrugged.

"They will put her on a boat to China," Kai Li explained gently. "She most certainly is a paper niece with no right to stay in this country."

Mei Ling sucked in her breath as if she'd been hit in her stomach.

"Nothing harmful is happening to her at this moment," Kai Li soothed. "She has a warm, dry place to sleep and food to sustain her. That won't be true if she is sent back to China."

Mei Ling sighed. He was right. The American police wouldn't help them. The rage inside her melted away, replaced by despair.

"I'm sorry, wife. We won't give up on her, but I don't know what we can do in this moment to secure her permanent release to us."

Mei Ling nodded and tried to offer him a reassuring smile, but her heart was so heavy it weighed down the muscles of her face.

~

A foul mood settled upon her and caused her to be a rude wife and mother. Dreams of Siew crying for help disturbed her sleep, making her tired and impatient with the children. Too many mornings she woke up to find Kai Li gone already. She'd slept past the time to make him breakfast like a good wife should do, not rising to make tea. She was making their home so unpleasant, she was driving Kai Li away.

More nights he came home late, returning after the sun had set like when they were in San Francisco, which made her have more time alone with the ghost. She prepared their evening meal to be ready to eat at the usual time, but it would be cold by the time he finally walked through the door. He attempted to eat it, but only managed to swallow a few bites.

He couldn't be peddling goods after dark. When she commented that he had been working too hard, hoping to get an explanation for his frequent absences, he deflected her observation. She looked for signs of an explanation—the smell of alcohol on his breath or the scent of perfume—but she only noticed the smell of garlic and ginger, leaving her with the suspicion he was eating in a restaurant before he came home.

Mei Ling wanted to provide a cheerful home for her husband and children, but it was impossible with the angry ghost following her everywhere she went. The spirit now put disturbing thoughts about Kai Li into her mind in addition to haunting her about Siew. *Maybe he is looking for a new wife . . . a better wife who can cook and be a kind and gentle companion like the Rabbit he was promised, not a raging Dragon like you.*

~

Weeks later Kai Li came home excited, looking like he had when he told her they were moving to Oakland. Perhaps he wanted to move again—this time to Alameda.

"Wife, I have good news and I have bad news. Which would you like to hear first?" He smiled.

She stared at him, confused and nervous. She wasn't confident she would agree with his feelings. Alameda was too far from Siew. It would take her too long to walk to the altar each day.

He chuckled, raising a fury in her chest.

He clarified, "It's an American saying. The bad news is I will be working in the evenings."

A pain shot through Mei Ling. She was going to have even more hours alone with the ghost and the children.

"How late?" she whispered, working to keep the despair out of her voice.

"I will be working as a cook, making dinner," he replied.

"In a restaurant?" Her heart quickened. She could fight the ghost on her own for his dream.

He explained, "Not in a restaurant—a home. But I can bring you dinner each night; that is part of the good news."

"A home?" she questioned. He was becoming a domestic servant again. Mei Ling was confused. "That is good news?"

He shook his head slowly. "The good news . . . ," Kai Li said, his voice drawing out in anticipation, "is that my cooking will earn Siew her freedom!" He stared at her, excitement shining in his eyes.

Her heart quickened. "What? How?"

"I have been going to the Pardee home in the evenings. First I spoke with Miss Haw, and talked my way into the kitchen. Fortunately they were in need of a better cook. I demonstrated my skills. After I won her over, she brought my food to the Pardees. They agreed they would like me as their dinner cook." He grinned.

A chill ran down her arms. "Oh, husband, that is wonderful news!" she exclaimed.

"We can bring her to live with us tomorrow."

A surge of energy rushed through Mei Ling's body. Siew would be here starting tomorrow! She threw herself at Kai Li and squeezed him tight.

"Why would you do this, husband? For a child you hardly know?" she asked.

"For your happiness, wife," he declared.

She studied his face. He was hiding something.

"My happiness is your only motivation, husband?" she asked.

A strange look filled his eyes. Sorrow? Uncertainty? He looked down, holding an argument in his mind. Finally he spoke, his voice tight with held-back emotion.

"I was an indentured servant, and I wasn't treated well." The pain in his voice shot through Mei Ling. She waited for him to go on.

When he didn't speak she asked, "Where? When?"

"San Francisco. When I was a boy, nine years or so. I'm not certain."

"But you came here when you were sixteen . . . and lived with your father," she said, confused.

He shook his head. "That is a falsehood . . . another lie."

Mei Ling's Dragon roared. Without meaning to she'd believed the book and all that she learned from it. She was foolish for doing so. She started to speak out, then stopped herself before she caused harm. Her husband was offering Siew her freedom. She took a deep breath.

He went on, looking as sad and afraid as she had ever seen him. "I was very young when the bandits came." His voice was a tight whisper. She leaned in to hear him.

"Five years, maybe. So little I still fit under the couch. That's where I hid." He stared off, his eyes glazed over as he spoke. "It happened so quickly I didn't understand all I had lost until it was over. Though maybe it took a long time. I don't know how long I hid on the ground, certain my mother would find me. But she didn't. She couldn't. When I finally crawled out they were so still. Lying there with the blood. I remember the blood. I don't remember any sounds. Was it guns? Or a knife? I try to remember, but . . ."

He looked at her, confusion on his face. "I can't say how my whole family was killed. I'm ashamed that I didn't pay more attention. It seems I should have cared more."

Tears streamed down Mei Ling's face. She couldn't stop them even if she tried. She imagined him, a little older than Bo, crawling out to find the still warm, utterly motionless bodies.

"I . . . ah," he stuttered. Mei Ling waited patiently, giving him room to continue. "A missionary found me. I went to an orphanage. When I was eight or nine I became a paper son, paid for with my own future labor." Kai Li filled in more details. "Seven years I earned nothing but food and a place to sleep, my clothes the discards from the sons in the house."

He stopped. Mei Ling breathed in the information that explained so much. Pieces of a mystery fell into place. She imagined his loneliness and fear. And his determination to make a good life for himself, for his first wife, then for her, and for the children. He'd overcome so much by himself and somehow was still one of the kindest people she had ever known. Her heart swelled up in love.

"Thank you for telling me, husband," Mei Ling said, hoping he could hear the respect in her voice.

"I don't remember my full name. I cannot say what clan I am, but I'm not an Ox," he said, looking pained. "My mother called me her little Rat."

"Rat," Mei Ling smiled. "That is a good sign to be, husband. Resourceful, flexible, and kind."

"I suppose, though, perhaps not the best match for your Rabbit." He looked at her. "I'm sorry I lied to you, wife."

Guilt sped up Mei Ling's heart. He was being honest, and she was still deceiving him. She snorted without thought. Hurt crossed over

Kai Li's face. Despite her fear and embarrassment, it was time she showed him the same respect. She wouldn't continue her charade.

"Excuse me, husband. My outburst was . . . You have lied to me, yes. But I haven't been entirely honest with you either." A chill passed through her. "Our wedding was the first time I had ever been in a church," she stated, staring at him, waiting for his reaction to her revelation.

His lips turned up at the edges. "I could tell you didn't know the liturgy when we first went."

"You don't mind that I'm not a Christian . . . or was not?" she asked. "I'm beginning to be both."

"There is no harm in anything that brings us peace . . . and instruction for living."

She nodded. Relief soared through her to have finally spoken out loud about her combined faith. But she had a bigger secret from her husband. How could they be in harmony with her deception between them? She cleared her throat, took a deep breath, and steeled herself to make the confession that gnawed at her soul.

"I'm not Yu Ling," she said. Relief poured through her as she said her Jah Jeh's given name.

His eyebrows knit together.

"That is my elder sister," she explained. "My sister became too ill to travel the day after the contract was signed, but the matchmaker wouldn't refund the dowry to my parents. She asked for me instead."

"Why hide the substitution?" Kai Li wondered.

"The matchmaker convinced us you would reject me because we would be incompatible."

"Oh." He leaned back as he understood the implication of what she was saying.

Mei Ling swallowed hard and bit her lip, waiting anxiously for his response.

"What is your name?"

"I'm Mei Ling," she told her husband.

"Mei Ling," he repeated. "That is a beautiful name."

Her skin tingled at the sound of her name in his voice. It had been so long since she'd heard her own name.

"What are you?" he asked, curiosity filling his face. She knew what he meant.

"A Dragon," she said, a challenge in her voice.

He laughed. "Of course you are a Dragon," he replied. "I don't know how I could have seen you as otherwise."

She studied his face, searching for his feelings about her revelation.

"Wife, I'm sorry that our marriage was begun by lies. However, I'm relieved that I'm not the only one who has been deceitful . . . and I believe that Rats and Dragons make excellent companions."

She smiled at him. "That they do, husband."

He smiled back, gazing into her eyes. She saw love. And respect. He knew her name and the truth. The wall of lies that separated them fell away. Her spirit soared.

Her husband accepted her *and* had found a way to fulfill her deepest desire: to rescue Siew. Her chest filled with love.

She leaned in for an embrace and he wrapped her up in his arms. She savored the warmth and the strength of him. Mei Ling felt closer to him than even the night that Joy was born. And after the children were asleep, she showed him.

CHAPTER 21

Oakland
August 1924

The ghost woke Mei Ling up with a command: *Get her now!* Adrenaline surged through her veins. She sat up slowly, protecting the dreams of her family. Darkness hid the tree on the other side of the window. *Not yet,* she chastised the ghost. *Soon, though. Very soon.*

Mei Ling tried to sleep again. She lay quietly, but dreams wouldn't transport her away. Instead, she planned for this special day. Kai Li was going to rise at the usual time, get his produce, and then return with the cart. All of them would walk to the Pardee mansion bearing bright oranges.

She rose and put water on to boil. Mei Ling pulled out the remainder of the peony tea she had saved from China. She warmed up the jook—adding a little cinnamon in recognition that this was a special day.

She dished the porridge out for Kai Li, placing his food on the table. Then she spooned out another portion to put on the altar along with an orange. She kowtowed in thanks and hope to their ancestors.

On this morning, Kai Li knelt down beside her. When she finished her last bow, she looked over at him on the ground next to her. She smiled and leaned her head on his shoulder. He kissed the top of her head before he rose and crossed to the table for his morning meal.

By the time he returned with his daily portion of produce, she and the children were waiting on the sidewalk.

~

The same White woman opened the door. Mei Ling bowed and held out four pieces of fruit. A genuine smile covered the woman's face. She looked like she was holding back tears.

Kai Li said, "Thank---------.---."

Be patient, Mei Ling told the ghost. *She will be here soon.* But Mei Ling felt the same urgency as the spirit. She wanted to see Siew too.

The woman walked away and returned a few minutes later with Siew. The girl's eyes opened in delight when she saw them. The little girl looked at the White woman, who nodded in approval.

Siew looked back at their family and exclaimed, "We get to visit? Today isn't Sunday!"

Mei Ling's heart skipped in excitement. She looked at Kai Li, who nodded at Mei Ling—wordlessly encouraging her to explain the good news.

Mei Ling crouched down in front of Siew. She took her small ward's hands and said, "Not just a visit. You get to come live with us!"

Siew froze, her face going stony. Mei Ling's heart sank. She'd assumed Siew wanted to live with them, but perhaps she was wrong.

"-- -- ----?" Siew asked the housekeeper.

"---, --- --- ---- ---- ----," the woman replied.

"------?" Siew asked.

"Yes." The woman smiled. "------."

"I ------- I ---- -- ---- -- ---- -- ---- ---------!" Siew said.

The woman's face fell; she looked like she would cry.

"--- ---- -- ------- --- -- ---. -- Chinn ---- --- ---- -- -- ------."

Siew started shaking. Was she afraid?

"What's wrong?" Mei Ling asked Kai Li. "She doesn't want to live with us?"

"Miss Haw just told her she won't be working here at all anymore. I believe Siew is overcome with happiness and shock."

Mei Ling exhaled in relief.

Siew put her hands on Bo's shoulders. Beaming, she exclaimed, "I get to live with you again!"

Mei Ling grinned at the excitement on the children's faces.

"--'- --- ---- ----------," Miss Haw said. "----- --- ---- -- ----?"

"Go with Siew to get her things," Kai Li translated. "Bo and I will stay out here."

Siew took Mei Ling's hand and brought her into a large storage pantry. One side had shelves of canned goods and baskets filled with bright fruits and vegetables. The other had cleaning supplies—buckets, mops, brooms, and bottles.

They passed through a door into a kitchen. Around the edges were counters, a sink, a brand-new stove, and . . . an electric refrigerator. Mei Ling had never seen one in person, only in advertisements in the newspaper. This is where Kai Li would earn Siew's freedom.

Suddenly ashamed, Mei Ling told Siew, "Our house isn't nearly as nice as this one."

Siew shrugged in reply. She led Mei Ling into a passageway. On the right was a built-in wooden table with benches. A large, dark, built-in wooden cabinet filled the other side. Stacks of plates, bowls, and cups in various sizes showed through the beveled-glass doors, and presumably silver filled the drawers. Siew ducked under the table on the right side. Mei Ling bent over to see where she'd gone.

It took a moment for her eyes to adjust to the darkness. Mei Ling's throat welled up at the sight. This cubbyhole was where Siew slept. On the ground, against the wall, was bedding and an open suitcase. The little girl was stuffing things into the small container. As Kai Li said,

Siew had been warm and dry, but she had to be terribly lonely. The child reached for the paper Quan Yin that Mei Ling had torn out of her notebook on Angel Island. It sat on a brick next to a dried flower. Mei Ling was hopeful that the goddess had provided some comfort to Siew.

The girl closed the lid and clicked it tight. She pushed the bedding out of the way and slid the small case across the wooden floor.

"Let me help you." Mei Ling reached for the handle.

The girl froze and put her hand out to block Mei Ling's hand. "I'm okay. You have Joy on your back."

"I can do both—help you and carry Joy," Mei Ling said.

Siew nodded and let Mei Ling take the suitcase out of her way.

Miss Haw was waiting nearby.

"You --- ---- --- -----," the White woman said.

"Thank you," Siew replied.

To Mei Ling's surprise Siew hugged the woman before they left.

~

Mei Ling looked at the bush with the altar as they passed by. She wouldn't need to return here each day anymore. *Thank you. Thank you,* the ghost chanted as they walked. Mei Ling shared the spirit's pleasure and was happy for Siew's mother to enjoy this journey, but she hoped the demanding spirit would leave once they got home.

At the doorway of their apartment, Siew hesitated, but Bo pulled her in, practically running to the living room.

"This is our couch," he announced, pointing to it. Then he tugged her through the arch. "This is the kitchen." He stared at her face for approval. When she nodded he led her into the bedroom. "We sleep here. Mah-ma and Bah-ba sleep there." He pointed to each mattress. "Joy sleeps anywhere she wants."

Mei Ling laughed. Kai Li did too.

"I'm going to work now," Kai Li said.

"I'm ready," Siew said, dropping Bo's hand. "Bye, Bo. See you after work!"

Mei Ling shook her head. "Siew, you'll stay here with me and the little children."

"Oh." Siew's face fell.

"Do you wish to leave?" Mei Ling asked.

"No!" Bo shouted.

Siew shook her head. "I'll do whatever you say."

Mei Ling studied the eager-to-please girl, fearing that Siew's experiences had made her meek. While she valued obedience, she wanted Siew to have her passion, her Dragon nature.

"Stay with me," Bo shouted.

Mei Ling said, "I'll appreciate your help here."

Siew stared at Mei Ling. Doubt and fear hid in her eyes. Then she nodded. Kai Li waved in the Western fashion and left. Bo took Siew's hand and led her to the last room.

"Ta-da!" he said as he opened the door with a flourish. Mei Ling laughed. She didn't know where he learned that phrase—perhaps from June's children. Siew gasped when she saw the toilet and bathtub. She looked around, confusion on her face.

"What are you searching for?" Mei Ling asked.

"The other family," Siew replied.

"What other family?"

"The one in the other bedroom that uses this bathroom."

Mei Ling smiled. "I was amazed too when I realized that is our very own bathroom—just for the five of us."

"Wow," Siew said. "You are rich."

Mei Ling smiled. She hadn't needed to worry that Siew would judge them as lacking.

"Yes, we are," she replied, and she felt the ghost's approval.

~

Later that day Mei Ling brought out the nearly finished bright-red gown. After weeks of work, only the trim at the bottom remained. Siew walked up to it, awe on her face.

"That is soooo beautiful."

"Thank you. It's for the bride in a wealthy San Francisco family. She's going to be married during the Autumn Moon Festival. We'll bring it to her next week."

Siew was obviously resisting the urge to feel it.

"If you wash your hands you may touch it gently."

Mei Ling spread the gown out to its full size across the couch. The girl ran her cleaned fingers across the bright colors. She petted the huge tail feathers on the peacock and stroked the neck of the peahen on the back. Her eyes traveled over the pink lotus flowers on the bottom of the skirt and the intricate green vines that edged the entire gown.

"Will you teach me?" Siew asked.

"Yes," Mei Ling agreed. "But not today. You keep Bo and Joy occupied while I work. If I get enough finished, we can walk to the park. Maybe Auntie June, Dorothy, and Tim will be there."

With the children occupied by Siew, Mei Ling accomplished much more than she usually did in a morning. She heard squeals of laughter from the bedroom and an occasional fuss from Joy, but otherwise she was left alone to stitch and think. Contentment settled in her heart. After months of distress, her soul was at peace.

~

On the way to the park, Mei Ling stopped at their favorite store to introduce Siew to the owner, Mrs. Wan, and let the children choose a treat. She pressed a round coin into each small palm. Bo skipped to the candies, pulling Siew along.

"What do you want?" he asked his new sister. "I like peppermint best."

The girl stared at the assortment of jars, her head moving back and forth. She shrugged. She looked at the coin in her hand.

"You can choose one long stick or four little ones," Mei Ling explained.

"No, thank you," Siew said. "You can have mine." She handed the coin back to Mei Ling.

Confused, Mei Ling asked, "You don't like candy?"

Siew shrugged.

Mei Ling suddenly understood. "You've never had any?"

Siew shook her head, almost imperceptibly.

"Then Bo and I will choose for you," Mei Ling said. "Is there any fruit you like?"

Siew shrugged, looking as if she was about to cry.

Keeping her tone light, Mei Ling named a few. "Orange, apple, banana, grape . . ."

Siew shrugged again. "Pineapple?"

"Yum," Mei Ling said. "I love pineapples too. They were the best treat on the ship, right?"

Siew nodded with a small smile.

Mei Ling asked Mrs. Wan for an assortment of candies, including pineapple. Mrs. Wan added passionfruit and lychee for good luck for the newest member of their family.

"Do you want any hell notes?" the storekeeper asked. "For the Hungry Ghost Festival?"

"Yes, please," Mei Ling agreed. "Two packs." They would burn the paper and give food as offerings to all their ancestors, including Bo's and Siew's first mothers.

As they walked away from the counter Mrs. Wan said, "Anytime you need anything, Siew, you come here. I will always help you."

Siew nodded with a little bow. She hadn't lost all of her Chinese ways.

As they walked out of the door, the girl whispered to Bo, "She's very nice."

He nodded as he sucked on his peppermint stick.

~

"We must register Siew too," June declared. "Today I will take you to Lincoln School to put her name down. Maybe they put her in Miss Chew's class. She is the Chinese teacher who went to Mills College, so all the little girls believe they will go there too."

College. A chill went down Mei Ling's spine. The ghost woke up with a sudden urgency. Apparently she hadn't gone far. *My daughter will go to college,* the spirit demanded.

Mei Ling looked at the children playing in the distance. College? Mei Ling had never met a woman who had been to college. Could they really dream of that for these children? The thought seemed entirely out of their reach, but finding Siew felt impossible not so long ago, and now she was living with them and chasing after Bo only twenty feet away. Why not aspire to have her children go to college? All three of them.

She struck a deal with the ghost. *Yes, we will dream of that for Siew—but for Bo and Joy too.*

~

Mei Ling stepped carefully as she carried the pot of steaming water. She set it on the ground below the finished gown hanging in the doorway. It was time to inspect it, cut off loose threads, and steam out the largest wrinkles. Siew had walked Bo to the park. Joy was tied to her back where she wouldn't get burned or muss up the red silk fabric. The baby peered around her shoulder, wanting to see what Mei Ling was doing.

"This is a pink peony," Mei Ling told the girl. "Here is a purple butterfly . . . and a yellow one."

Mei Ling snipped off the last few threads as she spoke. When she was done, she folded the gown, wrapped it in paper, and placed it in a box. She would deliver it to Mr. Young, the shopkeeper, today.

The last time she delivered hats and runners to him, he mentioned her items weren't selling as quickly as they had in the past. Her embroidery was losing its appeal. She harbored a small fear that he would no longer want this gown—or more work from her in the future.

When Mei Ling picked up Bo and Siew for the journey to San Francisco, June was at the park, gossiping with the usual gathering of Cantonese-speaking immigrant women.

"Show, show," June insisted.

Mei Ling looked at the circle of women who were becoming her friends. What if June, or someone else, ruined it? She was hesitant to pull it out of its protective wrapping.

"It's nothing, not worth bothering your eyes with," Mei Ling said.

"Not true!" June declared. She grabbed the box from Mei Ling's hands.

Mei Ling took the package back. She wasn't risking four months of work to careless handling.

"I will show you, but you may not touch the gown." She was adamant.

June nodded and said to the others, as if it was her idea, "We just look. Not touch."

Mei Ling set the box on June's lap. Excited and nervous, she opened it carefully and gently pulled out the gown by the shoulders, holding it high off the ground. It was a modern gown, cut in the style of the flappers with a drop-waist skirt and sheer fabric over a chemise, but traditional Chinese in red silk with Yue embroidery.

Mei Ling studied the faces of the women in the circle, looking for reassurance that she had succeeded in her combination of American and Chinese. Mei Ling heard a gasp. Her lips tugged up in a smile.

"Oh, beautiful," Fen Wai cried out. "Mei Ling, it is stunning!" Her hand covered her chest in amazement.

Mei Ling's heart unclenched. She smiled and bowed at her friends. If these women were any indication, Mr. Young's daughter would be pleased, though women in San Francisco were more discerning about fashion. And the endorsement of these immigrants did not guarantee that an American-born bride would approve of her work.

"As I said, it isn't worth troubling your eyes," Mei Ling said.

"Mei Ling." June's bossy voice came at her. "You must show to Mrs. Tsou. She will want a gown like this for her daughter. Come, come. Before you go to San Francisco we will go to her shop."

"Yes," Fen Wai agreed.

June led Mei Ling and the children over to the store. She was right: Mrs. Tsou ordered one on the spot. "Just the same, but less purple and more yellow." She needed it by the New Year in February.

"I will find you lots of customers in Oakland. No need for someone talented like you to go all the way to San Francisco," June declared. "Leave it to June to set you up."

Grateful for her encouragement and support, Mei Ling smiled at her friend. Customers in Oakland Chinatown would be wonderful, and June was just the person to help her find them.

CHAPTER 22

San Francisco and Oakland
August 1924

"Stay close," Mei Ling reminded Bo and Siew as they skipped onto the ferry. They were excited for this adventure, but Mei Ling's nerves were taut. Despite the enthusiastic reception from the ladies, she feared Mr. Young wouldn't be pleased with her work.

They stood at the railing, watching the distance grow between the boat and the shore.

"There's the tower!" Siew said, pointing to a spot in the distance.

Mei Ling searched the land until she spotted it: the Campanile at the University of California in Berkeley.

"You remember?" Mei Ling asked.

Siew nodded. "After you left I looked for it whenever they took me on a walk, because you said you would be near there."

Mei Ling's heart welled up with emotion. "I'm sorry we had to leave you behind," she said to Siew.

Siew shrugged but didn't look at Mei Ling when she said, "It was fine."

The girl must have been sad and afraid for a year . . . more than a year. Mei Ling liked to believe Siew had been too young to be affected, but if she remembered the tower, she remembered everything.

"It's behind you," Mei Ling said in a rush. "You are in our family now. Forever. You understand?"

Siew nodded, but the tight, bittersweet smile on her face told Mei Ling that she didn't believe her. Mei Ling's instinct was to reassure her it was true, but she had doubts of her own, and so did the ghost.

"There was a tall tower at the church by the Pardee mansion," Siew said. "I pretended I climbed it and could see you. Then I knew where to find you."

A rush of emotions rode a wave through Mei Ling's heart: guilt, anger, affection all mixed in.

Mei Ling told Siew, "I dreamed of finding you too, almost every night in my sleep." She smiled and left out the detail that she saw Siew in her nightmares.

She took a deep breath to calm herself. It was over, they were together, but neither of them fully trusted the situation.

"Did you ask Quan Yin for help?" Mei Ling asked.

"Every night, like you said," Siew said.

"She brought us back together," Mei Ling replied. "Did you work hard, be kind, and be humble?"

Siew nodded.

"And you were rewarded." Mei Ling smiled.

Siew smiled back with a nod.

Mei Ling wished she believed success was as simple as those words from her mother. She wanted Siew's challenges to be behind her, but was skeptical that the girl's—or even her own—path would be so easy.

She looked out at the water. An image of Jui Lan's face bobbing in the salty waves filled her mind. *No.* Mei Ling pushed those thoughts away.

"How long has it been since you were in San Francisco?" Mei Ling asked Siew.

The girl shrugged.

"You don't remember when you moved to Oakland?"

She shrugged again. Siew never had answers when Mei Ling asked about the time between Angel Island and her returning to them. No matter how Mei Ling asked, the little girl just shrugged, but Mei Ling couldn't shake off the feeling that Siew harbored a terrible truth.

Mei Ling admired the clock tower as they pulled up to the Ferry Building. They walked on Jackson Street, up the steep hill toward Mr. Young's store, passing streets and alleyways packed with people and goods. It was much denser than Chinatown in Oakland, filled mostly with men who had just arrived in the United States.

Just before they got to Grant they came to a standstill; a cart blocked the road and the sidewalk. Mei Ling glanced into Bartlett Alley and saw the women. Wanting to draw the children's attention away from the prostitutes in their cages, she pointed to the top of the building ahead. Bo followed her distraction, but when she looked at Siew, her eyes were glued to the scene down the alley. The girl walked into the narrow passageway.

"Is that you, Siew?" a woman called out. "I'll see you soon!"

Mei Ling sucked in her breath as if someone had punched her in the gut. She rushed to Siew, grabbed her hand, and pulled her into the street, away from the voice. She marched them downhill, away from the cages. She pushed Siew against a brick wall and crouched down in front of her.

"How do you know that woman?" Mei Ling demanded. "How does she know your name?!"

Siew's eyes were full of tears. She shrugged.

"She's a bad woman. You stay away from her and anyone like her. You understand?" Mei Ling shouted at Siew, her heart racing. "That isn't your future!"

Mei Ling wiped her eyes hard, refusing to cry in front of the children, and she stared at Siew until the girl finally nodded.

"You aren't like her!" Mei Ling announced. Then she stood up and strode a different route toward the store, the children running to keep up with her. She didn't care if she was frightening them. She was so upset she wanted to scream.

Mei Ling had been right. The fact that woman had met Siew confirmed Suk Suk's ultimate purpose in bringing her to San Francisco.

She'd walked so fast that she was panting when she arrived at the store. Pausing outside to calm herself, Mei Ling noted that the runners she'd made were no longer in the window display; nor were they close to the front of the store. Mr. Young had spoken the truth: her work wasn't valuable to him any longer.

They walked to the register. "I'd like to speak with Mr. Young. Please tell him that Mrs. Chinn is here with the gown," she told the unfamiliar cashier. Annoyance flashed on his face; the man looked her up and down, making her uncomfortable. She averted her eyes and smiled at Bo, who was holding her hand. The man left.

She placed the box on the counter, her heart pounding. They hadn't spoken of a price; she'd been afraid to ask for fear of seeming greedy and ungrateful, but she had put many weeks of work into this gown. She hoped to get at least seventy-five dollars for all of her hard work; the silk fabric alone had cost fifteen dollars. They needed to make so many purchases to see them through the winter, including warmer clothes and fuel for heat.

"Stay close," she told the children. Fragile items were displayed all along the aisles. She didn't want to pay for trinkets damaged by Bo or Siew.

The man returned but didn't say anything. She waited, feeling awkward.

Eventually Mr. Young came out.

"Hello, Mrs. Chinn," he greeted her warmly. Then he held out his hands in two tight fists. He opened them slowly. Each palm revealed a small animal carved into wood: a monkey and a tiger. "Take them," he encouraged the children.

They looked at her, and she nodded her approval. Bo and Siew each bowed with a smile and accepted their gifts. Siew immediately began acting out a scene with her animal, and Bo joined in.

"Let's see what you have for me." The man smiled at Siew.

Mei Ling opened the box and carefully pulled the gown out by the shoulders, making sure it didn't touch the ground. She studied the man's face. He nodded slightly with his lips pulled down, indicating mild satisfaction.

"It will do," he said, and he sighed.

Mei Ling hid her disappointment as she returned the gown to its packaging.

Mr. Young picked up the box with a nod and said, "My daughter will appreciate your gift to her on her special day."

Gift!? This was hours of work and one of Ahma's precious gold coins. She stood by, stunned as he turned away with the box. She wanted to protest but feared she would alienate her only source of income. If she spoke up, he might stop buying her work altogether.

She looked down and saw Siew staring up at her. The girl was watching to see what she would do.

Mei Ling's Dragon stirred to life. She remembered June's assurance that she would find customers in Oakland Chinatown. While she couldn't entirely count on that, she refused to let this man exploit her in front of Siew.

"I'm sorry, sir," Mei Ling countered. "I must not have been clear. As much as I would like this to be my gift, I must ask for payment for my work. To feed my children. I'm sure you understand."

He stopped and turned around slowly, his face hard.

"Are you certain about that?" he asked, a slight threat in his voice.

Her heart pounded, and she tasted metal in her mouth. The normally jovial man was angry.

Despite her discomfort at challenging him directly, she nodded and swallowed hard.

"I don't believe this is worthy of payment," he declared.

Her head spun, but she replied, "Then it isn't worthy of your daughter on her special day." She felt Siew's hand slip into her own. It gave her strength. June's certainty about her work gave her courage. She reached out her free hand, arching her eyebrows. The man stared at her. She stared back at him, looking him directly in the eyes, waiting for him to hand her the box.

"Very well," he said. He pulled out money and placed some on the counter.

She stared at the four five-dollar bills, an insulting amount of money for four months of work that did nothing to assuage her Dragon. She stepped past the counter and grabbed the box from his hand.

"We're leaving," Mei Ling said to the children. Her heart pounded fiercely as she stormed through the store. "Be careful!" she hissed to Bo and Siew. Shame and fury burned in her. She'd been foolish to invest so much time and money into this one project hoping for a good return. She'd have to find a buyer. Perhaps it would fit Mrs. Tsou's daughter, though the colors were wrong.

"Please wait." A woman's voice broke through her thoughts.

Mei Ling stopped short. She took a breath before she turned around.

"Let me see." A woman in her late thirties with hair pulled into a bun walked toward them from the back of the store.

The elegant woman took the box and gently pulled out the gown.

"Remarkable!" the woman exclaimed. "It is stunning, more than worthy of our eldest daughter. She will be as pleased with your work as I am."

She smiled. The word *stunning* pierced Mei Ling like a thrilling arrow.

The woman continued, "My husband doesn't understand the importance, but I do."

Mrs. Young walked away with the box. Mei Ling stifled a protest as she watched her walk to her husband. She said something to him so quietly that Mei Ling couldn't understand it, but she heard a hiss in the woman's voice. He reached into his pocket. Mrs. Young took all of the money and pulled out individual bills. Mei Ling counted as each one was removed. At ten bills a chill ran down her spine. By fifteen she thought her heart might burst. The woman stopped at twenty. Mr. Young's face was pale.

The mother of the bride returned to Mei Ling.

"Two hundred dollars. Under one condition . . ." She paused to let that number sink in. "You won't make another for any bride in San Francisco for one year." Her eyes opened wide and her chin tipped down in a question. She held the money close to her own heart, waiting for Mei Ling's response.

Two hundred dollars! Mei Ling's head nearly exploded at the thought of so much money. She nodded in affirmation. The woman held out the bills. Mei Ling took the money from her hand.

"You are very talented. I wish you the best," Mrs. Young said with a respectful bow. Mei Ling watched her walk past her husband.

Mr. Young shrugged at Mei Ling as if to say he tried, but no hard feelings. Mei Ling wanted to roar at him, but she kept her outward equanimity. She just put the money in her bodice, turned, and walked away from the store.

That man had tried to trick her, to make her believe her work wasn't of value to him. She nearly believed his carefully crafted lies, but she had bested him and come out ahead. *Humble*—her mother's word echoed in her mind. Humility in this situation wouldn't feed or clothe her children. Pride in her own work and her friend's faith in her gave Mei Ling the necessary strength to fight for her family.

She looked down at Siew and smiled. Humility hadn't saved Siew. Mei Ling's listening to the ghost and persistence had rescued this precious girl from a wretched life. And being honest with her husband. *Work hard—yes. Be kind—yes.* But Mei Ling was less certain that being humble would always lead to a harmonious life. Like the gown she just made, she might need to be both: Chinese and American.

Her body thrummed in excitement as she walked downhill toward the ferry home. Bo and Siew skipped alongside her, picking up her good mood.

She couldn't stop smiling as she pictured the look of surprise and delight on Kai Li's face when she showed him this money. She wouldn't squirrel any of it away; instead she would impress him with all of it.

CHAPTER 23

Oakland
September 1924

Mei Ling was startled awake by loud cries. She sighed and went to Siew for the fifth time that night. The girl lay in bed, sleeping with Bo curled up close.

Siew shouted at an invisible demon, "No, no, no. Go away. Leave me alone."

"You're dreaming," Mei Ling soothed. But the girl continued to shake her head and yell, growing more frantic.

Mei Ling patted Siew's sweaty forehead, but the girl slapped her hand away and yelled, "No!"

Then Siew bolted upright. Panting, she looked around, tears seeping out of the corners of her eyes.

They'd been through this ordeal once or twice most nights in the weeks since Siew lived with them. The sleeping girl couldn't hide the strong emotions that proved she'd been harmed in the previous year. Mei Ling had quizzed the girl, hoping Siew would disclose more in this half-asleep state than she'd revealed when she was awake. But the little girl responded to Mei Ling's inquiries about Suk Suk, Bartlett

Alley, or who she lived with with a shake of the head. The answers to her most burning questions were lost.

Mei Ling had learned what to do to soothe the agitated girl. "It was a dream. You're safe now."

Siew blinked, looked at Mei Ling, nodded, and lay back down. Mei Ling gently rubbed the girl's hair and whispered the story of the Rabbit Moon into her ear until the soft sounds of sleep came from her.

With the first day of school tomorrow Siew was more anxious than usual, though she didn't say so during the day. Mei Ling felt a large measure of compassion for the child—and she was exhausted. So she lay down by the seven-year-old, hoping her presence would be soothing enough that all five members of their household would sleep for the rest of the night.

Too soon the morning came. Despite the wakeful night, Mei Ling rose to make tea and jook for Kai Li before he left for work. Then she woke the children up to get Siew to her first day of school on time; no longer could they sleep as long as they wished. Their lives would be controlled by school hours.

Siew bolted into action, getting dressed, washed, and ready to leave in a rush. Mei Ling insisted she sit to eat breakfast, but the girl hardly ate anything. June had told Mei Ling to "pack a lunch" because Siew would be gone through the midday meal, unlike when Mei Ling was in school. Mei Ling filled a metal pail with rice, tofu, and bok choy. She placed a pear in it as well.

With memories of her own schooling bolstering her, Mei Ling set out with the children, excited and hopeful that Siew would enjoy this time of life as much as she had.

As they came closer to the building, they joined a stream of people heading to the same place. The children were dressed in Western clothing, though most of them were Chinese. The boys wore dark pants and the girls were in colorful skirts. Mei Ling was glad she had pulled Siew's long hair into a bouncy ponytail like so many of the girls wore. She measured Siew's clothes against the other girls'. The clothes that Mei Ling had sewed for Siew would allow her to fit in, something that had concerned Mei Ling as a young student.

They followed the crowd to the yard and then stopped. Children were marching into already-formed lines of students, but Mei Ling didn't know where Siew belonged. Her confidence wavered.

They stopped walking and Mei Ling looked around for a hint. Siew stared at her, doubt on her face.

"I will find someone to ask for help, but you will have to ask the question in English. Can you manage that?" Mei Ling asked.

Siew nodded.

Mei Ling saw a blond White woman standing at the front, talking with the students at the head of the line.

They walked up to her. "Excuse me." Mei Ling said one of the few English phrases that she knew with a slight bow.

The woman replied, "Yes, --- I help ---?"

Mei Ling smiled and looked at Siew.

Siew said, "I ---'- ---- ----- -- --."

The lady smiled and reached out her arm. "-'- ---- ------."

Siew bowed, then took the woman's palm in a Western handshake. "-'- ---."

The blond asked Siew, "------- -- ------- ------. --- --- --- ---?"

"-----," Siew replied.

"---- --- --- ---- --- ---- --- -- -- -------- ------," the woman said. "- ---- ---- -- -- ---- -------, --- ------. -----, I --- -- ----- ----."

Then the woman took Siew's hand and gestured with her head that Mei Ling should follow them. Shame burned in Mei Ling as she walked behind them. She hadn't imagined that she would feel so foreign at school. Her mother, having never been a student, must have felt like this—like she didn't belong. Mei Ling resolved to keep up her English studies at church, even though it was an exceedingly frustrating language and it seemed futile at times.

They were led to the front of a different line, where another White teacher was standing, her brown hair bobbed in the modern fashion. The two women spoke, then the first lady said something to Siew. She waved goodbye to Bo and Mei Ling, then returned to her line.

"Hello, I'm Mrs. Bartley," the woman said in Cantonese. Relief mixed with surprise at the sound of Mei Ling's own language coming out of that mouth. "I will be Siew's teacher this year. Welcome to Lincoln School."

"Thank you," Mei Ling replied with a bow. The White teacher bowed back.

"Return here at two thirty," the woman explained and then turned away from Mei Ling.

They had been dismissed. Mei Ling froze. Siew looked at her from the front of the line, appearing calm to the world, but Mei Ling recognized the hint of alarm in her eyes. She gave a little wave with her fingers, and Siew nodded back, her eyes glossy with unshed tears.

Please watch over her today, Mei Ling asked the ghost, and then she walked away from Siew. Ten paces later, she realized Bo wasn't at her side. She turned around to see him clinging to his foster sister. The girl crouched down, said something into his ear, and pointed in Mei Ling's direction. Bo looked at Mei Ling, who pointed sharply at the ground in front of her feet. She would be humiliated further if she were forced to retrieve him.

Slowly he trudged toward Mei Ling, occasionally glancing back at Siew, his protruding lip his only protest. Mei Ling shared his sorrow at leaving Siew behind, so she just took his hand without chastising him. She scanned the playground, hoping to spot June, but didn't see her friend, so they went home.

The apartment was too quiet without Siew. In only a few weeks it had become so normal to be with her that it was unsettling to be separated. Mei Ling's mind continuously traveled to thoughts of the girl. Seemingly every ten minutes Bo asked for her. Mei Ling reassured him that they would fetch the girl before the end of the day.

Without Siew to distract and watch the little ones, getting her work done was very difficult. Mei Ling had bought the silk for a new gown after getting measurements from Mrs. Tsou. She needed to begin now because she had already gotten a second order from Mrs. Tsang, an acquaintance at church. True to her word June had found her work by spreading the word in Oakland Chinatown that Mei Ling was available for the "best, best" wedding gowns.

Mei Ling put the children in the bedroom and told them to stay there. Bo stared up at her, looking as if he wanted to protest, but she reiterated her instructions and closed the door. He was going to have to be more responsible.

Through the door she heard Bo bark like a dog, followed by Joy's giggles. After a pause her son crowed like a rooster, and her daughter laughed again. Mei Ling smiled to herself. Bo was entertaining Joy in the same way Siew had amused him—with the sounds of the animals in the zodiac.

She pulled out the roll of butcher paper and spread it on the ground of the living room, leaving no gaps where dirt could touch the silk. She laid the bright fabric on top of the barrier and then placed a homemade paper pattern on the silk. She weighed it down with smooth, clean rocks, and then very carefully she cut it around the paper. She finished cutting before lunch. While the children napped she started stitching the seams together. When they woke up it was time to get Siew.

~

"This is my new friend, Mimi." Siew beamed as she introduced a petite girl with shiny black hair pulled back into a high ponytail.

"Nice to meet you," Mei Ling said, glad to see Siew looking so happy after her first day of school.

Bo threw his arms around his sister and patted her back.

"This is my brother, Bo," Siew explained to her classmate. "And this is Joy!"

Mimi bowed her respect.

"Bye!" Siew said as she waved to her teacher.

"----bye, Siew," the friendly woman replied. "--- you --------. Goodbye, Mrs. Chinn."

Mei Ling watched the conversation, feeling self-conscious again. She appreciated that the teacher included her by saying goodbye in Cantonese.

June invited Mei Ling and the children to the park after school. She agreed, even though there was work to be done in the garden at home. She felt like she belonged, gossiping with the other mothers while their children played. Next time she would bring her embroidery so she could be productive and visit with her friends.

As they walked home Siew told Bo about school. She explained about the carpet, the chalkboard, and the names of the students. Once they were in their apartment, she took the younger children into the bedroom to play. Through the open door, Mei Ling listened in on their game. Siew instructed Bo to sit on the ground and spoke to him in English, as if she were the White teacher and they were new students. Mei Ling smiled to herself, remembering that she and Jah Jeh did the same thing so long ago, but not in English. Her heart filled with love for the three children.

Guilt and sorrow rose inside her. It had been too long since she had written to her old home. Her focus on their life in California was so consuming that her family in China didn't press on her mind and heart as they once had. She'd had a recent letter from them that she had yet to reply to. It was bittersweet to realize that Oakland was more her home and these people were more her family than the ones she had left behind in the village.

The note she'd received last week was dated from May. The information from China came slower and slower. She didn't know if that was because the mail was delayed or lost in transit, the postage was too expensive for her family to afford, or if her family was too busy to write. She didn't allow herself to imagine it was because they didn't care. Whatever the cause on their end, she'd lost the habit of writing every week, though she honored them in her devotionals each day.

She put down her needlework and picked up a pen.

> September 2, 1924
>
> Dearest family,
> Thank you for your recent note—I treasure every detail.
>
> Our exciting news is that Siew, the little girl who we met on the boat, is living with us permanently. Our life is very busy and happy with three children. Our foster daughter is very helpful with Joy and Bo.
>
> Kai Li is as hardworking as ever and now has two positions. He peddles fruits and vegetables from early in the morning until the afternoon. Then he cooks dinner for a prestigious family, the Pardees. The arrangement with them allows him to bring us dinner as well so we enjoy his cooking and his company most nights.
>
> I continue to contribute to our family finances with the embroidery skills that I learned from Mahma and Ahma. I have found an excellent market for wedding gowns right in Oakland which I sell directly to customers. In addition a nearby store sells any

table runners I have time to make. I honor you all with every stitch.

Siew began school today. I believe she will be eager to be a good student, and I am happy that our family's tradition of educating girls will continue in our new home.

The dream of a public-funded school system is a reality here. Our friend June insists that our daughters will have an education equal in every way to our sons. She brought us to the University of California last week to remind our children to work hard in school so that they can qualify for admission and become successful in life.

When we rode up the tall tower in the center of campus, the elevator operator told us that fossils from wooly mammoths and saber-toothed tigers are stored on the floors that we passed by. They were found in a tar pit in Los Angeles. We didn't actually see them, but I believe he wasn't teasing us. June questioned the attendant to prove to us that there are many, many women and many Chinese who attend this prestigious university.

The view from the platform was breathtaking. We could see across the sparkling water all the way to San Francisco. In the middle of the bay were the famous islands: Alcatraz, where the prisoners are kept, and Angel Island, where we were detained. My heart stirred for all those detained there, though the numbers have dwindled enormously since the implementation of the new immigration laws.

> We couldn't make out our home in the crush of similar buildings, but it was there, just past the tall buildings in downtown Oakland.
>
> At last we will enjoy tea from our ancestral chrysanthemums. The cutting took root in our small garden, and we have so many beautiful golden blossoms. We harvested and prepared them as you taught me, so we will enjoy them all winter—and perhaps all year. I sent honor to you as we prepared them—just as I honor you and our ancestors each morning.
>
> Your devoted Mei Ling

She considered how much money to send to them and settled on twenty dollars rather than the ten she had sent the past few times. She hoped her family would take it as a sign of reverence and care, not ostentation. Mei Ling was acutely mindful that the news from China wasn't nearly as cheerful or interesting as hers. She hoped her letter would be received by her sister with interest rather than resentment.

~

The Autumn Moon Festival was just a few weeks after the start of the academic year. Lincoln School held a gathering to celebrate it. Families were invited to come in the evening to see short plays.

Because Siew was bilingual, she played the part of the translator. She'd practiced so much that Mei Ling had memorized her lines too—the ones in English as well as the ones in Cantonese. Mei Ling's ability to speak English wasn't progressing as fast as she would like, but she was understanding more and more.

It felt like a holiday as the five of them set out as the full moon was rising over the hills to the east. Mei Ling stared at the shiny orb and thought about how far her life had come since the last harvest moon. A year ago she'd been looking for shelter in case Kai Li turned her out for having a daughter. Back then she'd known so little about the man who had brought her to this new home and didn't trust him to stand by her. A year ago she hadn't met Joy outside her body, which seemed unfathomable, and her dreams had been haunted with images of Siew nearly every night.

"Can you see the rabbit in the moon?" she asked Bo, pointing to the glowing orb.

They stopped walking and all stared upward.

"I see it," Siew declared.

"Ummm . . ." Bo looked up, then a grin split his face. "Me too!"

He reached into his pocket for his little wooden rabbit. He held it up to the moon.

"Same, same," Siew said. "See, Joy?"

Mei Ling felt, more than saw, Joy nod her head.

Bo nodded and returned the carving to his pocket. It still traveled with him most of the time, his connection to his first mother, but he kept it tucked away now, not clutched in desperation.

Mei Ling glanced at her husband, her son, and her daughters. The harmony between them was palpable. Her heart filled with love and gratitude. She looked at the moon and telegraphed blessings to her family in China. Tears pushed at the corners of her eyes.

Kai Li noticed, and his eyes furrowed.

"I'm happy," she reassured him. "So happy."

His face relaxed, and he nodded and smiled. "Me too, wife. Me too."

~

After the skit they ate moon cakes in the schoolyard under the bright orb and colorful paper lanterns.

June exclaimed to Siew, "You speak so loud and clear in both languages."

"Thank you, Auntie," the girl replied with a smile.

Proud, Mei Ling nodded and patted Siew's back. She had done especially well. In such a short time, she had made the adjustment to this new life.

"May we go play?" Siew asked.

Mei Ling nodded and Siew ran off with Bo. The Cantonese-speaking families clustered in a circle. Though their children all went to school together, the parents self-segregated by language: the immigrants speaking Cantonese, the American-born Chinese speaking English with each other, and the non-Chinese with their own circle of conversation.

When Siew, Bo, and Joy were adults they would join the American-born Chinese, regardless of their birthplace; their English would be pure. No matter how long she lived here or how much English she learned, Mei Ling's accent would always mark her as foreign. Her children would be at home here in a way she never would. That realization was at once reassuring and disturbing.

Mei Ling watched Siew playing tag with a group of children. The girl held fast to Bo's hand even though it made it harder for her to run. A Negro and a White child, as well as a Japanese girl, played too—all of them here for the Autumn Moon Festival. It was a beautiful, if strange, sight; the children had their own world, separate from their parents.

Mei Ling felt the energy of someone staring at her. She turned her head.

Suk Suk glared at her! He turned his head to look to where Mei Ling had been watching. His eyes went wide in surprise and then shrank in fury, his jaw tightening until it pulsed. He must have seen Siew. He turned his head back slowly to stare threateningly at Mei Ling. He leaned forward as if he were going to attack.

Adrenaline flooded her body, her mouth suddenly tasted like metal, her chest tightened, and her Dragon woke. She took a deep breath to calm herself.

He stormed toward her but stopped before he reached Mei Ling. Suk Suk pointed at her and then balled his hand into a fist. He spun away and walked to the playing children. He grabbed Siew's friend Mimi by the arm. The girl flinched and dropped her head in submission. Suk Suk dragged her away from her friends; the little girl was forced to run to keep up with the large man's pace. He yelled across the yard. A woman in the American-born circle stopped midconversation and followed him out to the sidewalk.

Mei Ling stared at the spot where they vanished. Her heart pounded fiercely in her chest. She shouldn't have been surprised to see him, but she was. *Leave!* the ghost yelled in her mind. *You must protect Siew.*

CHAPTER 24

Oakland
September 1924

Mei Ling wanted to leave that very night, but Kai Li insisted that there was no need. Siew was safe in their home, and they had done nothing wrong by bringing her to live with them. Miss Haw had the right to allow Kai Li to fulfill any obligation Siew had to work. The housekeeper was very pleased with their arrangement and frequently told Kai Li so. He assured her that men like Suk Suk hated to be caught off guard, but that he had no reason to harm Siew. He had most likely acted threatening out of embarrassment.

Mei Ling wanted to believe her husband, but the ghost filled her head with the demand to *protect Siew*. Her fiercest desire was to keep the girl close at all times, but Kai Li didn't want Suk Suk to interfere with Siew's education. Mei Ling reluctantly agreed, but the next morning she instructed Siew not to leave school with anyone other than Mei Ling. Not even June or another trusted adult. Only Mei Ling.

In the afternoon Mei Ling arrived at Lincoln School so early that the yard was empty. She stared at the direction Siew would be coming from, her heart pounding in fear that the girl would never come out, certain she'd been snatched by Suk Suk. But soon enough Siew was waving and skipping toward them from her classroom. Jack Wong, Suk Suk, was nowhere in sight.

Refusing the children's request to play in the park, Mei Ling took them straight home where she felt marginally safer once the door was locked with Siew inside the house, but she was still agitated.

~

In the waking world Siew was safe, but it was otherwise in Mei Ling's dreams. Too many nights she woke with an image of Siew's face behind the cages, or Siew's head bobbing in the salty bay by the Golden Gate, or Siew pleading to live with them. There were many flavors to her dream, but in all of them Siew needed her help, and Mei Ling had failed her.

She'd wake in a panic, her heart beating hard. Sometimes tears wet her cheeks. After confirming that Siew was safe in their home, she would lie back down, but most of the time sleep eluded her.

Fear and exhaustion were Mei Ling's constant companions. Days passed with the same routine: Mei Ling reminding Siew to only come home with her, coming straight home, and locking the door.

She told the children it was because she had to work, but they could tell that her mood was sour. They retreated to the bedroom each afternoon, leaving Mei Ling alone while the ghost hissed in the background.

As the days grew shorter with the changing season, the bad dreams and the images of Suk Suk intruding upon their home came less frequently. Weeks went by without any sight of him. Her concern for Siew hadn't dissipated entirely, but perhaps Kai Li was correct and the man wasn't going to disturb them any further.

Each time fear arose, Mei Ling prayed to Quan Yin, *May Siew be free from harm.* Mei Ling remained alert but optimistic that their lives weren't going to be destroyed.

~

A pounding on the door roused her from a deep sleep. Mei Ling sat up, fear exploding in her heart and radiating to the tips of her fingers. She frantically shook Kai Li's shoulder.

"Someone is here!" she said. "Wake up."

His eyes popped open.

"Let me in!" a man's voice shouted as he pounded again.

Kai Li leaped out of bed and rushed to the living room. Mei Ling followed as far as the bedroom doorway. She peered past the crack between the door and jamb.

"Who's there?" Kai Li asked, his voice rough.

"Me," a deep voice answered. "Jack Wong."

Mei Ling's stomach lurched. She left the bedroom, closing the door tight behind her. The children, especially Siew, mustn't learn he was a threat. Kai Li looked at her, an unspoken question on his face. Despite her fears, she wanted to discover what this man wanted. She nodded her consent and Kai Li opened the door.

Suk Suk stood in the doorway, drunk and disheveled, reeking of alcohol. He hung an arm along the door frame, leaning into their home but not coming inside. His blurry red eyes slowly looked around. Mei Ling would have pitied him if she weren't so frightened and angry at his intrusion.

"Where is she?" Mr. Wong demanded, looking past Kai Li to stare right at Mei Ling.

Despite her fear, she came closer to him and whispered, "Siew is asleep. It's late."

Suddenly the man appeared confused. He looked at Kai Li, then back at Mei Ling. He took in a deep breath and exhaled, nodding.

"Shhh." Suk Suk put his finger to his lips and slurred out, "Don't wake her. She's just a little girl."

Her Dragon, ready to fight, was thrown by his changed demeanor. He took in a deep breath and closed his eyes. His breathing, slow and heavy, made Mei Ling wonder if he was falling asleep. Suddenly he opened his eyes, anger simmering in him.

"I never wanted to see her again. Look what you've done!" He hissed, "She was supposed to work there until she was fourteen so I wouldn't have to think about her, but now . . . you ruined it." He glared at Mei Ling. "I blame you. *You* ruined it. My daughter plays with her!"

Mei Ling felt his fury like a physical blow.

"I don't know how you got her away from that house. She can stay here for now," he declared, "but she has a debt to pay when she's older. You"—he pointed at Mei Ling—"can't change that. No matter where you go, the tongs will find you." He slowly moved his head back and forth, each word enunciated and definitive. "There is no escape. Chinnnaaa. Ammmerrricaaa. It doesn't matter. No escape."

He spun around and left. Mei Ling collapsed onto the couch, tears streaming down her face. She could hardly breathe. *Siew isn't safe. You can't keep her safe,* the ghost shouted again and again in her mind.

Kai Li sat by her side and put an arm around her shoulder. She looked at him. The tenderness and fear in his eyes overwhelmed her. She sobbed against his chest, mindful of muffling her sounds because of the children.

When her tears stopped, she sat up.

"Will we never have peace?" she implored.

"We will think of something," he replied. "We have seven years."

Her Dragon exploded inside her. She leaped up, wanting to scream at him. *Think of something? That is your solution?!*

She heard the click of a door closing. Her head whipped around, and her attention immediately moved to the children; one of them was awake! She went into the bedroom. All three were in bed. Siew lay with her eyes closed, but her shallow breathing told Mei Ling she was only pretending to be asleep. She crossed to Siew's side and got down close. She rubbed Siew's back. Siew shrugged her off. The child had been listening. Mei Ling's Dragon growled with equal measures of sorrow and fury.

"We will protect you," Mei Ling said, her voice hoarse and tight. "I promise. We will."

But Mei Ling wasn't certain of her own pledge.

~

Mei Ling stared at the photograph. Her fingers ran across Mui Mui's sweet little face. She was the only one grinning in the photo, her cheeks high and her teeth bright. She was close to Siew's age when they took the picture. None of them had any idea that in less than a year she would be gone forever.

She looked at the only other photograph in their home. Bo was hardly recognizable. Siew and Joy were missing altogether. *Take another,* now. The urge to preserve her family in a photo overwhelmed her. She wanted to do it that very moment, but Kai Li was still working.

On the way home from getting Siew at school, they stopped at the photographer's studio. Mei Ling nearly changed her mind when she heard the price, but her desire was so strong that she was willing to spend the money. She made an appointment for Sunday.

Mei Ling paced around the small apartment in the dark, waiting for Kai Li to return. By the time he arrived, the children were asleep. This time of year, *the holidays* as the Americans called it, the demands on him were continuous. He left early and returned late so that they didn't see him when they were awake at all.

"We must have a photograph," she declared as soon as he walked through the door. "Of the five of us!"

His dirty fingers rubbed his eyes and he exhaled hard. He stared at her, looking too weary to fight. He nodded and said, "I will make an appointment for after the Western New Year. The extra work from the holidays will give us the means."

"No. Now," she said. "I made an appointment for Sunday."

"Wife, why the urgency?" he asked.

Now, the ghost demanded. Her eyes welled up as she was flooded with sorrow.

"What if we aren't even left with a picture of her? She will fade from our memories as if she never existed," she whispered, her voice squeaky and her chin quivering.

"Oh, wife." His face contorted in pain. "Is this what you do, when it's dark and the children are asleep?"

She nodded.

He took her hands, looked right at her, and said, "We can find a way to take care of this. Siew will not be forced into prostitution or lost to us."

"How can you be certain?" she asked.

"I found her. She's living with us."

Mei Ling nodded. It *was* astounding that Kai Li had discovered a way for Siew to be with them. She wanted to believe in her husband and his capacity to keep their family whole, but she knew too well that parents couldn't always protect their children.

Mei Ling vowed to herself and to the ghost to do whatever it took to keep Siew safe.

CHAPTER 25

Oakland
January 1925

"He's come again," Mei Ling told her groggy and confused husband.

Kai Li sighed and left the bed. Mei Ling sat up and listened to the sounds from the living room. Jack Wong's slurry speech was too muffled to make out specific words, but Mei Ling knew what he wanted: forgiveness and understanding. He'd shown up in the middle of the night many times over the past few months. Each time Kai Li learned more of the story. Suk Suk insisted he was simply a go-between, not a gang member or leader. He claimed the gangsters forced him to bring Siew into the country to cover a gambling debt.

When the tong leaders had learned he was going to Guangzhou, they arranged for the papers that said Siew was his orphaned niece. Suk Suk arranged the indenture where she lived now and gave them the payment from it to cover her travel expenses.

He insisted that Siew would have been dead by now of starvation or disease had he not brought her away from the streets of Guangzhou. He even suggested that they should thank him for saving her. If Mei Ling wasn't terrified for Siew, she might have felt sorry for the man.

Kai Li returned in just a few minutes.

"He's gone already?" Mei Ling asked.

"No," he replied. "We are going out."

"What!?" Outrage woke her up entirely. She sat up and glared at the man in front of her.

"I do this for . . . her." His voice broke.

Furious, Mei Ling replied, "Becoming his friend will do her no good! You keep too much peace, husband. Sometimes fighting back hard is the solution, not being . . . submissive." The contempt in her voice was obvious.

Kai Li stared at her, his neck pulsing with pent-up anger. He looked as if he would argue back, but he closed the door and left her simmering in the dark.

Mei Ling took some deep breaths, hoping to calm her hammering heart. Her anxiety was destroying the harmony in their home. She hadn't felt any true peace in months. Mei Ling feared she would be bitter and angry for the rest of her life if they lost Siew.

Quan Yin, help me find a measure of peace even if . . . She could hardly let herself think it. If they lost Siew she didn't want to ever feel harmony again. Then she looked at Joy and Siew and Bo in bed. Somehow her parents had found a way to continue without being consumed by dark thoughts after they lost *two* children.

Quan Yin, help me find peace and strength.

~

Mei Ling came out to the living room when Kai Li returned from his outing with Suk Suk.

"What more did you discover, husband?" she asked as respectfully and as calmly as she could muster.

They sat close on the couch.

He recounted what he'd learned from his outing. "His gambling debt is to a San Francisco–based tong. To pay in full he must deliver Siew when she becomes a woman."

As he spoke a pit opened in Mei Ling's belly.

Kai Li continued, "He wants my reassurance that we won't hide Siew from him."

"What?" Mei Ling asked, outraged that Suk Suk wanted them to quell his fears.

"The Pardees paid the indenture fee to Suk Suk, which he gave to the tong to cover the expense of bringing Siew here. He knows we can topple his delicate plan. If I stop working for them, the Pardees will expect Suk Suk to refund their payment, and he does not have the money."

"Oh," Mei Ling replied, more fully understanding the bind she had placed Suk Suk in.

Kai Li added more: "He also mentioned he is terrified the tong will discover Siew is living with us, then seemed to regret he said it out loud."

Mei Ling's lips pulled up into a smile. "The tong doesn't know where she lives?"

Kai Li nodded slowly.

Mei Ling's understanding of their situation transformed entirely. Her body buzzed with hope and opportunity stirred as she realized their advantage over Suk Suk.

"He needs us to cooperate with him!" she declared.

Kai Li agreed. "He's afraid we will leave with her and he won't be able to find Siew, but if he takes her now he'll have a very large debt to pay—to a well-connected White family."

Mei Ling scoffed. "He and I fear the same thing: Siew disappearing."

Kai Li nodded. "He's also frightened for his own life. The tong will be furious if they learn Siew is living with a family that cares about her future well-being. Their power comes from secrecy, staying in the shadows. He's betrayed their way of doing business and put them at risk. They don't want the attention we'll bring to them if they claim her. A girl with a family is safe. We're the sunshine they fear."

"Oh, husband," Mei Ling exclaimed. "This is very good news. Thank you."

Kai Li said, "Siew isn't entirely safe, but I'm reassured that we have time to secure her future."

Mei Ling nodded and smiled weakly. She was relieved that Suk Suk, not the tong, was the primary threat to Siew, but she couldn't allow this situation to go on for years. The fear and uncertainty would destroy her. Something had to be done before Suk Suk, in his weakness, revealed Siew's location to the tong.

~

Mei Ling carefully opened the envelope addressed in the American fashion to *Mrs. Kai Li Chinn*. It was dated November 15, 1924—eight weeks ago and many months after the date on Jah Jeh's previous letter. Had her sister really gone so long without writing?

> Dearest sister,
> I write to you with the happiest and the saddest of news. Our beloved Ahma became ill after the Autumn Moon Festival.

Mei Ling's heart clenched, anticipating the painful news to come.

> Despite our care she joined the spirit world. Our hearts are weak with missing her.

Tears filled Mei Ling's eyes, blocking her vision. Anxious to learn more about her family, she smothered her sorrow by squeezing her lids tight to clear them enough that she could keep reading. She made out the next line through a misty veil.

> You can take comfort that the picture of your growing and beautiful family arrived before she departed. That she could see your daughter, the grandchild that she named, gave her great joy.
>
> Our happy news is that while we said goodbye to one family member we will be welcoming another. If all goes well my child will be born in the year of the Ox. I am excited and nervous at the idea of motherhood and so very grateful that I am near Mah-ma. I think of you, so very far away, and wonder at your strength.

Jah Jeh is carrying a child?! Mei Ling hadn't known she was married. That news must be contained in a letter that had been lost in transit. Though her mind and heart were reeling, Mei Ling didn't allow herself to stop reading. She pushed on, eager for the news.

> We thought the life that you are leading was meant to be mine, but I don't believe that was ever meant to be. I could not have survived, let alone thrived, as you have. A bold Dragon needed to make that adventure, not a gentle and cautious Rabbit like me.

The note continued with sweet details about Dai Dai, their parents, and Renshu, who must be her husband.

When she finished reading the letter, Mei Ling allowed the swirl of conflicting emotions to overtake her. The paper pressed against her chest while sobs poured out. Tears streamed down her face and sounds she had never heard before escaped her covered mouth. She'd known in her mind that she would never see Ahma again, but her heart railed against the loss—made more outrageous by the fact that it had happened months ago, and Mei Ling had yet to honor Ahma's spirit.

Jah Jeh was carrying a baby—a child Mei Ling might never meet. It was bittersweet news. Jah Jeh seemed to be living in the village with her husband, Renshu. Mei Ling remembered the shy boy from the village who had admired Jah Jeh from afar when they had come visiting. Jah Jeh had enjoyed the attention but never encouraged him. Now he was her husband. Mei Ling wished she knew more about the man her sister had married. Was he kind like Kai Li? Lost in his own thoughts like Fuchan? Or a different type of man altogether?

The happiest news was that her Jah Jeh had spoken so plainly of forgiveness. Mei Ling was greatly relieved that her sister was at peace, and even grateful, for each of their lives.

Sorrow and relief filled her as she walked to her altar and prayed: for her sister, for her beloved Ahma, and for herself.

Mei Ling thanked Ahma for all that she had given to her, most especially the precious gold coins. One had saved her on Angel Island. The rest helped her to feel secure when she first arrived in San Francisco and was so afraid that Kai Li would abandon them. She'd used one coin to buy the silk the first time she made a wedding gown. Her grandmother's wisdom, foresight, and generosity had brought security and prosperity to her life.

Mei Ling remembered Ahma's last words to her: "A wife obeys her husband, yes, but a wise woman earns her own money and saves for the emergencies that a husband cannot see coming. Give him most of your earnings but hold back a portion. A mother protects her children—always."

Ahma was still safeguarding Mei Ling . . . and by extension Bo, Joy, and Siew. Mei Ling bowed low to the ground and gave honor to her beloved grandmother's spirit.

Like her grandmother, she would protect her children, always.

~

When he returned from work Mei Ling told Kai Li the news from her family. She also had an idea to discuss with him. "Husband, I have been thinking about our predicament with Siew and Jack Wong."

Kai Li agreed, looking a little wary of the topic.

"Can we pay his debt to the tong, so that he won't seek her out in the future?"

He pulled in his lips and nodded. She was happy he agreed so easily. Then he confused her by shaking his head.

"I considered the same solution," Kai Li replied. "I asked him what he owes, and it's more than we live on in one full year."

Mei Ling's breath caught. She'd been so hopeful she'd found the solution for their predicament.

Kai Li looked chagrined. "I wish it were possible for me to quickly earn that much money. We can start saving with the hope that we'll have enough when the time comes."

Mei Ling's Dragon roared. Giving Suk Suk a year of income would end their own dreams. All their hard work would go to save Jack Wong rather than buying a house, sending the children to university, or opening their own restaurant. Her Dragon protested at the idea of making a huge sacrifice for Suk Suk's weak character.

CHAPTER 26

Oakland
February 1925

The loud banging on the door woke her up, but this time she did not rouse her husband. She had expected Suk Suk would come again, and she was ready to protect her family. *Quan Yin, guide and safeguard me.* The ghost walked with her as she left her sleeping family.

She opened the door just enough for him to see her. Suk Suk's red-rimmed eyes looked her up and down. Before he could say anything, she whispered to him.

"The others are sleeping," she cooed in the way that flattered men. "Can we . . . speak? Just you and I? Outside?"

He nodded.

"Let me get dressed more appropriately," she replied with a seductive smile. She slowly shut the door. Mei Ling exhaled, leaning her head on the painted woodwork. She took in a steadying breath to slow her heart rate. Then she quickly but quietly went into action, getting the supplies she had left in the entry closet—warm clothes, shoes, and a full bottle of whiskey.

When she was ready she walked past him without saying a word. He followed her down the stairs, clumping so loudly she feared he would wake up all those who slept in the building. Suk Suk lurched in a drunken stagger next to her in the foggy night. She steeled herself and then looped her arm through his. He smiled and pulled at her, wanting to stop.

"This is goo—" he started to say.

"Shhh," Mei Ling replied, putting a finger to his lips. "We need more privacy."

She tugged his arm, guiding them down Webster Street. They walked five blocks until they came to the estuary. The street turned into a wooden wharf leading to the bridge that Kai Li crossed each day. She led him to the right side of the wharf. Mei Ling's heart beat hard and fast as she folded her legs underneath her until she sat on the edge of the wharf facing north, the bay straight ahead. She demurely patted the spot next to her. Suk Suk collapsed onto the wood, his feet dangling over the dark water moving below. He leaned, his moist lips puckered.

She ducked her head, held up the bottle of whiskey, and said, "A little more?"

"Ladies first," he slurred out.

Mei Ling sighed. She unscrewed the cap, put the bottle to her lips, and pretended to drink three large gulps.

"You're a thirsty one!" he declared with a grin, taking the bottle.

"I am . . . unaccustomed to being in such a situation," Mei Ling said, hoping the fear in her voice sounded demure.

Jack Wong looked at her, his expression unreadable.

"I'm not a bad man," he said. "You know that, right?"

Mei Ling nodded, though every fiber of her being wanted to scream at him: *What kind of man besides a bad one takes an orphan into bondage?*

"I wish I could save her," Suk Suk slurred out, practically in tears. "But *they* are bad, bad men." He leaned in and whispered very loudly,

"They will kill me if I don't deliver." His head dropped forward, his chin bouncing up and down.

"You understand, don't you? I'm a good man." Suk Suk pointed to his chest, emphasizing each word with a thrust of his finger, as if the motion would force goodness inside of him. He waved his finger around and slowly shook his head. "But . . . I have no choice."

Mei Ling nodded, not defending Siew or arguing back. She simply nodded and kept encouraging Wong to sip from the brown bottle, occasionally bringing the container to her own lips without swallowing. Mei Ling shivered in the night, the damp fog penetrating deep into her bones.

"I'm a good man, but an unlucky one," Suk Suk continued. "She was the only way to pay my debt."

He sighed and moaned and drank. Eventually his dark head fell forward and he slumped sideways onto her. Mei Ling wrapped her right arm around the man, holding him like she would comfort a child—Bo, or Joy, or Siew. His head rested against her chest, over her heart.

"I'm not a bad man," Suk Suk whimpered. "Only a practical one. She is just a girl. An orphan. Of no value."

Of no value echoed in Mei Ling's mind. A flash of anger roared through her body.

"Did you bring her to Bartlett Alley?" she asked while she could, though she was terrified of the answer.

Suk Suk slowly turned his face and eyed her sideways. He seemed unable to hold his head upright. He gave one slight nod.

Mei Ling felt ill.

"Did . . ." She swallowed hard. "Did any man touch her?" Mei Ling steeled herself for the answer.

"No!" he declared, managing to wave a finger for emphasis.

She studied his face, looking for deceit, but saw none. Relief and gratitude ran a chill through her whole body. Mei Ling's worst fear was not true. Siew hadn't been brutally violated.

"She is a little girl. No. No. No." Suk Suk shook his head. "We aren't monsters."

She stared at him. Disgust in her voice, she whispered, "You can tell yourself that, but that doesn't make it true. You are a coward and a monster to force Siew to pay for your weakness."

He closed his eyes and turned his face away. He had the decency to look ashamed, but he seemed oblivious to the danger he was in. He'd entirely underestimated Mei Ling.

Suk Suk brought the bottle to his lips, tipping it back until it pointed to the sky and his head bent all the way back.

"Bah!" He growled at the empty bottle. He tossed it into the estuary. Mei Ling watched it float away, toward the bay.

He draped his arm over her shoulder like he owned her. She tensed but resisted the urge to push it off. His breathing grew heavy. His arm dropped away and his head fell forward.

Still she waited. When she heard soft snores, she gazed around to confirm they were alone. Then she reached behind him and firmly wrapped a hand around each of Suk Suk's arms and ever so slightly leaned him forward. She studied him for a reaction or resistance, but there was none. She tipped him farther, his weight pressing at her fingers. She paused at the last possible moment, knowing this was her final chance to change her mind. Her heart beat hard; her hands were moist. Siew's other mother whispered, *You must save Siew*.

Mei Ling looked up to heaven and said, "God, forgive me if you can. If you cannot, I won't regret this choice as I burn in hell . . . or I'm haunted for all of eternity."

The ghost commanded, *Do it!*

She tipped Suk Suk farther forward until he fell through her fingers. Her chest exploded.

She heard a loud splash in the estuary and then a feeble cry. "Help. Help me," Suk Suk's frantic voice called to her.

"I'm coming," she spoke to the darkness. "I'll get you out."

But she didn't move. Mei Ling stayed on the edge of the dock, her legs dangling over the side. Her body pounded with emotion while tears poured down her face, and her shoulders shook with each sob.

"Help!" Desperation filled the drowning man's voice. She imagined the burning in his chest as it filled with water. Compassion welled up in Mei Ling, even though this man had been willing to trade Siew to ensure his own well-being.

"Coming . . . ," she lied once again, her voice shaking. She pictured the terror on his face, his head bobbing up and down in the salty water.

Coughing, splashing, and *help* echoed up at her, a little farther away now. The current was carrying Suk Suk toward the bay as he drowned.

"You gave me no choice," she whispered, though only the ghost could hear her. "You aren't worthy of Siew's life, of our family's future."

She sat there, listening to the sounds of the drowning man grow faint. It felt like hours, but was probably only minutes, of splashing and coughing interspersed with his desperate pleas. Then no words, just the coughing and finally a loud, powerful silence except the sound of her own jerky breaths.

Mei Ling spoke out loud to the ghost. "It's done. We do not have to be afraid anymore."

But neither she nor the ghost believed those words. There might still be an enormous price to be paid for her choice.

~

You took a life popped into her mind as she moved through a fog toward home. She forced the thought out and replaced it with *May*

Siew be safe from all harm. May Siew be free from all suffering. May Siew know joy. She couldn't ask for herself, but she extended the wish for Suk Suk's soul: *May he be safe from all harm. May he be free from all suffering. May he know joy.* She *did* wish him release from the cycle of suffering.

A dark and quiet apartment welcomed her back. Mei Ling's desire for equanimity wasn't to be. Sleep was elusive, with the fearful images of Siew replaced by Suk Suk's bobbing head and the sounds of his gasping. She consoled herself by chanting, *It was in service of her safety, in service of her safety,* but that thought didn't entirely drive away her fear that she would be caught and taken away from her family—perhaps forever.

~

In the morning she acted as if nothing had changed while she got the children ready for the day. She ignored the pounding suspicion that she must look different in some way. They would keep to their regular schedule.

"We'll go to the park after school," she told Siew.

"Hooray!" the girl replied.

After a long, tense day at home Mei Ling was glad to be outside. The air felt different as they walked the familiar route to fetch Siew.

"Did you play with Mimi today?" Mei Ling asked, hoping to learn if Suk Suk's family knew that he was lost to them.

Siew replied, "She wasn't at school today."

"Perhaps Mimi is ill," Mei Ling replied casually, though a pounding heart accompanied her reply.

Siew shrugged as they entered the park. June was in the midst of the Cantonese ladies, with all eyes on her as she told a story.

"Dorothy is getting the afternoon paper so we can learn more!" June declared with glee.

Joy wiggled on Mei Ling's back, signaling that she wanted to get down. Mei Ling loosened the material knotted against her chest and released the toddler onto the grass. The little girl waddled over to Siew.

"Learn about what?" Mei Ling asked.

June looked at Mei Ling, unspoken intensity in her eyes. Then she looked away and announced, "Jack Wong is dead."

Mei Ling's heart lurched. "What?" she blurted out, then remembered to add, "How?"

June shrugged. "Maybe the newspaper has the details."

Anxiety welled up inside her. How did they know? She had counted on his body being lost for days, if not forever, in the expanse of the bay.

Siew marched back toward their circle carrying Joy, the toddler dangling over her two arms clasped together, the little girl swinging from side to side with each step.

"She wants you," Siew declared as she plopped Joy next to Mei Ling.

Mei Ling smiled and nodded but couldn't speak. Her eyes welled up as she watched Siew skip back to her friends, her dark pigtails bouncing up and down. *Protecting Siew was worth his life,* she told herself.

Joy climbed onto her lap and leaned back to nurse. The little one grabbed Mei Ling's thumb and waved both of their arms back and forth as she cuddled close. Mei Ling smiled at her daughter, a ball of nerves growing in her belly. She looked at Siew, playing with her friends, and thought of the woman who had given her life.

She whispered a message to the ghost: *I kept her free. Now you keep me safe so I can watch over all of them.*

Dorothy returned with the newspaper, the one in English, the *Oakland Tribune.*

June commanded her daughter, "Look for the name Jack Wong. Find that one and read it to us."

Mei Ling intently watched Dorothy, her heart pounding so fiercely she could hardly hear the world around her. The girl scanned the front page, then opened it up. Her eyes moved back and forth and then down and over. She folded the paper.

"Found it," she announced.

All eyes jumped to her, all mouths closed, and all ears opened.

Chinaman found dead in Estuary

The body of Chinese businessman Jack Wong, 35, was found early Monday morning in the estuary at the foot of Chestnut Street in Alameda. Investigators believe the Chinaman's body had been in the water for only a few hours. He is described as being 5 feet 10 inches tall, 180 pounds with black hair. He wore brown trousers and a white collared dress shirt. Circumstances of his death are unknown and being investigated by the Oakland police.

June and Mei Ling exchanged a look. Mei Ling shook her head imperceptibly, signaling that she didn't want to speak in front of these women. Terror pushed at her to act, but she forced herself to remain at the park, looking calm to the world. She wondered if the police were looking for her. She fought the urge to rush home and lock the doors; she resisted the impulse to find Kai Li to tell him that she may have ruined their lives.

CHAPTER 27

Oakland
February 1925

Late in the afternoon a loud knock on the door of their home caused Mei Ling's heart to explode. Bo and Siew ran to open it, excited to have a surprise visitor. Mei Ling's throat closed up tight when she saw the uniforms. Two White policemen stood framed in the doorway. They must have discovered what she had done and had come to take her away.

"We'd like to ----- with your father?" the taller one asked the children in English.

They were here for Kai Li!

"He's at work," Siew answered.

Wanting to display the innocence that would come with being hospitable, in English Mei Ling said, "Come in." Her hand visibly shook as she gestured to the couch.

The men stared at her but didn't reply.

"My mother says come in," Siew repeated.

One of them answered, "No, thank you." They understood Siew.

Mei Ling's heart was hammering so hard that she could hardly hear.

"---- your father we have --------- we ---- to --- him."

Siew nodded, fear now shining in her eyes.

"Bye!" Bo called out as the men walked away, oblivious to the situation.

Mei Ling collapsed onto the couch. Her chest was so tight she could hardly take in any air. She tried forcing a breath, but it didn't work. Panic rose. *Kai Li isn't safe.* Her hands shook and her sight was blurry. The children climbed around her, but she couldn't attend to them. She closed her eyes and forced her shoulders to release. She tried a tiny breath. That worked.

Siew held a glass of water out to her. Mei Ling took it and managed to swallow a bit. Joy climbed onto her lap. She set the water down and cuddled the warm body. Bo's little hand patted her leg. He could tell she was upset, though he didn't know why. Siew studied her face, perhaps looking for reassurance. The girl asked no questions, an indication that she was scared too.

Mei Ling pulled up the corners of her mouth in a forced smile. She took in a deep breath and then let it out with a sigh. She took Siew's hand and squeezed.

"I'm fine, only surprised to see them in our home," Mei Ling tried to assure the children, but her words rang hollow. "What did they ask you to tell Bah-ba?" Mei Ling asked.

"They have questions they need to ask him," Siew replied.

The walls closed in on her. Kai Li wouldn't return home for hours. If the police questioned her husband at the Pardee home, he might be caught in a lie. He'd deny that Jack Wong had been to their home the previous night, making him suspicious.

Mei Ling couldn't wait for him to return. She had to warn her husband before the police found him. She bundled up the children and set out to find Kai Li.

They shivered as they walked through the foggy evening. Mei Ling was concerned, but not deterred, about how she would be received. His employer might prevent her to speak with him. He would be confused by their surprise visit . . . and then upset with the information she had to share with him.

The children were quiet, too quiet. They sensed her emotions. Joy kicked her legs out at her siblings, but no one responded to her bid to start a game. Joy laid her head against Mei Ling's back. She imagined the girl's thumb in her mouth, offering comfort in this strange situation.

They walked to the back of the building.

"Stay down here," she told the older children.

She walked up the stairs to the door on the right. Mei Ling paused for a moment and took a deep breath. After she knocked, her life might change entirely. *Watch over our family whatever comes,* she asked Quan Yin.

She knocked and waited with a hammering heart.

Her husband opened the door. His sweet face instantly changed from surprised to concerned. He stepped out into the moonlit night and pulled the door behind him.

"What is the matter?" he asked, his eyes wide.

"The police . . . they came to our home to question you," Mei Ling leaned in and whispered, protecting the children from their conversation.

His eyebrows knit together in confusion. Joy looked around from her back.

"Bah-ba!" The little girl squealed and reached out a hand.

Kai Li looked at his youngest daughter. He took her hand and kissed it with a tender smile.

"Hello, my Joy," he said softly. "Do you know why they wish to speak with me?" he asked in hushed tones.

"Jack Wong is dead," she replied. "I believe it might be about that."

"What?" he questioned.

She leaned in and whispered, "He came over last night." She paused, took a deep breath, and said, "I handled it."

"What have you done, wife!?" Mei Ling heard the emotion in his voice and saw it in his eyes. She steadied herself on the door frame.

"I . . ." Mei Ling started to explain what happened.

"Stop. Please. The less I know at this moment the better," Kai Li said.

Mei Ling nodded.

"He came over, drunk? Wanting our reassurance?" he asked.

"Yes."

He nodded slowly. Kai Li looked at Siew and gave her a tight smile to signal that all would be fine. Then he gestured at the children, beckoning them to come to the porch. Kai Li picked up Bo, still small enough for him to carry, turned around, and led them inside the mansion.

A pile of chopped vegetables sat on the small table. Kai Li put Bo down on a bench and motioned for the others to sit. He went to the stove, the newest model, and stirred something in a pot. Mei Ling couldn't read his expression, but suspected he was thinking.

"Wait here," he said, and disappeared into the passageway. Mei Ling's heart flipped. She looked at her daughter. The girl was staring at the spot where Kai Li vanished.

Then Siew looked under the table, her dark hair sweeping against the pale wooden floor. She stayed bent over, not moving, not speaking, staring at the place where she'd once slept. Mei Ling ducked down to see what the girl was seeing. Their heads nearly touched one another as they studied the tiny space.

Siew looked Mei Ling in the eyes and said, "It's so small."

A light chill passed over Mei Ling. They'd sacrificed much to rescue Siew from a life under a table. Even though she was terrified at the moment, she couldn't regret ensuring freedom for this child of her heart. They both sat up. She put her arm around Siew and squeezed.

Mei Ling said, "I'm so glad you don't live under there anymore."

"Me too," Siew agreed and smiled at Mei Ling.

Miss Haw walked into the kitchen.

"Hello Siew. It's ---- to --- ---," the woman said. "---- ------ -- ---- ---- ---- the -------," she continued. "----- --- ---- ---- --- -------- ----- we wait?"

"Yes, please," Siew said. Mei Ling understood her own child's English, but Miss Haw spoke with an accent that didn't make sense.

"What did she say?" Mei Ling asked.

"Bah-ba is speaking with someone. We're going to have hot chocolate while we wait."

"Who is he speaking to?" she demanded, wondering if the police had come here already.

Siew shrugged. Mei Ling took a steadying breath.

"Ask," she directed, working to keep her voice calm.

Siew spoke to Miss Haw. The woman replied. They went back and forth for a few sentences.

"The governor," Siew translated. "Bah-ba is talking with the governor."

Mei Ling questioned the wisdom of drawing his employer into their family concerns, but bonds were the path to success in China. It was likely that was true here as well, especially a man of high social standing—assuming the former governor would use his connections to help, not harm, Kai Li.

Miss Haw made the promised treat and finished cooking the meal Kai Li had started. She appeared to be accomplished in the kitchen, graciously declining Mei Ling's offer of assistance.

After the hot chocolate was gone, Kai Li returned to the kitchen. He and the governor would meet at the police station in the morning. Miss Haw said something. She bowed to Kai Li before they left. Mei Ling was touched by her attempts to show respect and kindness to them.

They went home huddled together—walking in silence through the dark and foggy Oakland streets. Mei Ling begged Quan Yin to keep them safe from all harm.

~

The children were asleep when she told Kai Li what she had done the previous night, ending with the words, "I thought his body would be washed out to the bay and lost forever. I didn't count on a change in tides."

She studied his face for a reaction. Did he fear her now that he knew what she was capable of?

"We had time. I would have found a way to save her," Kai Li said, his voice tight and hard.

"Husband, the uncertainty and the fear were eating at my soul. I had to know I kept her safe, whatever the price." She stared at him, hoping for understanding but not regretting her choice if he didn't. "I'll go to the police; tell them it was an accident," Mei Ling stated.

Kai Li shook his head. "They don't suspect you. I will go."

"You don't need to pay the price for my choice."

"We will both be paying if one of us goes to jail," he said, sorrow filling his voice. The truth of his words hit her hard. A tense and poignant silence built between them.

Kai Li said, "Confess to being alone at night with a man who is not your husband?" He paused and shook his head. "We don't want that shame. I would rather go than have your reputation as a mother and a wife besmirched."

"I'm sorry."

He stared at her. So many emotions wrestled on his face that she couldn't read him. Obvious fear and anger. Was there any pride?

"No need to be sorry until we know the outcome of my interview," he replied. "Your action was rash, yes, but also brave . . . and honorable. You protected our family."

He tried to smile. Mei Ling's lip trembled and a tear slipped out. He wrapped his arms around her. She cried against his chest, terrified this could be their last night together. He held her tight, probably shedding his own tears, not attempting to comfort her with meaningless words. They clung to one another through the long night.

In the morning, Kai Li was awake before the sun rose. Mei Ling watched him kiss each child tenderly, so overcome with emotion that she bit her lip hard enough to make it bleed.

He came to her. They embraced, her head leaning over his heart and her arms wrapped around him. She clung to his shirt, not wanting him to leave. Taking in his scent, she asked Quan Yin and the ghost, *Please protect him. He is a good man and did nothing wrong.*

Kai Li would go to the produce stand to let Mr. Johnson know he would be away for the day, and perhaps longer. Mei Ling didn't let herself think too long about that possibility, but her body was on high alert. Her heart pounded in her chest no matter how many deep breaths she took.

Siew must have sensed the tension in the house, but Mei Ling didn't speak directly about their situation to any of the children. They followed their usual morning routine. The walk to school was a haze, and then Mei Ling was in a quiet house with little to distract her from her anxiety.

She didn't want to leave in case Kai Li returned. Minutes seemed like hours. She alternated between sitting in a stupor on the couch and pacing around the living room. Eventually she took the little ones into the backyard. She could prepare the garden for planting as they played. Using the small shovel she turned the dirt, digging deep to bury the shoots of grass so they would turn into nutrients for the soil.

The physical labor felt good for her jumpy body and investing in their future soothed her spirit.

A cry from Joy interrupted her project. The girl's dress was caught on one of the berry brambles that sprouted up in their yard. Mei Ling carefully separated the thorny vine and unhooked her daughter. A bright-yellow flower caught her eye. She bent over to look at it more closely; it was small, less than two inches, and all alone, but it shone up brightly at her, somehow surviving in this prickly patch, reminding her there would always be flashes of beauty even in the midst of pain.

When she finished working the garden bed, they went inside for lunch and naps. She tried to sleep with the children, but rest wasn't forthcoming.

She gave up on sleep and pulled out the book of Confucian wisdom from her father. She sat before their family altar and asked the ancestors to intervene on her husband's behalf. She was there, meditating and rocking, when she heard a sound in the hall.

Her head whipped around. Kai Li stood in the doorway. He looked right at her, nodded with a smile, and crossed to her side. She exhaled in relief and a chill raised her arm flesh. He knelt down so close that their shoulders touched.

"We must thank the ancestors," he said in a hoarse whisper.

They kowtowed to the altar in unison, waves of gratitude surging through Mei Ling. *Thank you for your mercy, Quan Yin.*

After they rose she asked, "What happened?"

He took in a deep breath and smiled. Then he shrugged.

"I'm free," he said. "Our family is preserved."

The knots in her shoulders loosened. "What did you say?"

He replied, as if recounting a story, "Jack Wong came over, already drunk. He and I went out as we had many times before. It was late when I headed home; he left as well. Perhaps he walked the wrong direction and stumbled into the water."

"They believed you," she replied.

Kai Li nodded. "Connections matter in every country. Governor Pardee and Mr. Johnson spoke on my behalf," he replied. "They testified that I'm a good man and could not possibly murder someone. It was the truth. I'm glad that I had no cause to lie to them about that."

Kai Li stared at her. Mei Ling nodded, steeled for his condemnation.

"Thank you," he said. "For your courage and strength."

She studied him, looking deep into his eyes for any sign of rejection, but only saw love and respect. A chill flowed through her whole body.

Is it really over? Mei Ling asked the ghost of Siew's mother. *Is our daughter really safe?*

Yes! came a loud and clear reply.

Mei Ling knew it was true: they had saved their precious Siew, the kind and resourceful little girl who slipped her way into Mei Ling's life as they journeyed across a vast ocean.

Thank you. Be well.

The ghost slipped away. *Goodbye.*

Mei Ling's soul opened up in gratitude, and her heart sang with the possibilities.

EPILOGUE

Berkeley
August 1936

Kai Li and I never spoke of what I had done again, though he alluded to it on the day we brought Siew to the University of California in Berkeley. We went with her to see the campus on the first day of classes. Kai Li hardly hid his pride. More than once on the Key System train from Oakland to Berkeley, I saw him wipe his eyes.

I fussed with Siew's clothes as we rode the elevator up the Campanile: Joy, Bo, Siew, Kai Li, and I. There must have been other people on that ride, but I only remember my family.

"Can we visit every week?" Joy asked in English. She was twelve, on the cusp of womanhood. I already missed my child even though she was standing right in front of me.

I tsked, shook my head, and replied in Cantonese, "You may come here when you are admitted. For now, Siew needs to study, not be distracted by little girls."

Joy's lip pushed out in a pout.

I relented with a small smile. "We can't come every week, but I suppose once each semester wouldn't be too much."

The elevator came to a jerky stop. The doors opened slowly. We stepped into a small hallway and climbed the stairs to the viewing platform. People, mostly White, but not all, stood at the open archways, looking out.

We turned left and walked to a vacant spot. Kai Li sucked in his breath as he peered out at the beautiful sparkling, clear day. He'd never been up here before or seen such a sight, a breathtaking view even grander than the one from the park in Hong Kong.

Bo, taller than both of us, scanned the horizon. Hidden in this smart and handsome sixteen-year-old young man was the little boy who had clutched a wooden rabbit in that tiny hovel in Guangzhou. He stopped carrying it years ago, but it still sits on his altar.

Bo pointed and said, "The Tribune Tower."

Kai Li nodded and added, "There's Alameda—and our house is between them." He looked right at me and smiled. I leaned my head on his shoulder, my love for him so deep.

"Where's our restaurant?" Joy asked.

"Ummm." Kai Li puzzled out the streets and then pointed. "Rabbit Moon is . . . somewhere over there."

I looked to where he pointed. It wasn't visible, hidden from view by other buildings, but I pictured the restaurant with its bright-red door.

We moved to the right and saw the new Bay Bridge and the nearly complete Golden Gate Bridge. The bay sparkled in the sun.

"Alcatraz!" Joy pointed.

"And Angel Island," Siew said quietly.

I asked, "Do you remember being there?"

She nodded. "I remember when we went on a walk and we looked out . . . at this tower." Siew's voice got high as she choked back tears. "You promised we would visit one day."

Intense feelings flooded my heart.

Siew cleared her throat. "That gave me so much strength." She looked right at me, like young Americans do, her beautiful brown eyes moist. "You have no idea how much those words meant to me. It kept me going when I was afraid and lonely. You kept that promise . . . and then gave me so much more."

My heart welled up with love and pride.

Siew looked at Kai Li, then at me again. "Bah-ba, Mah-ma, thank you," she said quietly. "For your hard work and . . . well, for everything. For all the sacrifices you made for me."

She didn't say anything else. Instead she bowed deeply and held it to show respect and appreciation to us, her parents, tears glistening in all of our eyes. Kai Li looked at me, and I suspected we were both thinking of the night I destroyed a life to save hers.

Kai Li leaned in so close I could feel his breath in my ear as he whispered only to me, "Thank you for your strength and courage, wife. She is worthy of your greatest sacrifice."

"Yes, she is," I agreed.

I remembered myself at Siew's age: forced to leave home to start a new life with a stranger in a foreign land. It was a leap I didn't know I could make. As my mother instructed, I took the first step, though I didn't believe I could do it. But once I took one step I knew that I could do the second. One stride at a time, I walked into a new life with strangers as my companions, strangers who became my world.

I looked at them, my strong and solid family, and saw no trace of our flimsy paper start. Each of these kind and hardworking children came to me in a different way, but they are all mine. I sent out a blessing to Bo's and Siew's first mothers: Wong Lew She, whose name I still carry, and the nameless woman I know nothing about—except that she must have loved our daughter well. Those two women bore precious children that I had the honor of raising. *Thank you.*

And my dear Kai Li, the kindest man I have ever met, who manages to love a Dragon like me. Why was I so blessed? Every day I thank the ancestors for all that has been and all that will be, for the miraculous and ordinary circumstances that are my life.

ACKNOWLEDGMENTS

I am deeply grateful to:

- Michelle Ma for hooking me up with Brendan Jiu. And for the resources that Brendan trusted me with—most especially a copy of his ancestors' interviews at Angel Island.
- Hannah, Tim, and Lola May. Because a puppy! And love.
- Kyle Fisher. Because I forgot you in *Mustard Seed* and our Scrabble games are a highlight of my days.
- Wes Cordez. Thanks for the information and culture at ChineseAmericanFamily.com.
- Kelli, Karen, and, most especially, Dorothy Eng. Dorothy's casual mention that she was in her mother's uterus on Angel Island got this story in motion.
- Woolseyville Compound, my solid foundation.
- Rinda, Maya, Kalin, and Wynnie—for laughter, encouragement, and not letting me take myself too seriously.
- Ori Tsveli for the challenge to insert Tong Len into my novels, and my life, however I can.
- Sheri Prud'homme for productive writing retreats at Hearthstone.

- UU Oakland for reminding me to seek out faith—especially when it's hard to find.
- Carmen, Bojan, and Nikola for the joy of sharing in the beginning of a new life.
- Tiffany Yates Martin, Jodi Warshaw, Danielle Marshall, Gabriel Dumpit, Nicole Pomeroy, Rebecca Brinbury, Michael Townley, and those on the Lake Union team whose names I don't know. I'm deeply grateful for your work to bring this story into the world.
- Terry Goodman. You have my never-ending gratitude for finding my needle in the self-published haystack.
- Readers: Gogi Hodder, Sheri Prud'homme, Margie Biblin, Darlanne Mulmat, Rinda Bartley, Linda O'Roke, Kayla Haun, Mimi Tsang, Claudine Tong, Daisy Quan, Lynna Tsou, Kathy Post, Kelli Eng, and Dorothy Eng. Your kind and honest feedback has made this a better story.
- Trente Moran and Tom Haw for the characters Pasha and Miss Haw, respectively.
- Judy Yung. Your work to uncover buried voices is a gift to me and the world.

RESOURCES

These resources were so valuable for my research:

- Angel Island State Park
- San Francisco Chinese Historical Society
- Oakland Chinese Historical Society
- *Making Waves*, edited by Asian Women United of California
- *Making More Waves*, edited by Elaine H. Kim, Lilia V. Villanueva, and Asian Women United of California
- *Unbound Voices* by Judy Yung
- *Unbound Feet* by Judy Yung
- *Angel Island: Immigrant Gateway to America* by Erika Lee and Judy Yung
- *Island*, edited by Him Mark Lai, Genny Lim, and Judy Yung
- *Hometown Chinatown: The History of Oakland's Chinese Community* by L. Eve Armentrout Ma
- *Fierce Compassion* by Kristin and Kathryn Wong
- *Oakland's Chinatown* by William Wong
- "Becoming American: The Chinese Experience," a Bill Moyers special
- *Bittersweet Roots: The Chinese in California's Heartland*

- *Chinese Village Cookbook: A Practical Guide to Cantonese Country Cooking* by Rhoda Yee
- *The Chinese Must Go: Violence, Exclusion, and the Making of the Alien in America* by Beth Lew-Williams

BOOK DISCUSSION

1. What frustrated, surprised, moved, or upset you about *Paper Wife*?

2. What did you like most about this book? Least?

3. Why did Mei Ling go along with her parents' plans for her to marry Kai Li and move to California?

4. Trust is an ongoing theme in the novel. Were you surprised, or not, by any of the various deceptions?

5. Do you think Kai Li and Mei Ling can be forgiven for lying to each other? For lying to the immigration officers?

6. The doctor on Angel Island asks Mei Ling if she is who she says she is. Do you think he could tell if she had ever been pregnant, or was he just venturing a guess to take advantage of the situation? Were you surprised when he sent her extra food?

7. Do you or your family have one or more immigration or migration stories? If so, what do you know about them? How do they compare to Mei Ling's story?

8. Did you learn anything new about US history from *Paper Wife*?

9. Which character did you identify with the most and why?

10. Which character do you dislike the most and why?

11. Do you believe he was lying when Mr. Young told Mei Ling that her work was no longer valuable to him?

12. Laila Ibrahim left unanswered questions about Siew's and Kai Li's pasts. Was that frustrating to you? Believable?

13. Do you believe the ghost was something internal to Mei Ling or an external representation of her internal state?

14. How do you think Mei Ling's childhood religion shaped her thinking? Do you see similarities or differences with how your beliefs shape you?

15. Were there any plot points that were left unresolved or not resolved to your satisfaction?

16. What ideas do you think Laila Ibrahim wanted to get across in this novel? Did she succeed?

17. What did you think of the ending? Could you imagine making the same choice as Mei Ling?

GLOSSARY

Angel Island Immigration Detention Center

Beginning in 1910, immigrants were detained and interrogated at this island in the middle of the San Francisco Bay to determine if they should be turned away or allowed to land in San Francisco. During the island's Immigration Station period, the island saw nearly one million immigrants from more than eighty countries. The majority were from China (70 percent), Japan, India, Mexico, and the Philippines. European and first-class passengers were inspected onboard the ship and rarely detained.

Because of the Chinese Exclusion Act, Chinese immigrants received the most scrutiny. Most were detained for a few weeks, though many were on the island for ninety days, and the record was two years. Many expressed their dismay at the hopeless conditions through poetry carved into the walls.

The immigration detention center was closed in 1940.

Asiatic Barred Zone

The immigration act of 1917 stated "the following classes of aliens shall be excluded from admission to the US . . . persons who are natives of islands not possessed by the United States adjacent to the Continent of Asia, situate south of the twentieth parallel latitude north, west of the one hundred and sixtieth meridian of longitude east from Greenwich, and north of the tenth parallel of latitude south, or who are natives of any country, province, or dependency situate on the Continent of Asia west of the one hundred and tenth meridian of longitude east from Greenwich and . . . south of the fiftieth parallel of latitude north . . ." This act did not apply to people from the Philippines, as a United States "possession," and Japan—though an informal agreement with Japan severely reduced immigration from that Asian nation.

Benevolent Family Associations
During the gold rush in California, these organizations began to provide social and financial support to Chinese immigrants living in hostile environments. Later, they served to make residency and citizenship easier for immigrants and acted as informal chambers of commerce for Chinese businesspeople. They continue to be an important social support for many people.

Burlingame Treaty
Passed in 1868, it guaranteed the right of free immigration and travel within the United States for Chinese people. American business leaders worked for and celebrated this treaty as a means to a plentiful source of cheap labor.

Chinese Calendar
As a lunisolar calendar it uses a combination of solar and lunar phenomena to determine dates. The new year begins on the second new moon after the winter solstice, which occurs in late January or the first few weeks of February.

Chinese Dialects
There are seven major dialect groups in China with hundreds of subdialects. Some of the dialects are more closely related than others.

Chinese Exclusion Act

Passed in 1882, this act reversed the agreements of the Burlingame Treaty. It is the only law passed by the US Congress that suspended immigration for a specific nationality. Senator John Miller, a Republican from California, introduced this ten-year moratorium on Chinese immigration to the United States Senate.

The Geary Act made Chinese exclusion permanent in 1902. Subsequent amendments to the law prevented Chinese laborers who had left the United States from returning. It was repealed by the Magnuson Act in 1943.

The passage of the act represented the outcome of years of racial hostility and anti-immigrant sentiment by many White American citizens and politicians. It set the precedent for later restrictions against immigration of other nationalities and started a new era in which the United States changed from a country that welcomed almost all immigrants to a gatekeeping one.

Chinese Zodiac

A classification scheme that assigns an animal and its reputed attributes to each year in a repeating twelve-year cycle. There are predicted compatibilities between potential spouses and other relationships. In order, the zodiac signs are rat, ox, tiger, rabbit, dragon, snake, horse, sheep, monkey, rooster, dog, and pig.

Coaching Books

Applicants of Chinese descent had detailed interrogations at Angel Island Immigration Center before being landed in the United States or returned to China. Testimony about family history, the layout of their ancestral village, and details about their dwelling had to match with the actual or paper family member they were joining. Any discrepancies in their testimonies could mean deportation. Chinese immigrants prepared for these interviews by studying coaching books purchased from immigration brokers.

Coolies

A dated term, now generally considered offensive, for Chinese men who did physical labor.

Donaldina Cameron

A Presbyterian missionary from New Zealand. She was assigned to the mission in San Francisco's Chinatown. She rescued more than three thousand Chinese immigrant girls and women from indentured servitude and forced prostitution. She was known as the "Angry Angel of Chinatown."

Golden Gate

The Golden Gate is the opening between the Pacific Ocean and the San Francisco Bay. One side is on the San Francisco Peninsula and the other on the Marin Peninsula. Since 1937, it has been spanned by the Golden Gate Bridge.

Johnson-Reed Act of 1924

The purpose of the act was to preserve the (perceived) ideal of American homogeneity. The law banned the immigration of Arabs and Asians to the United States and aimed to severely limit the immigration of Africans. In addition it limited the annual number of immigrants who could be admitted from any country to 2 percent of the number of people from that country who were already living in the United States as of the 1890 census, down from the 3 percent cap set by the Emergency Quota Act of 1921, which used the Census of 1910. It severely restricted immigration of Southern Europeans and Eastern Europeans. It set no limits on immigration from other countries of North and South America. Congressional opposition was minimal. This act put an end to a period in which the United States essentially had open borders.

Kowtow

A custom of kneeling and touching the ground with the forehead in worship or submission.

Kuomintang

A major political party in China. They advocated the overthrow of the Qing Dynasty and the establishment of the Republic of China. They ruled parts of mainland China between 1928 and 1949. They subsequently ruled Taiwan. Sun Yat-sen and Chiang Kai-shek were leaders of the party in the 1920s.

Matchmaker

A woman who arranges marriages as a formal occupation.

Missionaries

A member of a religious organization, sent into an area to proselytize or convert local residents to their faith.

Oakland Chinatown

Oakland's first Chinatown was settled by Chinese gold miners in the 1800s. The Chinese community in Oakland was relocated five times before being segregated to a designated "exclusion zone" in the current location of Chinatown in the 1870s. After the 1906 San Francisco earthquake, thousands of Chinese from San Francisco moved to temporary shelters in Oakland. Many stayed permanently. Zoning ordinances did not include Chinatown until 1931 when the newly created City Planning Commission designated the area as part of the light industrial zone.

Paper Wife/Son/Daughter

Paper wives, sons, and daughters used fraudulent documentations to immigrate to the United States. The practice rose in response to war and famine in China, the Chinese Exclusion Act, and the 1906 San Francisco earthquake in the United States. Purchased documents stated these immigrants were the blood relatives of Chinese Americans who had citizenships in the United States. This allowed individuals to immigrate to the United States to work, reunite with family, or start a business.

The fire after the earthquake destroyed most of the county records. Some men of Chinese descent living in San Francisco inflated the number of sons and/or daughters that they had residing in China. The cost for the documents was based on age—typically one hundred dollars per year. For example, $1,200 would be paid for a twelve-year-old.

Rickshaw

A light, two-wheeled hooded vehicle drawn by one person.

San Francisco Chinatown

A densely populated neighborhood in San Francisco that was the only area of the city where people of Chinese descent were permitted to own and inherit property. It borders the port of entry for Chinese workers who arrived starting in the mid-1800s for gold mining in the Sierra Nevada, building the intercontinental and other railroads, and farming in the California Delta.

Tien Wu

Worked as a translator as well as organizer with Donaldina Cameron at the Presbyterian Mission House in San Francisco's Chinatown.

Tongs

Chinese organized-crime gangs.

Transcontinental Railroad

More than three thousand male laborers were recruited by the Central Pacific Railroad Company to build the railroad between California and Utah. It was completed in 1869. Alexander Saxton, in *The Army of Canton in the High Sierra*, calculates that railroad companies paid Chinese labor two-thirds of what was paid to White workers.

Wong Kim Ark

Wong Kim Ark was born in San Francisco in 1873. After traveling to China, he was denied reentry to the United States as a citizen and was treated as a noncitizen. He challenged the government's refusal to recognize his citizenship. His case went to the Supreme Court, which ruled in his favor, holding that the citizenship language in the Fourteenth Amendment encompassed the circumstances of his birth and could not be limited in its effect by an act of Congress.

In addition, a child of a citizen, even one born in China, also becomes a US citizen at birth. This decision established an important precedent in its interpretation of the Citizenship Clause of the Fourteenth Amendment to the Constitution.

ABOUT THE AUTHOR

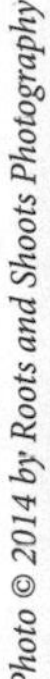

Laila Ibrahim spent much of her career as a preschool director, a birth doula, and a religious educator. That work, coupled with her education in developmental psychology and attachment theory, provided ample fodder for the stories in her novels, *Paper Wife*, *Mustard Seed*, and *Yellow Crocus*.

She's a devout Unitarian Universalist, determined to do her part to add a little more love and justice to our beautiful and painful world. She lives with her wonderful wife, Rinda, and two other families in a small cohousing community in Berkeley, California. Her young adult children are her pride and joy.

Laila is blessed to be working full-time as a novelist. When she isn't writing, she likes to take walks with friends, do jigsaw puzzles, play games, work in the garden, travel, cook, and eat all kinds of delicious food. Visit the author at www.lailaibrahim.com or at Facebook at www.facebook.com/lailaibrahim.author.